FATE OF THE FALLEN

ATLANTIS LEGACY, BOOK 2

LINDSEY SPARKS   WRITING AS   LINDSEY FAIRLEIGH

RUBUS PRESS

Editing by Fresh as a Daisy Editing
https://www.freshasadaisyediting.com/

Cover by We Got You Covered
www.wegotyoucoveredbookdesign.com/

ISBN 9781949485158

ALLWORLD ONLINE

AO: Pride & Prejudice

AO: The Wonderful Wizard of Oz

Vertigo

THE ENDING SERIES

The Ending Beginnings: Omnibus Edition

After The Ending

Into The Fire

Out Of The Ashes

Before The Dawn

World Before

THE ENDING LEGACY

World After

For more information on Lindsey and her books:

www.authorlindseysparks.com

Join Lindsey's mailing list to stay up to date on releases

AND to get a FREE copy of *Sacrifice of the Sinners.*

www.authorlindseysparks.com/sacrifice

To read Lindsey's books as she writes them, check her out on Patreon:

https://www.patreon.com/lindseysparks

ACKNOWLEDGMENTS

Thank you so much to everyone who has supported my work on this book, including my beta readers, LP, Sarah, and Jenna, and my amazing editor, Holly. Thank you to my husband, Adam, for watching our little gremlin while I hide away in my office.

And most of all, thank you to my Patreon Patrons, who support my work on a monthly basis:

Teri Lindley (Hi Mom!)
Tina Canon
Olivia
Carlotta Woolcock
Courtney Barry
Fred
Aisling Ó Béara
Cortney Robinson
Pamela Myers Scroggs

[1]

"We've *got* to be close," I said, smacking at a giant, blood-sucking insect snacking on the side of my neck. It crunched against my palm, sending a cascade of shivers down my spine. My upper lip curled in disgust, and I wiped my hand on a towering tree as I passed by, leaving a smear of yellow-green goop on the rough bark. So incredibly gross.

A howler monkey cried out in the distance, seeming to laugh at my discomfort.

Ahead of me, Raiden hacked through yet another bunch of vines with his trusty machete, clearing the trail through the rainforest's dense underbrush. The loaded pack on his back jimmied and jostled with each purposeful swing of his arm. His neck and arms were coated in a sheen of sweat, turning his tanned skin a shimmering bronze, and his gray T-shirt was soaked through, the cotton clinging to his torso, defining each and every muscle. I would have been able to appreciate the effect a lot more if I wasn't so preoccupied by my own sweaty body and my general state of misery. The GPS receiver tucked into the holster on Raiden's belt beeped steadily faster, signaling that we were closing in on our target. Finally...

The sights and sounds of the Amazon Rainforest had enthralled me—at first. The rainforest was alive with the thrumming, buzzing, and chirping of the creatures that inhabited it, the natural orchestra frequently cut through by a croak or howling cry. I had seen dozens of monkeys and even more vibrantly colored birds, but the novelty could only last so long.

The humidity quickly overwhelmed all other sensory information. It felt like a second skin—a suffocating, smothering second skin. My tank top was in a soggy state, and it felt like a sweat-soaked sponge was wedged between my pack and my lower back. The flyaway hairs that were too short or stubborn to be tied back in a ponytail were plastered against my forehead and the sides of my face. A dull headache had started behind my eyeballs. I blamed dehydration. We had only been out here for a few hours, and I had already drained two of my three huge water bottles. I was really starting to dislike this place.

It's just a short hike through the Amazon, I'd said. *We'll find it in no time,* I'd said. *Easy peasy,* I'd said.

I wished time travel was included in the grab bag of psychic gifts I inherited as Persephone's clone so I could go back in time and slap some sense into my past self.

The location marked by the holodisk I had found at the end of Hades' labyrinth pointed to a place in the heart of the Amazon Rainforest. Coming here had been the logical next step for Raiden and me, after we had found our way back through the labyrinth in Rome. Our moms were safe—or, at least, not in immediate danger—and the Custodes Veritatis was hunting us. Getting as far away from Rome as possible, as quickly as possible, was pretty much our only move.

We couldn't go home, much as I craved the peace and tranquility of Blackthorn Manor. The Order was sure to be monitoring the estate. But they didn't have any reason to suspect we would go to Brazil, so that was precisely what we did. Besides, we needed to find what Hades left at the location marked on the holodisk before the Custodes Veritatis found it. The Order had already proven its unscrupulous nature, and I agreed with Peri that it would be far too dangerous for any more Atlantean artifacts to fall into their hands.

Plus, Hades owed me some answers. Assuming Peri's hunch was right and Hades was still alive—as impossible as it seemed—I was determined to track him down and make him talk.

I just hadn't expected that following his trail would be so damn soggy.

I heaved a deep, miserable sigh. "Please let us be close," I muttered on the tail of my exhaled breath.

I doubted Peri would have been whining, but then, I wasn't her. I mean, I *was* her, biologically. I was her clone, and I carried her consciousness in my head, but none of that seemed to matter right now. I was hot and tired and possibly on the verge of tears. In the showdown between nature and nurture, nurture was definitely coming out on top.

Even Raiden, who was barely four days healed after being shot in the thigh *and* tweaking his bad knee in a car accident, was handling the slog through the jungle better than I was. I had had my brief, blazing moment of glory in the labyrinth, stepping into Persephone's kickass shoes, but as soon as I swapped those out for my mundane hiking boots, I had returned to my usual, useless self. I had even managed to reduce her awe-inspiring weapon to a glorified walking stick.

Something tucked under the winding roots of a nearby tree caught my eye, and I stopped mid-step. "Raiden!" I exclaimed, planting the butt of the doru into the soft earth and pointing to a small pile of shoebox-sized stone blocks with my free hand. The blocks of stone were weathered and worn, their surfaces almost entirely covered in a combination of lichen and moss, but there was no mistaking the perfectly rectangular shape. There was nothing natural about that shape. These blocks had been *made*.

As Raiden moved closer to the rubble, I scanned the area

surrounding us. It didn't take me long to find more evidence that people had once inhabited this place. Based on the aged state of the evidence, *once* was a very long time ago.

What appeared to be a half-collapsed wall off to the left was shrouded in vines and half-consumed by the underbrush, and when I squinted just right, an enormous boulder up ahead took on the unmistakable shape of a human face. Or, at least, a human*oid* face.

"Is this it?" I asked, glancing back at Raiden who was crouching in front of the pile of stone blocks. "Is this what we're looking for?"

Raiden checked the still-beeping GPS receiver and shook his head. "Unless these ruins spread out for miles…" He looked at me as he stood. "Sorry, Cora. We've still got a ways to go."

I let my head fall back and groaned in disappointment. But as we continued on, the increasingly elaborate ruins were enough to take my mind off my general state of misery. For a little while, at least.

The bones of structures left behind by people many centuries ago became more numerous and apparent until, suddenly, they were all around us. The soft earth and underbrush gave way to paving stones, and once massive stone structures soon surrounded us, bent and bowed by time. Tall kapok trees grew atop the buildings and free-standing walls in places, while the dense rainforest canopy concealed the ruins of the ancient city from anyone hoping to catch a glimpse of the Amazon's secrets from above.

We slowed considerably as we made our way through the long-abandoned city, taking it all in. I couldn't help but wonder if my mom had ever been here. Or was this a truly lost city? Was this the fabled city of "Z" or possibly even the mythical El Dorado? When I spoke with her on the phone this morning, she hadn't mentioned finding anything like this during the Brazil portion of her latest, ill-fated trip. But then, she and Emi had been more preoccupied with issuing warning after warning of all the ways the Custodes Veritatis might try to track or trap us.

"Can you mark our location?" I asked Raiden. I wanted to make sure we had it noted, both so I could ask my mom about it later and, if the opportunity arose, so she and I could return together and attempt to uncover some of the secrets hidden here, finally fulfilling the mother-daughter expedition she'd desired for so long.

Raiden pushed a button on the GPS receiver, and the device issued a single, lower-pitched beep. "Marked," he said without looking back at me. His eyes were constantly moving, less out of awe over our surroundings and more from increasing wariness of the dangers that could be lurking in the shadows and beyond, in the places he couldn't see.

"Who do you think built this place?" he asked as we continued on our current path through the city.

I paused, falling behind, and frowned as I studied the decoration at the base of a broad stairway branching off our path. Two huge snake heads had been carved from stone, their mouths open and fangs bared, like they were guarding whatever lay at the top of the stairs. The architecture looked nothing like what I had seen in photos from Machu Picchu or any other Inca sites. This reminded me more of the temple ruins of Ta Prohm in Angkor, what with the intricate stonework and the kapok trees invading the ancient city, their roots growing over and through the ruins. Except Ta Prohm was in Cambodia, clear on the other side of the world.

"Cora," Raiden called back to me. "We should keep moving."

After one last glance at the snake heads, I turned to follow Raiden, jogging to catch up.

"I have no idea who built this place," I told him as I fell into step beside him.

Another ten or fifteen minutes of walking, and we passed

through a partially crumbled stone gateway. The rainforest floor soon overtook the paved path, and vegetation hid all remaining signs of what must once have been a thriving civilization. As I ducked under a leafy branch Raiden was holding up to clear the way for me, I looked back one last time. But then Raiden released the branch, and the city was, once again, hidden from view.

We found a game trail that carved a path through the rainforest in the general direction we wanted to go, but after following that for a mile or two, we were back to bushwhacking.

"Hold up," Raiden said, raising a hand, fingers curled into a tight fist. I recognized the hand signal from countless movies and TV shows, but mainly from *Stargate SG-1*, the source of most of my knowledge about the military.

Raiden sheathed his machete and pulled the GPS receiver from its holster on his belt. The handheld device had gone quiet.

"Are we here?" I asked, sidling up to Raiden so I could get a look at the screen. I had assumed that once we reached our destination, the GPS receiver's beeping would bleed into one long tone, not stop altogether.

Much to my chagrin, the screen was black.

"It's dead," Raiden said, his voice gruff. He smacked the side of the device with an open hand, then shook it a few times.

I swallowed, thick saliva like paste coating my throat. Unable to hold out any longer, I propped the doru against the nearest tree and shrugged my pack off my shoulders. Squatting down, I pulled the remaining full water bottle free from one of the bag's side pockets.

"The battery died?" I asked as I stood and unscrewed the cap. I brought the bottle up to my mouth. "Didn't the guy in the shop say it was supposed to last seventy-two hours?"

"The battery didn't die," Raiden said, a hint of defensiveness in his tone.

I raised my eyebrows.

"At least, not on its own," he added as he tucked the defunct GPS receiver back into its holster and turned his wrist so he could see the face of his enormous, multi-function watch. Eyes glued to the timepiece, he turned toward me, frowned, and then turned back around.

"What?" I asked, lowering the water bottle. The dull headache was annoying, but the knots forming in my stomach told me we had a bigger issue. I could rehydrate later. "What is it?"

"My watch is dead, too," Raiden said. "And the compass needle is going crazy."

I narrowed my eyes, an idea tickling the edges of my mind. Back in Rome, when I first entered the labyrinth and found myself in near absolute darkness, I had pulled out my phone, hoping to use the built-in light, but the phone's battery had inexplicably died. And later in the labyrinth, when looting a corpse had landed me an antique compass, I recalled being intrigued by the way the needle spun around and around, endlessly searching for North.

"This is it," I said, my voice ringing with absolute certainty. "We're here."

Something about the technology Hades had built into the labyrinth—as well as whatever he wanted us to find here, it would seem—didn't jive well with modern electronics.

At Raiden's quirked eyebrow, I explained, "It was the same in the labyrinth. Didn't you notice it there?"

"I was a little preoccupied at the time," Raiden said as he lowered his wrist. He scanned the endless expanse of trees and vines and overgrown underbrush surrounding us. "I don't see any ancient alien buildings, so..."

I planted my hands on my hips, lips curving into a smirk. "That's because you're looking in the wrong place." I waited for him to look at me, for his eyes to lock with mine, and then I gave the rainforest floor a pointed look.

"Huh," Raiden said, scratching along his jawline. "Say you're right and whatever we're looking for is beneath our feet —how do we find our way in?"

If we hadn't stopped here, I never would have noticed it—the glint of gold beneath a swath of vine-like roots and massive fern leaves maybe a dozen paces away. I touched my fingertip to the pendant hanging on a chain around my neck, tracing a circle around the large, amber stone set into the pendant to deactivate the regulator. The stone shifted from subtly glowing amber to brilliant, electric blue, and the ancient device stopped suppressing my latent psychic powers. In a rush, my psychic senses awakened, and the world became so much richer than it had been just a few seconds ago.

I closed my eyes, taking a moment to quiet the sudden rush of foreign thoughts and feelings flooding into my mind from Raiden. Skepticism. Excitement. Worry. Determination. And much to my surprise, each and every one of those emotions floated on a deep ocean of contentment. At his core, Raiden was happy. Because he was with me.

My heart seemed to swell in my chest, and I opened my eyes, fully intending to tell him I felt the same. But when my eyes met his, a flush rushed up my chest and neck, overheating me further, and my heart lodged in my throat, blocking the words. I had a lot of weaknesses, but this budding relationship Raiden and I were *maybe* in had to be the thing I was the absolute worst at. Not like this was really a great setting for declarations of feelings, anyway.

I flashed Raiden an awkward smile, clearing my throat as I reached for the doru. I tucked the end of the staff under my arm and aimed the focus crystal atop the weapon at the roots covering the spot of glinting gold. If this was an Atlantean site, then it was safe to assume the buried artifact wasn't gold at all but nearly unbreakable orichalcum, the same metal that both the regulator and the doru were made of. Energy charged along the length of the ancient weapon, tickling my palms and humming through my arms. With the merest thought, I sent out three tiny energy bursts.

Blue fire blasted a pathway through the underbrush, sizzling over the roots and fern leaves, burning them down to little more than ash. When the smoke cleared, the golden object was barely visible, buried under a heap of soot.

Hurriedly, I picked my way through the smoldering underbrush, ducking under a branch here and a singed vine there. I crouched in front of the golden object, sweeping away the ash to get a better look.

I grinned. It *was* orichalcum, just as I had suspected. Which meant this really was an Atlantean site. Whatever Hades wanted us to find—and whatever I needed to protect from the Order—was here.

The exposed part of the orichalcum object, roughly the length and width of my forearm, had a curved symbol engraved into its face and was half buried by the singed earth.

I dug my fingers into the dirt. The energy blasts had heated the ground, leaving it hot to the touch. Gritting my teeth, I scooped the soil away, over and over, until I could see the rest of the symbol and make out the general shape of the golden object.

It seemed to be a solid block of orichalcum, symmetrical in shape but narrowing as I dug deeper. A quartzite block bordered it on either side, the stone glimmering a subtle pink beneath the dirt smudges. The symbol inscribed on the face of the orichalcum block looked an awful lot like the Greek letter *beta*. But I knew better. Thanks to Peri's presence in my mind—even at times like this, when she seemed to be slumbering—I could understand her long-dead language. This symbol wasn't from the Greek alphabet; it was Atlantean.

"What is it?" Raiden asked, close behind me, and I jumped. I had been so focused on digging out the mass of orichalcum that I hadn't heard him approach.

I turned my head slightly so I could see him in my peripheral vision, but never really took my focus off the gleaming symbol. "I think it's a keystone," I told him.

"Like at the top of an arch?" Raiden said, putting two and two together.

I nodded as I turned my full attention back to the orichalcum block. "You know how much Hades loves arches..." The labyrinth had been lousy with them. I traced the groove carved by the symbol with the tip of my finger. "Hopefully we just found our way in."

I stood and backed up a few steps, studying the ground around the keystone. "Nothing the doru can't handle," I said, thinking a dozen controlled energy blasts would create a deep enough crater to clear the dirt away from the front of the arch. "Come on," I said, turning and starting back along the trail I had burned through the rainforest.

I didn't hear Raiden following. He could be catlike in his movements, but out here, that didn't equate to silence like it did indoors.

"Cora..." The way Raiden said my name made it sound like a warning.

I spun around, shifting the doru into a defensive hold.

Sidearm in hand, Raiden swayed where he stood before crumpling to the ground. His head missed the uncovered keystone by mere inches.

"Raiden!" I exclaimed, taking a lunging step toward him. "What—"

Another monster bug chomped down on my neck, and I raised my hand to swipe it away. Instead, I pulled something long, hard, and cold away from my neck. I glanced down at the weird-shaped bug as I took my next step toward Raiden.

Without warning, my leg gave out, and I tumbled face-first into the scorched underbrush. I couldn't raise my hands to stop my fall. My arms weren't responding to my brain's order to move at all, and I hit the ground with a grunt, the doru slipping from my grasp. My other hand flopped out in line with my face, and a slender dart rolled onto the singed ground.

My thoughts grew fuzzy, darkness creeping in at the edges of my vision. The words *tranquilizer dart* formed in my dazed mind, but the logical part of my brain balked at the conclusion. Tranquilizer darts didn't work this fast, at least not in real life. Two-second tranq-outs were a myth relegated to the world of fiction. TV. Movies. Video games.

But not even the last few threads of reason and logic could prevent the inevitable, and darkness consumed the world around me.

[2]

I woke to the smell of a campfire, the sound of raucous, masculine laughter, and a throbbing frontal lobe. Beneath the woodsmoke, the subtle scent of rich soil and the not-so-subtle odor of urine flavored the air.

Foreign thoughts and emotions whispered through my mind, and I figured I must have conked out with my regulator deactivated. I reached up to touch the glowing blue stone, intending to mute my psychic senses. Or, at least, I tried to. My hands were stuck behind my back.

Not *stuck*—tied.

Adrenaline burned the final remnants of sleep from my mind.

Not *sleep*—drugs.

In a rush, I remembered what had happened to me. To Raiden. We had been taken down by some suped-up version of a tranquilizer dart. It was like something taken straight out of one of my games, a thought I was quickly growing tired of having. Risk-taking and life-and-death adventure were great when there was a video game controller and a screen separating me from the actual threat of death. In real life, it wasn't nearly as fun.

Groaning, I rolled onto my back, trapping my arms beneath

me. It wasn't exactly comfortable, but at least it took the pressure off my aching shoulder and hip. It didn't do much for my headache, though; that intensified with each beat of my heart.

I blinked, taking in my immediate surroundings. It was dark. Nighttime. Four walls of dirt surrounded me, maybe ten feet high and seven feet wide, and the night sky was barely visible through the thick rainforest canopy high overhead.

I was in a pit in the ground. Whoever tranqued me must have tied me up and dumped me down here. No wonder the whole right side of my body hurt; my attackers must have just rolled me over the edge and let me fall. That was probably the source of my pounding headache, as well.

Closing my eyes, I focused on the whispers from the unfamiliar minds of my captors above. I thought I sensed nine separate minds, but I couldn't be certain. A few were farther out than the others, alone and slowly circling. I figured they were probably on watch, keeping the camp safe from whatever other, wilder predators come out to play in the rainforest at night. The rest were clustered around a point closer to the pit, probably around a campfire. That was where my count lost its precision. They were too close together to differentiate with any certainty.

I rolled onto my left side, grunting from the effort. And then I froze, heart lodged in my throat. The seconds ticked by, and still, I didn't breathe.

Raiden lay face-down at the far end of the pit. He wasn't moving. I wasn't even sure if he was breathing. I couldn't feel his mind at all. I could feel whispers of thoughts and emotions from above—nothing concrete, but enough to know our captors were there—but I couldn't feel Raiden. Not at all.

Was it the tranquilizer, muting his brain activity? Or was it more than that?

Panic flitted around in my chest like a caged bird. I inched my way closer to Raiden until I was near enough to lay my head on his back. I pressed my ear against the back of his ribcage, just below his shoulder blade, and inhaled deeply, holding my breath.

Thud-thump. Thud-thump. Thud-thump.

"Oh, thank God," I whispered on my exhale.

Raiden was alive. The drugs must've been responsible for his mental muteness, then.

Raiden's T-shirt was still soaked with sweat, but I didn't mind the damp warmth one bit so long as I could hear the steady beating of his heart. I closed my eyes and simply listened, basking in the relief flooding my body.

"Peri," I whispered, keeping my eyes closed and focusing my thoughts inward. "Are you there?" I waited a few seconds, then added, "I could really use your help…"

At least a minute passed, me thinking Peri's name, over and over. But she didn't respond. It was like she wasn't inside my head at all. I figured the drugs in the tranquilizer dart must have subdued her as well.

I blew out a breath and opened my eyes, awkwardly elbowing my way up to a sitting position. Raiden would wake up eventually. I had to believe that. The least I could do was gather what information I could while I waited for him to come to.

I picked one of the captors circling the camp and concentrated, skimming what I could from the surface of his mind. I wasn't able to get much. My psychic senses felt dulled, like they, too, had been muffled by the drugs. It was like trying to hear what someone was saying underwater.

I could tell the captor was male, and that he was a soldier for the Custodes Veritatis, a position that gave him confidence and made him feel strong and powerful. But he was afraid—of me, and also of *them*. Not of his companions, and not of the Order. Something else scared him. Something *other*.

They were shadows lurking around his mind. A ghost story told around the campfire. The Order's version of the boogeyman.

I frowned. That was all I could get from him, so I hopped to the next captor's mind.

It was another man, this one more angry than afraid, though the fear was there feeding his anger. He wanted to be sitting around the campfire, clinging to false bravado with the others. He told himself he was pissed off because it was unfair that he was patrolling while his buddies were bullshitting. But really, his anger stemmed from his fear—of that mysterious *them*—and he longed for the comfort of his peers. Safety in numbers, and all that.

I shifted my focus again, locking on the third mental signature circling the perimeter. This captor was female.

"Well, well, well…"

The sound of a masculine voice so close shattered my concentration, and my eyes popped open, my stare locking on the silhouetted man towering over me from the edge of the pit above. I could make out the shape of a rifle held across his body.

"Look who's awake," he said, his voice like crunching gravel. He crouched, resting the rifle on his knees, and cocked his head to the side. "And I came over here expecting to find the big guy up. We dosed *you* real good. A normal chicky your size would be out for hours, yet." He shook his head, a low laugh rumbling in his chest.

Hatred radiated from him like heat from a flame. It was so intense, it drowned out all other thoughts and emotions, and I couldn't pick up anything else from his mind, not even his name.

The man stilled, his focus on me becoming razor sharp. "But then, you aren't exactly *normal*, are you?"

I backed away, scooting on my butt, my stare never straying from his shadowed face. My ponytail was a joke, tilted off to the side of my head, barely holding half of my hair. I hid behind the loose strands, letting the dirty curtain of hair fall in front of my face. But still, I watched him.

He shifted the rifle, aiming it at me.

I pulled my knees up, using my legs as a shield, and squeezed my eyes shut, angling my face away from the man who could end my life with the twitch of a finger. Inside my head, I screamed Peri's name over and over.

"Just a scared little girl," the man muttered, a sneer audible in his voice though it was too dark for me to make out his expression.

I heard the *thwap* of intense air pressure releasing and felt a sharp prick on the outside of my thigh. Almost instantly, my thoughts grew fuzzy and the world darkened. He must have shot me with another of those impossible tranquilizer darts. The darkness closed in faster this time.

With the last threads of consciousness, I skimmed the source of all that hatred from his mind. He, too, was afraid. *I* scared him because I threatened everything he believed in simply by existing. He wanted to fix that by erasing me from existence. If I overdosed on the tranquilizer, I wouldn't be a problem any longer.

I felt a second prick of pain, this time in my shoulder.

And then there was only darkness.

[3]

I cracked my eyes open and was once again greeted by the dark of night, though whether it was the same night, or another, I couldn't say. I was still in the pit, huddled against the dirt wall with my wrists tied together behind my back, my shoulders and arms cramping from spending far too much time locked in the same position. But that ache paled in comparison to the charley horse sending bolts of lightning through my hamstring. Tears welled in my eyes, and I gritted my teeth, straightening my leg. I sighed as the intense pain quickly faded until it was little more than a memory.

The cobwebs cleared faster this time, and I felt less fuzzy-brained. I wondered if I was building up a resistance to the tranquilizer. Maybe I could use that to my advantage. I could trick our captors into thinking I was unconscious and then…

I blinked, looking around. My heart dropped, and any thoughts of plotting our escape vanished as dread took root in my belly. Raiden was gone.

I scrambled to my feet, fingers digging into the dirt wall at my back to steady me. I still felt a little woozy.

"Raiden!" I called out. I could just barely sense his mental signature a short distance from the pit. Pain radiated from him—they were hurting him—and icy dread warred with fiery rage within me. "Raiden! Can you hear me?"

"Cora!" Raiden shouted. "I'm—"

His words cut off abruptly, replaced by a guttural grunt and the bruising sound of flesh hitting flesh.

"Another word, and I blow your fucking head off," a man said. I recognized the voice; it was my visitor from the last time I had been awake, the one who had hoped to kill me—*accidentally*—by double dosing me with the tranquilizer.

I could sense his current intent, not because my psychic senses were all that much clearer than before, but because his conviction ran bone deep. He was interrogating Raiden, trying to force Raiden to reveal what I was, where I came from, and whether there were any more like me—so he could hunt the others down and destroy them.

While I was unconscious—the second time—this man had convinced the rest of the team to hold off on delivering me to the Primicerius, the leader of the Custodes Veritatis who I had met in Rome, who just happened to be waiting for me at some mansion in Rio. This madman had gone rogue and was determined to shirk his orders and execute me, right here, right now. And his companions were more afraid of him, in his manic state, than they were of the Primicerius and *his* wrath should they return empty handed.

"No," the rogue leader snapped, responding to something I hadn't heard. "Stay here," he ordered. "Keep him down." After a thud and a grunt that brought to mind a combat boot making contact with Raiden's abdomen, he said, "I'll take care of *it*." And by *it*, he meant *me*.

Heart hammering in my chest, I backed into the corner farthest from my captor and hunched in on myself. "Peri," I whispered, breaths coming short and fast. Fear was a block of ice in my belly. "If you can hear me, now would be a really great time for you to come out…" I was so scared, I was practically panting. "Please, Peri, I need your help!" I hissed.

"Praying isn't going to save you," my captor said, coming into view as he neared the edge of the pit.

This time, he faced the campfire, and the flickering light allowed me to get a better look at him. His stubbled, square jaw and boxer's build made him look like the career soldier he clearly was. A wad of chew bulged in his lower lip, accentuating his cruel sneer, and his eyes burned with fanaticism. He gripped a pistol in his right hand, the gun held close to his thigh, pointed at the ground. I could just make out the name stitched into the patch on the chest pocket on the left side of his tactical vest: *Davidson.*

"God created man in his image. You—" Davidson spat down into the pit, the sickly yellow goop nearly hitting the toe of my hiking boot. "You're just an abomination. He doesn't listen to the likes of you."

I glared up at Davidson, jaw clenched and chest heaving. He believed himself to be a devout man—a *godly* man. He was fanatical in his faith. Nothing would stop him from destroying any and all threats to his worldview. Nothing would stop him from destroying me. He had done far worse in the past. I picked up on flashes of memories from his mind. Moments when his fanaticism had made him do terrible things. Dogs, the elderly, children—none were immune to his righteous wrath, not if hurting them provided a means to his desired end. In his mind, any and every despicable action could be justified.

If Peri wasn't going to step in and save me, then for once, it was up to me to save my own damn self.

Thinking fast, I grasped at the first idea that came to me. I could appeal to Davidson's core values, and maybe he would relent. Probably not, but it was worth a shot. At least, keeping him talking might buy me some more time to come up with a better plan.

"Thou shalt not kill," I said, my voice raspy.

Davidson tilted his head to the side, angling his ear toward me, and narrowed his eyes. "What did you just say to me?"

I cleared my throat and squared my shoulders as best as I could. "Thou shalt not kill," I repeated, my voice stronger this time.

Davidson raised his eyebrows and shook his head, a dry, humorless laugh rumbling in his chest. His headshake turned into a nod. "That's what I thought you said," he murmured, crouching and placing his hand on the earthen lip of the pit. In one smooth motion, he jumped off the edge and dropped down to my level.

He landed with a grunt, then straightened and looked at me. "Thou shalt not suffer a witch to live." He spat again, this time aiming for my face.

The instant the spittle struck my cheek, rage ignited within me. I suddenly felt electrified. Energy crackled over my skin, making the hairs all over my body stand on end. The dark strands that had slipped free from my ponytail lifted off my shoulders, floating around my head.

Davidson's eyes widened, and he raised his sidearm, aiming at my head.

"Go to Hell!" I screamed down the barrel of the gun.

As the final word left my mouth, Davidson pulled the trigger. The crack of gunfire was deafening, but the blast of electric-blue energy that exploded out of me like a mini supernova drowned it out, muffling the world with the crackle of static. The psychic energy dissolved the bullet mere inches from my face. A fraction of a second later, my wrists were free.

I watched, horrified, as waves of electric-blue energy coated Davidson. It sizzled over his clothing and skin, eating away at everything it touched like acid. Fabric and skin dissolved, leaving exposed muscle and bone for the energy to consume. He screamed, but the static muted the sound.

I felt Davidson die, felt his consciousness extinguish. By the time his body hit the ground, he was little more than a pile of rapidly disintegrating bones.

I sucked in a breath, and the deadly energy whooshed back into me. I stared at the dissolving remains of Davidson, horror widening my eyes. Tears streamed down my cheeks, and my stomach twisted into knots. I did this. I killed him. Not Peri. *Me.*

I swallowed repeatedly, suppressing the urge to vomit. How many others had I killed?

"Raiden!" I screamed his name as loud as I could. "Raiden! Answer me!"

I started shaking, anticipating the worst. If I had killed Raiden like I just killed Davidson…

Large tremors made me shudder. My teeth chattered, but still I screamed, "Raiden!"

"I'm here!" he shouted back. "I'm all right, Cora." His voice sounded rough, hoarse. "I'm okay. Just, hang on a sec."

I retreated deeper into the corner, huddling away from the pile of steaming bones, away from the man I had just killed. I brought a trembling hand up to the regulator, activating it to suppress my frightening psychic powers. The pit looked the same, untouched by the psychic energy. It was almost like the energy had had a mind of its own, only destroying the immediate threats of Davidson, his bullet, and the bindings around my wrists.

Above, I could hear rustling and heavy breathing. From the sound of it, the only person moving was Raiden. I couldn't sense any other minds. The knots in my stomach twisted and tightened. I couldn't help but suspect why I couldn't sense any other minds —my energy blast must have killed all our captors. *I* had killed them. All of them.

Though they had drugged us and were holding us prisoner in a literal hole in the ground, and though they had clearly been torturing Raiden and intending to kill us both, I hoped my suspicion was wrong. I hoped the energy blast had only destroyed Davidson.

What qualified a person as a mass murderer? More than a handful of kills in one go?

My stomach, already unsettled, boiled with nausea. My abdominal muscles convulsed, and I bent over, vomiting a bitter yellowish slime. My stomach heaved three times, leaving me doubled over and panting.

The sound of boots hitting the dirt inside the pit drew my attention. I lifted my head a few inches.

The relief that flooded my body as I looked at Raiden was more potent than any drug.

He paused, staring at the steaming pile of bones that had once been Davidson. Then his eyes shifted to me, locking with mine, and he stepped over Davidson's remains to crouch in front of me.

Raiden was in rough shape, pain radiating off him in waves. The leg of his army-green cargo pants was saturated with dark blood, and he had knotted a strip of black fabric around his thigh, a makeshift bandage over the reopened gunshot wound. His face was a mass of red, mottled splotches, and his right eye was swollen shut. His lower lip was split, and a trickle of dried blood stained his chin.

"Are you all right?" Raiden asked, his hands settling on my upper arms.

I almost laughed. *He* was asking me if *I* was all right. Had he seen himself?

I let him pull me up, so I was standing more or less upright. "Did they hurt you?" Raiden asked, concern furrowing his brow. His hands slid up over my shoulders and settled in the crook of my neck. He turned my head this way and that, then scanned the rest of my body, giving me a quick but thorough once over.

I grasped his thick wrists. "Hey," I said, then cleared my throat. "I'm all right, okay?" I rubbed his wrists with shaking hands. "I'm all right," I repeated, but the words came out wobbly, and my chin started to quake. I was on the verge of breaking down. I cleared my throat again and jutted out my jaw to stave off the emotional tsunami.

Raiden pulled me to him, wrapping his arms around me and crushing me against his chest. "I was so scared," he said, his voice tight with emotion. One hand curved around the back of my neck, and his chin rested atop my head.

I embraced him just as ardently. For a moment there, I had thought he was dead, and it felt amazing to hold him in my arms. To feel his solid strength. His warmth and vitality. His steady heartbeat.

"I thought I'd lost you," I said, my voice tremulous.

"You and me both," Raiden said. "Thank Peri for me. That was one hell of a save."

I grasped the back of his soggy T-shirt, my hands balling into tight fists. "That wasn't Peri," I told him and sucked in a shivering breath. "That was me."

[4]

"Any idea of how to get back to the arch?" I asked Raiden across the campfire, between spoonfuls of a barely edible MRE.

I could not, for the life of me, understand how the slop in the package received the label of *Chicken Fajita*. I choked it down nonetheless. It had been well over a day since I had last eaten anything, and after multiple rounds of tranquilizers and the energy explosion, my body was in desperate need of fuel to regain its strength. Raiden was already digging into his second MRE. *Chili and Macaroni*, according to the label. It looked a lot better than mine.

Raiden paused, considering my question, his brown plastic spoon hovering in front of his mouth. He shrugged, then ate the bite and dug the spoon back into his MRE pouch. He set the pouch on the ground and leaned back against the boulder he was using as a back rest, stretching his arms over his head. He had already cleaned and bandaged the reopened wound in his leg, and he had swapped out his filthy, sweat- and blood-soaked T-shirt and cargo pants for a cleaner set of clothing from one of the dead commando's packs. Our own packs were here, too, but better to burn through the Order's supplies first.

I had traded up, clothing-wise, as well. But my change of attire came from my own stash. I now sported Peri's ancient hoplon suit, and the channels running the length of the full-body suit glowed a subtle amber. The garment fit like a wetsuit but offered more protection than any body armor ever created by humans. Plus, the hoplon suit had a built-in temperature regulator, making me forget all about the hot, humid air.

I was secure enough with my shortcomings to admit I should have been wearing the hoplon suit from the get-go, but I had resisted out of pure, obstinate stupidity. Because the hoplon suit belonged to Peri.

While physically, I *was* her—thanks to ancient Atlantean cloning technology—wearing her hoplon suit made me feel like a little girl playing dress up in mommy's clothes. I was a poser. Every part of the suit fit perfectly, boots and all, but it felt off. It made me hyperaware of just how different I was from Peri. How much *less* I was in almost every way.

Unable to stomach another bite of the MRE, I set the pouch down on the ground and picked up the canteen I had swiped from another of the commando's bags. *Greer*. That was the name printed on the patch on the front of the bag, though it was impossible to say which of the bodies had been his. I wondered if there was a Mrs. Greer who would be waiting for her husband, or any little Greers, to come home. A mother? A father? Brothers and sisters?

My stomach twisted as my thoughts strayed along that dangerous path, and I choked down a gulp of water.

Raiden brushed off his hands, then turned partway, placing a palm on the boulder. He shifted his weight, planting one boot on the ground, and winced as he stood. "We should get moving," he said, limping the few steps it took to reach his pack. He crouched in front of the bag and started stuffing in pilfered supplies. "We need to leave this area," he added. "The Order is bound to know the location of this camp, and it won't be long until Henry sends another team after us…if he hasn't already."

I grimaced. Looked like we were back to running. With one hand, I rubbed the nape of my neck. This stupid lingering headache was making the muscles in my neck and shoulders tighten with tension. At least it seemed to be fading.

I heaved a breath, my shoulders rising and falling dramatically, then lowered my hand and leaned forward onto my knees. "So, where to?" I asked, my voice oozing defeat as I stood up.

Raiden paused his packing, an unopened MRE in hand, and looked at me. "We're not giving up, Cora," he said, his expression earnest. "We'll come back, and we'll find whatever Hades hid here. We'll get your answers, but we have to be smart about it. We won't find anything if we're dead."

We. He kept saying *we*. Like he needed to be here, risking his life. For me.

Raiden would never leave me to deal with this on my own. The thought had never even crossed his mind—and I knew it with absolute certainty because I had seen inside his head. I wasn't connected to his mind at the moment; the regulator was in the amber, active mode, and I planned on leaving it that way unless it was an emergency. The residual thoughts and feelings my psychic senses picked up from Raiden would be too much of a distraction.

Besides, after the devastating psychic explosion, I was too afraid to deactivate the regulator and unleash my powers. I really didn't want to blow anyone else up today, least of all Raiden.

I felt like a ticking time bomb. I needed to find whatever Hades had hidden at the location marked on the holodisk, and sooner rather than later. Hopefully it was Hades, himself. I felt certain he could help me get a grip on my alien nature.

But Raiden was right. I wouldn't find anything if I was dead. Or if Raiden was, because without him, I was essentially useless. Oh, I was plenty dangerous, but I was unpredictable. My powers were spiraling rapidly out of control. I needed Raiden. To guide me. To ground me. To save me…even if the person he was saving me from was myself.

I nodded to Raiden, letting him know I agreed. Move now. Stay alive now. Get answers later.

Raiden returned his attention to his pack just a moment before something slammed into my chest.

"Ouch!" I exclaimed, glancing down to see what had struck me. Despite my reaction, it hadn't really hurt—just surprised me. Not much could actually injure me through the nearly impenetrable hoplon suit.

An arrow lay on the ground at my feet. Not a modern hunting arrow made of carbon fiber and steel. This arrow was constructed of wood and stone, with genuine feathers for fletching.

Brow furrowed, I looked from the arrow to Raiden. I watched as another arrow buried itself in the top of his pack, mere inches from his bowed head.

Raiden froze, and Peri took over, wresting control of my body away from me—control I would have given freely. But there was no time for a gentle passing of the reins. In the blink of an eye, I became her avatar, ready to speak and move at her direction. Even my emotions synced up with hers. Only my thoughts remained my own. The sensation was both terrifying and thrilling.

But most of all, I was just glad Peri was back. The tranquilizer had muted her presence, and the mental seclusion had been surprisingly lonesome. It was astounding how quickly I had grown accustomed to having her there, a mostly silent presence residing in my mind.

At her direction, I deactivated the regulator and thrust my hand out toward the doru, which was propped against a nearby tree trunk. It flew into my hand, smacking against my palm. I curled my fingers around the golden staff, feeling the energy flow out through my arm to charge the weapon. With a flick of my wrist, a sizzling barrier of energy sprang up around us, protecting us from the barrage of arrows that followed mere seconds later.

Raiden was still in the process of drawing his sidearm from the holster on his thigh as I started toward him.

"Let me know when you're ready, and I'll drop the shield," I said, Peri's accent making my voice sound strange to my ears. I stopped in front of Raiden and glanced down at his bandaged leg. "Can you run?"

He had cleaned the reopened wound and stitched himself back up, but he was still hurting pretty badly. I could feel his pain, even if he wasn't showing any signs of it.

Raiden stared at me—at us—for a long moment, processing the shift that had just happened within me. I wasn't Cora anymore. I was Peri. His mind rejected the possibility at first. I knew this because Peri was paying very close attention to his thoughts.

Finally, Raiden came to terms with this new reality. He inhaled deeply through his nose and nodded. "I can run," he said, then tilted his head to the side. "Not fast, but I *can* run."

"Good. I'll grab Cora's bag," I said, feeling strangely out of body as I referred to myself in the third person. "Then, we run."

Again, Raiden nodded. "Where to?"

"The Beta Site."

Raiden cocked his head slightly, an eyebrow raised in question.

"The arch," I said. "The symbol on the capstone marks it as the entrance to one of my people's settlements. We will be safer down there than we are out here."

I wasn't so sure, but at the moment, I hardly had any say in the matter. My vocal cords were Peri's to command.

Raiden frowned. "Is that why Hades marked this location?"

I shook my head. "Something else, I think."

In Peri's thoughts, I could see her reasoning—there was nothing notable about the place she called the *Beta site*. If Hades had, for some reason, wanted to direct humans to one of their settlements, he would have chosen the Alpha site, located near the earth's southern pole. That had been their main settlement on this planet.

"Do you know what they want?" Raiden asked, looking out through the glowing blue energy barrier. "Or who they are and why they're shooting at us?"

I shook my head. "I cannot sense anything beyond the barrier. I may be able to pick up something once we are on the move." I stretched my neck and adjusted my grip on the doru. "Are you ready?" I asked Raiden.

With a grunt, he hoisted his pack onto his back. After a moment of resituating the bag's straps on his shoulders, he gripped his pistol in both hands and glanced at me sidelong. "Ready as I'll ever be."

I moved closer to the energy barrier. The arrows had stopped coming after the living shield obliterated the first wave. My knees bent in preparation to make a dash for my pack, sitting at the base of a tree about ten paces away. With a mere thought, Peri lowered the shield.

And we ran.

I slid on my hip beneath a whizzing arrow, slipping my arm under one of the pack's straps and spinning onto my knees. I was already up and running by the time I had the other strap situated on my shoulder.

I veered to the left, dodging a pair of arrows, then ducked behind a narrow tree trunk as another arrow flew past my right ear. I spotted one of the bowmen up ahead—a short man who looked like he had stepped straight out of a documentary on the tribes living in the Amazon Rainforest, scant loincloth and all, save for the golden skullcap covering his hair—and made a sharp right.

An arrow struck a tree right in front of my face, stopping me in my tracks. I turned on my heel backtracking a few paces.

Raiden altered his trajectory to follow.

Peri had a destination in mind, like she could sense the arch marking the entrance to the Beta site. Within her thoughts, I saw that she could do just that. Orichalcum had elemental properties that resonated with psychic energy. So long as the regulator was deactivated, she—*I*—could feel the location of the golden keystone, like a beacon guiding her onward.

What she couldn't feel was a single thing from the minds of our attackers. I skimmed the reason from Peri's thoughts. Their strange headwear was made of a hybrid metal, a combination of orichalcum and true gold. The alloy blocked their thoughts from Peri, rendering her psychically blind.

A bowman stepped out from behind a tree barely three paces ahead, blocking the only passable route. His bow was drawn, the arrow in line with my right eye.

I skidded to a halt, then backed up a step, the doru upraised but not charged. Peri didn't want to hurt these people. *We* were intruders on *their* land—dangerous intruders, based on the scene we had left behind at the Order's camp. These people's reaction was not just understandable, it was warranted.

We weren't running because they were attacking us. They weren't any real threat to us. It would take little more than a thought for us to destroy them. But Peri didn't want that. We were running because Peri was trying to save them. To her, human life was a precious, fleeting thing, made all the more valuable by her relative immortality. These people had one shot at life, and the last thing she wanted was to take that from them.

I looked to the left. Even in the darkness of night, I could see that a few paces away, the ground cut off in a steep cliff, the endless sea of the rainforest canopy stretching out far below until it melted into the starry horizon.

Raiden huffed to a stop behind me, his gun trained on the bowman targeting my head.

"Don't shoot him," I said, arm outstretched as I glanced at Raiden over my shoulder.

"You know something I don't?" Raiden asked between heaving breaths.

I stood up straighter, planting the end of the doru in the soft earth. Peri was making a show of relaxing my stance. Of disarming. Of standing down. "I know that if this man wanted me dead, I would already be dead," I said quietly.

Without warning, the bowman shifted his aim a full ninety degrees and loosed his arrow. I followed the trajectory of the arrow, watching it *thunk* into an enormous ceiba tree some twenty paces off to my right.

I stared at the quivering arrow for a moment longer, then returned my attention to the bowman.

He lowered his bow and raised one arm, pointing to the arrow.

"He wants us to go over there," I murmured to Raiden.

"No shit," Raiden said.

While I would have chuckled, Peri was unamused by Raiden's sardonic remark. At Peri's direction, I turned toward the arrow-marked tree. With short, controlled energy bursts, I burned a path through the dense underbrush. I looked at the bowman again, meeting his eyes just for a moment, then stepped onto the smoldering trail.

Raiden grabbed my arm, stopping me mid-step. "Why do we care at all about where *he* wants us to go?" he asked, nodding toward the bowman.

I met Raiden's questioning stare, then glanced at the bowman —at his strange golden skullcap—for a fraction of a second. I read Peri's thoughts, loud and clear. Orichalcum was a difficult metal to manipulate. It was volatile and unpredictable. Crude technology, as would likely be employed by people who looked as primitive as the bowman, wouldn't be capable of creating an alloy using the rare metal. It would be far more trouble than it was worth to create ornamental headgear from an orichalcum alloy, unless these people knew the true value of the metal. Unless they knew, somehow, that the orichalcum-alloy skullcaps would protect them, not physically, but psychically.

To Peri, it was obvious that there was more to these people than their primitive appearance let on. She wanted to know what, exactly, they were hiding.

I recalled the *them* haunting the minds of the Order's commandos, and I couldn't help but wonder if the bowman was one of them.

Annoyed by Raiden—a *man*—second-guessing her, Peri yanked my arm out of his grasp and turned my back to him. At her direction, I followed the trail cut by the doru's blasts, making my way to the broad base of the tree marked by the bowman's arrow.

The base of the ceiba's trunk was as wide as a bus, and its roots rose out of the earth like giant ribbons. I picked my way around the tree at the outskirts, where the roots were still low enough to step over. Slowly, I made my way around the enormous tree. Small noises alerted me to the presence of more of the bowman's people, hidden by the dense foliage and the darkness of night, minds masked by the orichalcum alloy.

Raiden followed me, mirroring Peri's annoyance. I had to remind myself that just because he was annoyed with Peri, didn't mean he was annoyed with me. Even if the emotion was aimed straight at me.

As I rounded the far side of the tree, a hollow between two towering roots came into view, cutting deep into the trunk of the massive tree. I moved closer, charging the doru with enough energy that the focus crystal glowed brighter. Electric-blue light cut through the even deeper darkness within the hollow, illuminating the ground's sharp downward slope further in.

"I don't think we should go in there," Raiden said, just a few steps behind me.

I inhaled deeply, sighing on my exhale.

Apparently, Peri and Raiden weren't destined to be best friends. They were both too alpha, their personalities guaranteed to clash.

I stopped in my tracks and spun around to face Raiden. Peri used my voice to spit a curse at him in her native tongue, then unceremoniously handed control of my body back over to me.

I stood there for a moment, staring wide-eyed at Raiden, stunned by the sudden shift back into the driver's seat.

The corners of Raiden's mouth tensed, and he stood a little straighter. His handgun was still drawn, but he was aiming at the ground. "Are you done insulting me?" he asked, raising one eyebrow defiantly.

"Yeah." I said. "I mean, it's me," I added, feeling awkward. I hugged the doru and kicked the side of a root. I averted my gaze to the hollow in the base of the tree, glancing at Raiden sidelong. "Sorry about that." I flashed him a weak smile. "She has kind of a strong personality."

Raiden snorted. *Strong* wasn't the word he would have used to describe Peri.

"I agree with her, though," I said before his thoughts could convince Peri she needed to teach him a lesson in respect. "There's a lot more to these people than it seems." I shot a pointed look to the dark hollow. "We should find out what it is they want us to see."

"Don't you already know?"

I shook my head, quickly explaining about the orichalcum alloy used in their skullcaps.

"Huh." The corners of Raiden's mouth turned downward in a curious frown. "That *is* interesting..."

I raised my eyebrows. "Yeah," I said with a nod. "So..." I looked from him to the mouth of the hollow and back.

Based on a combination of curiosity and the simple fact that he couldn't see a clear way out of our current predicament, Raiden nodded. "You've got the light," he said, giving the glowing doru a pointed look as he extended his arm toward the dark hollow. "After you."

[5]

The headache was worse again, but I pushed the pain to the back of my mind as we entered the hollow in the base of the massive ceiba tree. The glow from the focus crystal cast the interior of the hollow in an eerie blue light. Energy hummed along the length of the doru, gently reverberating up my arm.

Two steps into the hollow, the ground sloped downward at an angle steep enough to warrant stairs, though there were none, and the walls transitioned from wood to earth. This was no natural cavern. It had been tunneled out.

I held the illuminated end of the doru out in front of me like an old-fashioned torch and slowly made my way farther into the hollow. The temperature dropped the deeper we descended, and the hard-packed dirt floor gave way to stone stairs, looking to have been carved into the bedrock. With the stairs, came stone walls, chiseled into a rough arch shape that reached its apex several feet over my head.

After fifteen or twenty steps, the floor leveled out. The walls of the tunnel still bore chisel marks, but not everywhere, and the way ahead snaked gently in what could only be a natural pattern. At some point, this cave must have been widened to allow for comfortable passage. But when? And by whom? By the people who drove us into the hollow?

Or by Hades?

Raiden and I had been walking underground for about ten minutes when the cave widened and the illumination from the doru's focus crystal seemed to dim, the change almost imperceptible.

I glanced at Raiden over my shoulder. "I think it's getting lighter in here," I said.

Raiden nodded, gun drawn and eyes scanning everything. "Anything could be up there," he warned. "Be ready."

I gulped and nodded, returning my focus to the way ahead.

After another minute or two, we rounded a sharp bend and the light source came into view—starlight flooding in through an opening at the end of the cave. The floor dropped off right after the opening, and all that was visible beyond the mouth of the cave was a distant rock wall that shimmered faintly, reflecting the starlight. It looked like the tunnel was leading us to an immense cavern—one that wasn't entirely closed off to the aboveground world based on the silver light splashed across the rock wall.

I picked up the pace, eager to find out what lay at the bottom of the cavern. I didn't stop until I had reached the opening and had stepped out onto the ledge. Standing with the toes of my boots mere inches from the edge, I stared around in wonder, lips parted and eyes opened wide.

The cavern was enormous. High above, a hole in the cavern's ceiling—maybe twenty yards across—opened up to the rainforest. Vines and other, leafier vegetation spilled over the lip, and trees surrounded the opening like a crown, leaving a tiny patch of the starry night sky visible.

And what lay far below was no less remarkable. A pool filled the center of the cavern, crystal clear and still as glass, the water glowing with a strange bioluminescence that lit the cavern with a haunting silver glow. It looked incredibly deep, immense rock formations barely visible at the bottom, arching and twisting, hiding whatever secrets lay at the furthest depths. The pool was surrounded by patches of ferns, tall grass, and flowers scattered about the cavern floor, the flowers' vibrant pink, purple, and red hues muted by the silver light. Huge, pale waterlilies broke up the lily pads floating near the pool's edge. The scene was magical, looking like it belonged in some fantasy realm, the kind of place populated by faeries and elves, not here on Earth.

"Damn," Raiden said, coming to stand beside me on my right. He shook his head slowly, his expression displaying the awe I sensed emanating from him. "Have you ever seen anything like this?"

I shook my head, no clue why he was asking *me* that; *he* was the one who had traveled the world. I looked beyond him, to a stairway carved into the cavern wall. It was narrow—no wider than my shoulders—and far from even.

"Looks like that's our way down," I said, my heart rate increasing at just the thought of attempting to navigate that deathtrap. I quickly activated the regulator to mute my psychic senses, and the glow in the doru's focus crystal extinguished. The stars and sliver of a moon provided enough light to see by, and I would need every ounce of concentration to make it down to the bottom of the cavern alive.

"Lovely," Raiden said, his voice dry.

We exchanged a look, and I cleared my throat. "After you," I said, tucking the doru between my pack and my back.

Raiden shook his head again, then shrugged out of his bag and set it on the ground. Crouching down, he untied a coil of rope from the side of the pack. He created a loop at the end of the rope, knotting it tightly, and secured it around the base of a thick stalagmite near the opposite side of the ledge. He lifted his pack, resettling it on his shoulders, then wrapped the rope around his waist, pulling the loose end until the length between his body and the stalagmite was taut.

Raiden tossed the long tail of the rope over the ledge, watching it dangle over the surface of the pool for a few seconds before looking at me. "With the way the stairs follow the cavern wall, the rope won't reach all the way to the bottom," he cautioned me. "We'll have to make it down the final ten or fifteen feet of steps unsecured. And if you do fall," he added, "don't let the rope stop you completely, just let it pull you over the pool so you can drop into the water. You don't want to end up with internal damage or a broken back out here in the middle of nowhere."

Wide eyed, I nodded and backed up a step, clearing the way for Raiden to reach the stairs. I didn't want to end up with internal damage or a broken back *anywhere*, but I figured that was stating the obvious, so I didn't voice the thought.

Raiden passed me and started picking his way down the narrow, curving stairway. "Once I release the rope," he said without looking back, "wrap it around yourself and follow me."

I watched Raiden, breath held for longer than was comfortable. His pace was slow and steady, and he only had one scare, when the outer half of one step crumbled away underfoot. After that, he hugged the cavern wall even closer. By the time he released the rope, my heart was hammering and I felt like a sweaty mess, even with the hoplon suit's temperature regulator. Apparently it didn't do much for stress sweat. And I hadn't even stepped foot on the narrow stairway.

I waited until Raiden reached the floor of the cavern to start my own descent. I hugged the wall as closely as I could with the bulky pack on my back. The bag made me feel top heavy—not the best balance distribution for this situation—but wearing it was the only way to get it down without dropping it into the pool, and its contents were too precious to risk letting them sink to the farthest depths of the pool and out of reach of a free dive. I was the better swimmer between the two of us, but I was nowhere near that good.

As I made my way down the precariously narrow stairway, I steadily released slack to the rope encircling my waist, alternating which hand held the dangling tail end in a death grip. With every step, I held my breath, slowly easing my full weight onto the next stair, hoping the stone wouldn't break away underfoot. It made for extremely slow going.

I stared at the string of stone steps stretching out before me, knowing that looking over the edge to the bottom of the cavern would make it much more likely I would slip or trip and end up taking the fast way down.

"You're doing great, Cora," Raiden called up. "Just like that, one step at a time."

A laugh escaped from my throat, high-pitched and thready. My heart was a thudding lump in my throat, my ribcage a vice around my lungs.

I was almost to the part of the stairway that had crumbled out from under Raiden's boot. I paused two steps up, staring down at the five or so inches of stone stretching out from the wall, all that remained of the stair.

I swallowed roughly, then licked my lips. "Just do it," I said under my breath.

Two quick steps. Right foot. Left foot. Pause. It was over in a matter of seconds. Breathing hard, I leaned against the cavern wall, forehead resting against the cool stone.

The next few steps were comparatively easy, and my pace increased along with my confidence. The hardest part was behind me. It would be smooth sailing from here on out.

I had just released the end of the rope when the lip of a step crumbled under my boot. My heel slipped off the step, and I tried to regain my balance using my left foot, but the crumbled stone was like marbles beneath the soles of my boots. My feet slipped out from under me, and I landed on my butt, sliding down the remaining stairs with bruising efficiency.

I skidded to a halt with my butt on the second to last step, the heels of my boots finally finding purchase on the relatively flat cavern floor.

Raiden rushed toward me, slowing as I came to a stop. "Well, that's one way to get down…" He stood at my feet, arms crossed over his broad chest. "You all right?"

I blinked up at him, a deer in the headlights, not quite sure what just happened. Unexpectedly, laughter bubbled up from my chest and burst out of my mouth. I dropped my head back, relaxing against my pack, riding the wave of adrenaline making my blood seem to hum in my veins. Raiden's laughter joined my own, creating a chorus of hysteria-tinged hilarity that echoed throughout the cavern.

Once the adrenaline surge faded from a high to a low and I was left feeling shaky and slightly nauseated, my laughter died out. I stared up at the stars through the hole in the cavern ceiling and focused on taking deep, even breaths.

"All right, all right, enough lounging around," Raiden said, holding his hand out to help me up. "Besides, you're going to want to see this…"

I placed my hand in his and raised my eyebrows. "See what?"

"This," he said, grunting slightly as he hoisted me onto my feet and turned me ninety degrees. He pointed across the pool, toward the opening we had passed through high up in the cavern wall.

Dusting off my rear end, I followed his line of sight.

There, on the far side of the pool, beneath the ledge jutting out high above, an archway had been carved into the cavern wall. Tucked back under the ledge as it was, it would've been almost impossible to see from the hole in the cavern roof unless someone looked down at just the right angle, and even that was a stretch. A shorter, broader stairway carved into the stone wall lead up to a small landing in front of the archway. The archway itself looked strikingly similar to the entrance to the labyrinth in Rome, all the way down to the slab of stone blocking the opening.

My lips curved into a broad grin, and I tore my gaze from the archway to look at Raiden. "This has to be what Hades wanted us to find," I said excitedly.

Raiden nodded, the corner of his mouth lifting in a small but pleased smile. "My thoughts exactly."

Giggling, I jogged past Raiden and raced around the edge of the pool, pack bouncing against my back. I reached over my shoulder to pull the doru free and used it as a walking stick, helping to propel me up the stairs.

I stopped on the landing, doru planted on the stone floor, chest heaving with each quick breath. Slowly, I reached for the stone slab blocking the archway. Fingertips a hairsbreadth from the slab, I held my breath and moved my hand forward.

My fingers passed through the stone like it was no more substantial than air, and a faint tingling sensation danced over my skin.

I grinned ear to ear and pulled my hand back. "It's a hologram," I told Raiden, bouncing a little on the balls of my feet. I turned to look at him, assuming he had followed me up to the landing, but he wasn't there.

He had hung back, standing at the base of the stairs, his pack on the cavern floor. He was watching me, hands on his hips, no sign of following.

"What are you doing?" I asked, walking to the edge of the landing. "Get up here."

Raiden shook his head. "We don't know what's on the other side of that hologram."

"I know," I said, nodding. "That's why we need to go *through* it…"

"After we've rested," Raiden said, crossing his arms over his chest. "Let's take a second to clean up, have a bite to eat, refill our water bottles, and just breathe for a few minutes. A lot has happened in the last 24 hours, and we could both use a little R and R."

I turned back to the hologram and stared at it longingly. With a groan, I turned away and headed back down to the pool. My feet felt leaden as I plodded down the stone steps, and I admitted —reluctantly—that maybe Raiden had a point.

I rested the doru against a stalagmite near the cavern wall—I definitely didn't want it slipping into the pool and sinking to the bottom—then shrugged the straps of my pack off my shoulders and lowered the heavy bag down to the floor.

Raiden had already shucked his pilfered cargo pants and was perched on a stool-sized rock formation near the edge of the pool, wincing as he peeled off the blood-soaked bandage wrapped around his thigh. He must have popped some of his fresh stitches.

"Why didn't you say anything?" I asked, hurrying over.

"It's nothing," he said, cheek twitching as he peeled the final piece of gauze from the reopened bullet wound. The skin around the wound was red and puffy.

"Bullshit," I spat, stopping in front of him. It was my turn to plant my hands on my hips. "That's infected."

Raiden glanced up at me for the briefest moment, but his look said *"I know"* better than words ever could. "There's a broad-spectrum antibiotic in my first aid kit. That should knock it out," he said and returned to doctoring the wound.

I bit my lip, not feeling the same level of certainty he was projecting.

I would have offered to help, but Raiden had a lot more knowledge and experience with this sort of thing, so I made myself helpful in other ways. I prepped an MRE for each of us and filtered water from the pool to refill our water bottles. The water was cool and refreshing, and with every slow ripple, it beckoned me to dive in and wash off the sweat and grime I'd been unable to wipe away after my time trapped in the pit.

I finished refilling the water bottles and glanced over at Raiden. He was still perched on his rock, painstakingly redressing his wound. He wasn't paying an iota of attention to me.

Taking advantage of the relative privacy, I stripped out of the hoplon suit and down to my bra and underwear, then waded into the pool. The cool water spurred a wave of goose bumps, and I savored the chill.

I floated on my back in the center of the pool, staring up at the tiny patch of night sky visible through the hole in the cavern's ceiling. The old, familiar stars were right there, peeking through the leafy canopy, yet I felt like we had traveled to an entirely different world.

In my thoughts, this cavern existed in some fantasy land, plucked straight out of *Elder Scrolls*, my all-time favorite video game franchise. I was a wood elf taking a break from my quest to enjoy a dip in the healing waters of a mystical pool. I imagined the water, itself, was alive, healing my wounds and replenishing my strength. My health meter would be full by the time I left the pool, and I would feel like a whole new me.

If only that fantasy were further from the truth. Over the past week, my world *had* transformed, filled with aliens and psychic powers, and I *had* become a whole new me. Or rather, I had returned to being an *old* me. The original me. At least, part of me had. The Peri part of me.

But right now, regulator activated and Peri silent, I just felt like me. Like Cora.

I heard splashing near the edge of the pool and raised my head to glance Raiden's way. He had stripped out of his shirt, leaving him in just his boxer briefs as he stood knee deep in the water. His muscled torso was mottled with bruises from being beat on by Davidson and his buddies.

Raiden wadded up his dirty T-shirt and was repeatedly dipping it in the water, then wringing it out. After doing that a few more times, he dunked the T-shirt again and started wiping himself down. Water trickled over defined muscles, accentuating his honed, masculine physique.

Nothing more had happened between us since that night in Rome, and even that had been relatively innocent. I wanted more, even though the thought of being so intimate and exposed terrified me. Maybe when things calmed down and we were no longer running for our lives…

As my thoughts descended into the realm of all things scandalous and naughty, my concentration wavered, and my feet sank into the pool like stones, ruining my peaceful backfloat. I flailed and kicked, spluttering as I regained my bearing and attempted to keep my head above the water.

My neck and cheeks were on fire, and as I treaded water, I turned away from Raiden, hyperaware not only of his near nudity, but also of my own. I had been so focused on getting into the water while Raiden was distracted that I hadn't spared a single thought for how I was going to get back out. In my underwear. Practically naked. Even in the dim starlight, I felt extremely exposed.

Figuring I might as well get it over with, I spun around in the water and swam a lazy, head-up breaststroke toward the edge of the pool. Once my feet could touch the bottom, I stood and waded back to the place where I had left my discarded hoplon suit, a good thirty or forty feet away from where Raiden waded. I hastily swiped as much of the water off my skin as I could, purposely not looking in Raiden's direction, then wriggled into the hoplon suit. I was pleased to discover that the same moisture wicking properties that kept me more or less sweat-free in the suit also dried me off relatively quickly.

I headed back over to my pack, where I had left the MREs, and sat on the ground, using the cavern wall as a back rest. I picked up one of the warmed meal pouches—*Cheese Tortellini*, according to the label—and took a hesitant bite. A little bland, but not that bad. Not nearly as gross as the quote-unquote *Chicken Fajita*.

I took another bite. As I ate, I stared at the hologram tucked away under the arch at the top of the stairway, contemplating what might lie beyond. I was not watching Raiden dress out of the corner of my eye. I was *not*.

Raiden was soon fully clothed and heading my way. His limp was more pronounced than before, and I hoped the antibiotics kicked in soon so he wouldn't be so uncomfortable. As he sat on a squat boulder, I handed him his warmed MRE pouch—*Veggie Omelet*. Not one of Raiden's favorites, if his expression was any indication. Seeing the coagulated goop on his spoon, I could hardly blame him.

"Thanks," Raiden said anyway. He barely chewed, swallowing quickly, then picked up a water bottle and gulped down a few swigs. He set the water bottle down and cleared his throat. "Have a good swim?"

"Mmhmm," I mumbled, before spooning another bite of tortellini into my mouth. My neck and cheeks heated as I imagined him watching me in the water. It wasn't like he hadn't seen me in a swimsuit a hundred times before, but now it felt different. Now, him watching me meant something more.

"How's the leg?" I asked, avoiding looking his way and hoping it was too dark for him to see my blush.

"Good as new," Raiden lied. I didn't need to read his mind to know that.

I stared at him for a long moment, frowning, letting him see I wasn't buying his tough-guy act. Was his face slightly flushed? Was he sweating more than was warranted? I didn't know all the signs of sepsis, and I suddenly wished I had spent more time—or any time at all—studying first aid.

"We'll get you to a hospital as soon as we get back to civilization," I told him.

Raiden took another bite, murmuring his assent. I should have been happy he was complying, but it only made me worry more.

"Any guesses as to what we'll find in there?" I asked, figuring we both needed the subject change. I spooned another bite of tortellini into my mouth.

Raiden turned his head, glancing at the archway before meeting my eyes. "No way to say," he said. "And only one way to find out."

[6]

Standing before the hologram, I exchanged a look with Raiden. Only his eyes were visible above the respirator covering the lower half of his face. With the mask, his loaded pack, and his general soldier-y appearance, he looked like he had just walked straight out of the *Fallout* wasteland.

We had come prepared. The mold in the labyrinth had nearly taken me out, and Raiden had experienced the joys of inhaling hallucinogenic spores firsthand during our escape from the Custodes Veritatis. Whatever lay on the other side of this holographic stone slab, we were ready. Or, at least, as ready as we could be.

My regulator was deactivated, the stone in the pendant glowing electric blue. The channels running the length of my hoplon suit and the grooves carved into the doru as well as the focus crystal atop the staff glowed the same unnatural color.

I could feel Raiden's anxious anticipation, almost like it was my own. He put on a good show of stoic ambivalence, but he was just as curious as I was to find out what Hades had hidden on the other side of the hologram and just as eager to get to that fated prize before the Order found it. I also sensed he had been downplaying how much pain he was in—massively—and I was even more determined to complete our quest ASAP and get him to a place where he could receive the medical attention he needed.

I stepped through the hologram first, doru in hand and focus crystal charged, ready to blast any threat into oblivion. The holographic stone offered zero resistance, humming over my skin as I passed through it, the fuzzy static making my hair stand on end. The sensation lasted for a fraction of a second and was over almost as soon as it started. It was replaced by cool, dry air, a drastic change from the humid heat pervading every inch of the rainforest, even at night.

I looked around, heart sinking as disappointment settled in. The arched hologram was a dead ringer for the one beneath Vatican City. The resemblance didn't end there.

"Another labyrinth?" Raiden said, joining me on this side of the holographic barrier. He scanned the passage ahead, then turned to touch the hologram. His hand didn't pass through. It was solid. Which meant that, once again, the only way out was through.

The entry corridor looked the same as the one in Rome, all the way down to the iridescent spores floating through the air and the patchy layer of mold carpeting the ceiling.

I took a step forward, deeper into the corridor, and a pair of torches burst into flame from sconces set in the stone walls on either side of me. Two more lit further down the corridor, and two more after that. It was just like in the labyrinth in Rome, archways and crisscrossing passages and all.

Which meant more games. More riddles. More tests.

I closed my eyes, taking a deep breath of filtered air as I reined in my frustration. What was the point of all this? Was it just a wild goose chase? Was Hades playing an elaborate, millennia-spanning prank on humanity? On *me*? From Peri's memories,

I knew that she and Hades shared a complicated past. Was this his way of punishing her for something?

"Where's the book?" Raiden asked.

He was talking about the *Liber Veritatis*, which I had found in the hands of a dead priest in the other labyrinth. Before he died, the priest had mapped out the labyrinth's maze of corridors on the inside of the book's back cover. There was no guarantee this labyrinth was laid out the same, but we didn't have anything else to go on.

"Front pocket," I told Raiden, turning to give him access to my pack.

With the sound of a zipper and a few tugs on my pack, Raiden had the book free. He flipped open the back cover and quickly traced a path to the center of the maze with the tip of his finger, then looked up, staring down the corridor. "This way," he said and started walking.

I followed a step or two behind, doru at the ready, just the teensiest bit amused by the roles we had slipped into. In a weird twist of fate, Raiden was the navigator for this mission, and I was the muscle.

We took a right, then a left. Another right. Two more lefts, and another right. I lost track of what direction we were facing compared to where we had started. So far, the only difference between this labyrinth and the one in Rome was the lack of dead bodies.

My gut told me we had to be getting close when Raiden rounded a corner ahead of me and stopped mid-step.

"What is it?" I asked, joining him. "Did we reach the—" The next word died on my tongue.

The walls of the passageway ahead were spattered and streaked with a dark residue that could only be long-dried blood. A sound whispered up the corridor behind us, and I spun around to peer down the long passageway. Torchlight flickered, but nothing else moved.

"What?" Raiden looked at me, then followed my line of sight. "What is it?"

I shook my head. "I thought I heard something," I said, laughing under my breath. I adjusted the respirator's strap, ensuring that it was snug. Some of the spores must have been sneaking through, allowing the toxin they carried to mess with my head. Those same toxic spores had made me see and hear all sorts of horrors back in Rome. "It was nothing," I said. "I'm sure."

Raiden's eyes narrowed minutely, and he doubled-checked the fit of his respirator as well. After a quick glance down at the map in the book, he pointed to the blood-spattered corridor. "We go this way."

He started up the corridor, and I turned to follow. But at the faintest ghost of a whisper, I froze, glancing back.

There was nothing there. Just an empty corridor.

Gulping, I turned and hurried up the passage after Raiden. "I'm not so sure the respirators are working," I told him.

Raiden paused in the intersection between corridors up ahead, and in a flash, his sidearm was drawn and aimed up the left-hand passageway. "I'm not sure, either," he said, his voice low and carefully controlled.

I jogged forward and skidded to a stop beside Raiden.

A woman stood in the middle of the corridor, maybe one hundred yards away, completely nude. She was lanky, all jutting bones and wiry muscles, and her hair was a wild, knotted black mane that reached past her hips. She looked like she would belong perfectly among the tribal warriors we had encountered earlier—or like she *had* belonged among them, once upon a time. Now, she looked like she belonged in a horror movie; her tan skin was streaked with fluorescent veins, the same eerie, irra-diated shade of yellow-green as the mold on the ceiling. She faced us, but her head was angled downward, hiding her features from view.

"Do you see her?" Raiden asked without taking his eyes off the horrifying woman.

"Yeah," I said, my voice barely audible.

I aimed the doru in her direction, feeling the orichalcum staff start to vibrate as I charged it with psychic energy. "I don't think there's anything wrong with the respirators," I said.

"No shit," Raiden murmured.

The woman raised her head, and I took an involuntary step backward. Her eyes glowed with that same unnatural, irradiated yellow-green. She opened her mouth in a yawning scream, but instead of emitting any audible sound, a cloud of mold spores projected out of her.

A moment later, another naked person raced around the corner, rushing past her. This one was male, and young—barely a teenager—but just as severely infected with the mold. And just as terrifying. He sped up the corridor, heading straight for us.

I didn't want to blast him. He was just a kid. I sensed Raiden struggling with the same thing, even as the nightmarish boy charged us. The situation hit too close to Raiden's trauma from the war, and his thoughts and emotions were stuck in a disturbing feedback loop. He was frozen, paralyzed by his memories, unable to act.

I waited for Peri to take over and do what needed to be done. It would be a relief to have her take the decision out of my hands. To feel like the burden of killing this boy was hers, not mine.

Seemingly beckoned by the woman's silent call, another naked, irradiated person rounded the corner and charged up the corridor. A little girl. A moment later, another person joined the charge—a man, older but not old.

And still, Raiden stood beside me, frozen by the memory of his hellish past, and Peri wasn't even a whisper in my mind. Panic flitted in my chest.

Recalling the shield Peri had raised back at the Order's camp to protect us from the barrage of arrows, I extended my hand out in front of me. I imagined a wall of electric-blue energy blocking the passage in front of us, shielding us from the rabid people charging toward us. The psychic energy tingled as it flowed down my arm and into my hand.

One second, I was staring into the irradiated yellow eyes of the teenage boy as he closed in on us, the next, I was watching him through a glimmering, semi-transparent barrier.

The boy slammed into the barrier but yelped and leapt back, shocked by the living energy. But he didn't flee. For a long moment, he stared at me through the energy shield, shoulders rising and falling with each heaving breath. Without warning, he turned and ran up the corridor to the left. The little girl course corrected to follow him, as did the man a moment later.

I watched them through the energy barrier until they were out of sight. I had the sinking suspicion they weren't running away, but looking for a way around. And if they had been trapped in here long enough to become these unnatural human-mold hybrids, then they probably already knew exactly where to go.

"Raiden," I said, grabbing his arm and tugging hard.

He continued to stare at the woman through the energy barrier, but he wasn't seeing her, not really. His mind was trapped in a town in the middle of a desert on the far side of the world.

"Raiden!" I screeched, pushing into his mind and giving him the mental equivalent of a slap. "We have to move!"

He looked at me, eyes haunted. "What?" he asked, blinking several times.

"We have to go—*now*!" I told him, starting down the corridor and dragging him along by his arm.

Raiden looked over his shoulder, seeing the woman through the energy barrier, and finally snapped out of his trauma-induced daze.

I released his arm, no longer needing to drag him. He ran on his own, slowed by his limp, but far from slow.

We slowed from a jog to a walk as we reached the next intersection of corridors. The way ahead was blocked by a wall. Our only options were the passage to the right or the passage to the left.

"Which way do we go?" I asked, looking in either direction before turning my attention to Raiden.

His head was bowed over the book, one fingertip touching a point on the map. Our location, I supposed.

"We go right," he finally said.

We started down the corridor but came to a skidding halt when the teenage boy rounded the corner up ahead.

"Is there another way?" I asked, holding my hand out in front of me, preparing to form another energy barrier.

Raiden returned to examining the map. After several painfully long seconds, he nodded, eyes still locked on the book. "I think so," he said, tracing a path with his finger. "Yes," he amended, glancing at me, then at the boy charging down the corridor. "It'll take longer, but we'll get there."

"Good," I said, erecting an energy barrier just as the little girl rounded the corner. As this new barrier formed, I felt the other one dissolve.

We spun around and raced down the opposite passageway. I followed Raiden around dozens of turns, always setting up an energy barrier when we passed through an intersection, ensuring they could not attack us from behind. It seemed to take forever, but we finally made it to the puzzle wall at the center of the labyrinth.

Or, at least, we made it to the place where the puzzle wall *should* have been.

Raiden rounded the final corner. I followed a few paces behind and nearly slammed into the back of him. He stood there, staring down the long, dead-end passageway.

With the flick of my wrist, I created an energy barrier to block the passageway behind me, then stepped around Raiden. My mouth fell open as I saw what had stopped him short.

The floor was covered in a mass of bones—all human, from the looks of them. Mold cascaded down the walls and hung from the ceiling in thick, lumpy columns scattered haphazardly throughout the corridor. The torches on the walls were no longer visible, long since covered by mold, and the whole corridor seemed to thrum with a pulsing, fluorescent light. The mold spores floating around in this corridor were so thick that the air had a foggy quality. The mold in the labyrinth in Rome hadn't looked like this. The fungus in this labyrinth must have mutated while trapped down here.

Moving slowly, I made my way to the first column of mold. My stomach knotted, twisting with nausea as the shape of a hand became impossible not to recognize under the thick blanket of irradiated yellow-green fuzz.

"It's a person," I said, my voice hushed by horror.

The body had been strung up and hung from the ceiling, left for the mold to consume. I looked past the poor desecrated corpse to the other columns littering the passageway. They were all bodies. All people.

A chill crept up my spine, and I shivered from head to toe. I enjoyed horror movies, but I generally avoided the body horror subgenre. The images of graphically violated bodies from those movies tended to linger in my mind far too long, disturbing my dreams for weeks on end. Now, I felt like I had stepped into one of those disgustingly horrifying movies.

Behind me, I could sense Raiden moving closer. I took a backward step, leaning my shoulder against him, seeking comfort in someone so solid. So familiar. So alive.

The hoplon suit acted like a psychic conductor, opening up a clear channel from his mind to mine. I sensed the goodness at his core and the slowly mending fractures in his heart. As his arm slipped under my pack, curling around my waist, and his fingers sprawled along my ribcage, I sank into his mind. He was just as horrified by this scene—by these mutilated bodies—but beneath that, I felt a startling sense of compassion. Of pity.

"Why would anyone do this?" I asked him over my shoulder, unable to look away from the mold-covered hand.

"Survival," Raiden said. "Those people—however they ended up in here, this must be how they've survived. Cannibalism would only feed them for so long. They would have starved as soon as the meat turned rancid, and I doubt the stream of explorers has been steady enough to provide them with consistent fresh game. But by doing this,"—he gestured to the mold-covered body hanging from the ceiling—"they can harvest more mold and, who knows, maybe it preserves the meat as well." After a moment, he added, "Like dry-aged beef."

My stomach lurched, and I couldn't hold back the nausea any longer. I bent over, breaking free from Raiden's loose hold, and ripped the mask from my face just a moment before I spewed barely digested chunks of MRE onto the bones riddling the floor.

As soon the vomiting spell had passed, I secured the mask over my nose and mouth and closed my eyes. Hands on my knees, I took deep breaths, hoping the filtered air would clear my lungs of the toxic spores I'd inhaled while exposed.

I felt it the moment the boy slammed into my energy barrier. My whole body stiffened, and I straightened, turning to stare at the wall of shimmering blue energy. I feared a hard-enough impact would weaken the barrier, or that repeated impacts would wear it down. For now, at least, the barrier stayed strong. In fact, if anything, the contact seemed to strengthen it.

I peered at the boy, echoes of Raiden's compassion and pity spawning my own. This was no kind of life. Maybe killing them would be a mercy.

"I wonder how they ended up in here," I said, glancing at Raiden.

"Don't know," Raiden said. "And right now, I don't really care." His fingers wrapped around my elbow, his only concern getting me to safety. "Come on," he added, pulling me past the first column of mold and deeper into the passageway. Bones crunched and crumbled under our feet.

I swallowed roughly, stare lingering on the boy. The monster. The survivor.

"Cora," Raiden said, tugging on my arm.

Finally, I looked at him.

"Let's get out of here."

[7]

A thick wall of glowing mold, the irradiated luminescence seeming to pulse out of the fungus in waves, blocked the end of the corridor. Raiden and I stood before the obstacle, Raiden with his arms crossed over his chest, me with a hand on my hip and the end of the doru planted on the floor. If this labyrinth was like the one in Rome, then there would be a puzzle wall at the end of this corridor, and solving the puzzle and heading deeper into the labyrinth was the only way out of this sickening place.

Behind us, all four of the mold-infected monstrosities stood at the shimmering energy barrier, perfectly still, watching us intently. I could sense their proximity to the barrier, as well as their stillness, like the electric-blue energy that made up the barrier was still a part of me. It was psychic energy, created by my body and directed by my mind, so technically, it *was* a part of me.

"If it's just a thin layer, maybe we can scrape it away," Raiden suggested as he studied the wall of mold blocking our way.

I glanced down at his sheathed machete, frowning as I considered the suggestion. Eyes narrowing, I flipped the doru around so the butt end was pointed toward the mold and stepped closer to the poisonous curtain. The end of the doru slid into the wall of mold fairly easily, but the resistance grew stronger as I pushed, as though the mold became denser further in.

When the doru was buried up to the halfway point, I sighed and pulled the staff back out of the mold. "I think it's safe to say that scraping it away won't work, but…maybe we can blast it away."

I flipped the doru around again, aiming the focus crystal at the toxic mass. With barely a thought, I charged the focus crystal and sent out a minor energy blast. The ball of electric-blue energy pierced the irradiated wall of mold, creating a deep dent and sizzling over the surface.

But in a matter of seconds, the mold closed up around the hole.

And then it started to grow.

Mouth gaping, I stood frozen in place as I stared at the impossible reaction. The energy blast hadn't damaged the mold; it had *fed* it.

Raiden grabbed my arm and pulled me back a few steps. Just in time, too, because the place where I had been standing only a moment ago was quickly swallowed up by the swelling mass of mold.

Raiden gripped the handle of his machete and pulled the long knife free. I sensed his intent to hack through the fungus, to clear a way through with brute force no matter how deep a tunnel he had to carve into the mold.

"Wait," I said, my hand covering his, stopping him from raising the machete.

I glanced back at the fearsome family waiting hungrily on the other side of the energy barrier. I focused on the sense of them—of the mold that pervaded their bodies—so close to the sheet of shimmering electric-blue energy. Close, but not touching, because the energy barrier *hurt* them. Why didn't that sustained energy field empower their mold-infested bodies the way the energy blast had strengthened the wall of mold? It was the same mold…

Both times the boy had slammed into the energy barrier, it had seemed to weaken him. And at the same time, the barrier had strengthened. It was almost like an energy transfer, like my psychic energy was feeding off the boy. Or rather, off of the mold saturating his body, much as the wall of mold had fed off the energy blast from the doru.

But why the inverse effect? The only difference I could see was that the barrier was constantly being sustained by me. If I created a new energy barrier, this one would fall. I may not have been touching it, but it was still connected to me.

I blinked, an idea lighting my thoughts. I quickly slipped the bulky pack off my shoulders and propped it against the wall, then looked at Raiden. "I'm going to try something," I said, releasing his hand. Taking two steps forward, toward the swollen wall of irradiated mold, I held out my hand, palm out.

Raiden snagged my trailing wrist. "Cora—"

I looked at him.

"I don't think you should touch it," he said.

I flashed him a weak smile. "I'll be fine," I told him, sounding a whole lot more confident than I felt. I wriggled my gloved fingers at him. "Nothing's going to hurt me through this," I added, hoping my faith in the hoplon suit wasn't misplaced. "This will work, Raiden. Trust me."

After a long moment of loaded eye contact, Raiden nodded and released my wrist. It was a good thing he wasn't the one who could read minds. I was fifty-one percent sure this would work. But I figured those odds were better than the near certainty we would end up as dry-aged cannibal food if we lingered in the labyrinth for too long.

Holding my breath, I pressed my hand against the surface of the mold. The gloves of the hoplon suit allowed for near complete tactile sensation, so I could feel that the mold was warm to the touch, and that its texture was both soft and slightly sticky, not unlike cotton candy. A strange, familiar energy vibrated through it. It felt similar to my psychic energy. Not the same, but close.

Drawn to the energy within me, the mold slowly climbed up my fingers. I could feel it trying to suck the psychic energy out of me. I gritted my teeth, focusing on blocking the energy suction.

After a few minutes, my entire hand was engulfed. Fighting the urge to shriek and run, I forced myself to take deep, even breaths as I waited until my arm was buried to the elbow. The greater my contact with the mold, the stronger the energy suction grew. I closed my eyes, concentrating on fighting it.

"Cora…" Raiden's voice was filled with concern. He touched my shoulder, and in an instant, his fear washed over me.

My concentration slipped, and my eyes snapped open as the mold took advantage of my weakened defenses, sucking the energy out of me like my arm was its own personal straw.

"Shhh," I hissed at Raiden, scrambling to regain my composure and stem the leak.

I squeezed my eyes shut and took a deep breath, saturating my hand and arm with as much psychic energy as I could. As I released the breath, I unleashed the energy, sending it into the mold like roots branching out of my fingertips.

For a moment, black spots danced on the edges of my vision, and my legs weakened. My heart beat lazily and I wavered on my feet, almost completely drained of psychic energy as I pushed everything I had out through my hand.

A strained heartbeat later, I flipped the switch, and energy was suddenly flooding back into me. Far more energy than I had sent out into the mold crashed into me, knocking me to my knees. My heart beat wildly, like it had received a direct injection of adrenaline. I arched my spine and threw my head back, overcome by the sheer force of the power flowing into me.

"Holy shit," Raiden whispered. Or maybe he just thought it. I couldn't tell the difference in the tsunami of energy. "It's working!" he exclaimed. "Cora, whatever you're doing is working!"

Behind him, I heard the mold-infected people shrieking, the sound like buzzing flies compared to the roar of the energy torrent raging through me. The influx of raw energy seemed to go on forever, cramping my muscles and lighting my nerve endings on fire.

Until, all of a sudden, it stopped.

I collapsed forward, curling over my knees and resting my cheek on the stone floor. I pushed the respirator off my face and gulped in a lungful of clean, spore-free air.

I felt electrified, and when I opened my eyes, the world was tinged aquamarine and seemed to spark and sparkle. I stared at my hand, flopped on the floor a few inches from my face. Lightning danced over the surface of my glove, straddling the line between green and blue, and the channels of my hoplon suit glowed that same strange color. It was almost like the energy from the mold had fused with my natural psychic energy, creating something different. Something new. Something *more*.

"Cora?" Raiden's voice hummed with tension, and his concern drifted over me, strangely comforting.

From his thoughts, I learned that the mold was gone. Dried up and flaked away. All of it. From the ceiling and walls to the passageway ahead of us, the once luminous mold was little more than gray dust piled up on the floor. What had been columns of mold scattered along the corridor just moments ago had reverted to corpses in various states of preservation, ranging from relatively plump and fresh to shriveled and mummified.

And the four creatures who had been stalking us throughout the labyrinth were now just people, lying unconscious on the floor. Not dead. I could sense their minds. Dormant, locked in a state of unconsciousness deeper than sleep.

"Cora?" Raiden said, repeating my name as he crouched beside me. He dropped to his knees and bowed lower to the floor until his face was nearly in line with mine. "Are you all right?" I heard the question both in my mind and through my ears, and the effect was dizzying.

I blinked, focusing on his question. Was I all right?

I was alive, but that was the only thing familiar about my current status. I felt supercharged, full to bursting with energy.

"I don't know," I whispered. Tears welled in my eyes. "*Am* I all right?"

Raiden's concern deepened. He reached for my shoulder, and the moment his hand contacted my hoplon suit, I went into sensory overload. Raiden's life flashed before my eyes, coupled with a stabbing pain in my skull.

I screamed, jerking away from him so fast I slammed my shoulder into the wall. I slid back down to the floor, brittle, discarded bones crunching and snapping beneath me.

It took all of my concentration to raise one trembling hand and touch a fingertip to the regulator hanging around my neck. I traced my fingertip around the stone, activating the device that would suppress my psychic powers.

The relief was intense and instantaneous. The blue-green tinge faded from my vision, and my mind was blessedly, blissfully quiet.

For a long time, I simply sat on the bed of bones and worked on taking deep, even breaths. It took a while, but I finally slowed my breathing, and my heart rate followed. I still felt the wild, foreign energy within me, but it was subdued. For now.

"Feeling better?" Raiden asked, stiffly regaining his feet.

"Yeah," I tried to say, but no sound came out. I cleared my throat and swallowed roughly, then tried again. "Yeah—more like me and less like…"

"A lightning rod?" Raiden provided, eyebrows raised.

I laughed breathily and nodded. My attention drifted to the wall at the end of the passage. The puzzle built into the stones was now plain to see. It was exactly like the puzzle wall in the labyrinth in Rome, from the number of stone blocks with divots carved into their faces to the arrangement of the blocks in the wall. I just hoped that meant the solution to the puzzle was the same, as well.

My attention shifted to the four people lying unconscious on the floor at the other end of the corridor.

"What do we do about them?" I asked, glancing at Raiden.

They were murderers and cannibals, but there was no saying how much of that had been the mold and how much had been them.

"We get them out," Raiden said. "We can hand them over to the natives and be on our way."

I nodded, gaze returning to the wall. "I'll get started on the puzzle, if you want to move them closer while I work…" I glanced at Raiden sidelong.

He nodded and stepped closer, holding his hand out to help me up.

I hesitated, just for a moment. When my palm touched his, a shock of electricity sparked between us. Just a normal shock, powered by built-up static electricity. At least, that's what I told myself.

Once I was standing, Raiden released my hand.

I retrieved the doru off the ground, grunted as I hoisted my pack onto my shoulders, and headed for the end of the corridor. It was time to find out exactly what Hades was hiding.

[8]

"Eternal life, priceless treasure, or the knowledge of the ages," the hologram of Hades said. "The choice is yours."

Bouncing on the balls of my feet, I waited as Hades finished his spiel. The choice he offered here was the same as the choice had been in Rome. Even Hades' speech was identical to the one given by the other holographic recording, all the way down to the language—Latin—though the recording itself, was different. Hades still wore his pristine silver-gray suit, and he was still larger than life, brimming with otherworldly, elven beauty, but there was now a shadow to his icy blue eyes that hadn't been there before.

I moved closer to the hologram of Hades, my eyes locked on his face. I could feel Peri within me. She watched through my eyes, her longing for the man she loved spilling into me. Her mental presence seemed to aggravate my headache, and I raised a hand to massage the base of my skull.

Hades seemed older here, though I couldn't put my finger on what gave me that impression. He looked tired, his pale eyes haunted and his serene expression strained. How many years had passed between the construction of the labyrinth in Rome and the building of this one? And why *two* labyrinths?

The closer I moved to the lifelike hologram of the man Peri loved, the heavier my heart became. Tears welled in my eyes, and sadness constricted my throat. Why had Hades gone to all this trouble? This time, the puzzle wall led directly into this chamber—no gemstone riddle at all. Had Hades been in a rush to finish this labyrinth? Was that why it was an abridged version?

And why build them at all?

"What happened?" I wondered aloud as I studied Hades' features, my voice the faintest whisper. Both Peri and I wanted to know—what happened not just to Hades, but to all the Atlanteans here on Earth after her death?

The entrance to the Beta site was buried. What about the Alpha site? Were there other settlements? Were our people still here, still alive, living in their high-tech underground cities? Or were Hades and I the last two left alive—if he even *was* still alive?

I was three steps away from Hades when the hologram of him winked out of existence. For a moment, I simply stood there, disoriented as I stared at the place where he had been.

"Straight ahead, right?" Raiden said from behind me.

I started at the sound of his voice and turned partway to look back at him. "What?"

Raiden set the little girl on the floor beside the woman—her mom, based on the striking resemblance between the two. The girl looked much smaller and younger now that she wasn't rabid and charging at us. She couldn't have been more than five years old.

"We're going through the knowledge door," Raiden said. "Straight ahead, right?"

I blinked, returning to the here and now, and looked at the doorway in question—the middle archway of the three set into the wall at the far side of the chamber. "That's the plan," I said, my mind on the task at hand, though my heart still felt a million miles—and thousands of years—away.

I crossed to the archway in question and stuck my hand through the subtly glowing hologram blocking our view of whatever lay beyond. The hairs along my arm stood on end, and that increasingly familiar gentle tingle danced over my skin.

I pulled my arm out and looked over my shoulder at Raiden. "It's a hologram," I told him, planting a hand on my hip. "I think it's safe to assume we won't be able to pass back through once we're on the other side." I shot a pointed look at the family of four lying naked on the floor. "How do you want to do this?"

Raiden crouched and scooped up the little girl, cradling her in his arms. He stood easily, like she was made of feathers rather than flesh and bone. He closed the distance between us, holding her body out to me. "Here, see if you can carry her."

Frowning, I tucked the doru between my pack and my back and held my arms out in front of me. The handover was a little awkward, but I was surprised by how light the little girl really was. She couldn't have weighed more than forty pounds. While she didn't stink, exactly, a strong odor wafted off her frail body, reminding me of how Tila smelled when she was past-due for a bath.

"I've got her," I said, adjusting my hold on the little girl slightly. I looked at the other three labyrinth-dwellers. "And them?" I asked Raiden.

"I'll push the man and woman through, then come through with the boy," he said, already making his way back to them.

"Sounds good," I said with a nod and turned to the archway. "See you on the other side," I called back to Raiden. And then I took a deep breath, held the little girl tighter against me, and stepped through the hologram.

The chamber beyond was cloaked in absolute, choking darkness.

"Damn it," I hissed, eyes instinctively opening as wide as

they would go in a vain attempt to see. But there was no light, save for the subtle amber glow from the hoplon suit, which didn't do much of anything to penetrate the deep darkness.

Darkness had never been something I feared, but then, I hadn't ever experienced darkness like this, absolute and surrounded by the unknown. This was the kind of darkness that turned a sane mind mad. This was the kind of darkness that birthed monsters.

Feeling with my boot, I shuffled to the side, out of the path of the archway. The floor was rough and riddled with uneven grooves. I carefully set the little girl down on the floor and reached over my shoulder for the doru, pulling it free. As I set the staff down beside the little girl and started to slide one shoulder strap down my arm, I heard a shuffling sound behind me. Logic told me it had to be Raiden pushing either the man or the woman through the archway, but there was no saying for sure without a light source.

Heart pounding, I shrugged off the straps of my pack and set the heavy bag on the floor. I could have deactivated the regulator with a touch and created a ball of brilliant psychic energy to light the space, but I was too afraid of what would happen if I lost control of all the excess energy I had soaked up from the mold.

I could still feel it within me, dormant and contained, but just barely. It was waiting for me to let my guard down. To let it out. That was something that absolutely could *not* happen until I had put some distance between myself and other people. Like, miles of distance. There was no saying what might happen once the energy finally broke free.

Suppressing the urge to panic, I turned my pack around and unzipped the front pocket where I had stowed some of the survival supplies we had stocked up on back in Manaus. I fished around in the pocket blindly until I found the bundle of glow sticks held together with a hair tie. Hand trembling, I tugged one glow stick free, snapping it as soon as it was out of the pocket and shaking it frantically. The glow stick illuminated almost instantly, and I held it out toward the scuffling sound.

Much to my relief, the sound was just Raiden pushing the unconscious man through the archway. The woman already lay on this side, only her feet sticking through the hologram.

I placed the glow stick in my mouth, holding it sideways between my teeth, and stood, heading back to the archway. I crouched down and lifted the man by the armpits, angling my face away from him and holding my breath to avoid the intense cloud of body odor surrounding him. Unlike the little girl, he *really* stank. Once he was through, I moved on to the woman and pulled her the rest of the way through to this side of the hologram.

Lightheaded from holding my breath for too long, I scurried off to the side, inhaling deep lungfuls of stale but less pungent air. I didn't have a lot of experience with BO, mostly because I didn't have a lot of experience with people, but I felt certain this odor would have been overwhelming to even the most worldly traveler.

Once I felt a little steadier, I pulled the glow stick out of my mouth and turned to survey the room, holding the neon green stick up so I could see my surroundings. My brow furrowed.

The room was about the same size and shape as the chamber at the end of the labyrinth in Rome—circular and maybe twenty feet in diameter—but that and the archway framing the exit hologram on the opposite side of the space was where the resemblance ended. The stone walls and floor bore chisel marks, thick and uneven, like they had been hastily done. There was no pedestal. No storage cube or other artifacts. No alien symbols.

There was *nothing*. The chamber was empty.

Confused, I moved closer to the nearest wall and ran my fingers over the rough chisel marks. After seeing everything else Hades had built in this labyrinth, as well as in the labyrinth in

Rome, it was hard to imagine him leaving this final chamber unfinished.

Had something prevented Hades from completing his work? Cold dread washed over me. Had something happened *to him*?

I turned away from the wall, scanning the empty space, searching for some sign that my—and Peri's—worst fears weren't coming true. When my eyes reached the ceiling, I frowned.

The stone overhead was smooth and polished but otherwise featureless. Why would Hades have completed the ceiling first?

I held up the glow stick as high as I could and peered at the juncture between the ceiling and the wall. A rough border had been gouged into the smoothed surface, the stone scarred with more chisel marks.

I narrowed my eyes, understanding giving rise to hope. Hades hadn't left this chamber unfinished. Someone else must have made it here before me—*way* before me—and robbed this chamber bare. It had been stripped of everything, down to the polished stone floor.

Frustration boiled in my blood. I knew exactly who was responsible for this. I had stood in the transplanted chamber mere days ago, clueless as to the significance of the space.

The Order. The Custodes Veritatis. Their vault hidden beneath Vatican City *was* the final chamber from this labyrinth. That explained the vault's striking resemblance to the space at the end of the Rome labyrinth. *This* was where the Order had found their precious Atlantean artifacts. Where they had found *me*.

Which meant there hadn't been any point in us coming here. The geomarker in the holodisk had led us on a big, fat wild goose chase, and I was no closer to understanding anything. I was no closer to discovering Hades' fate. I was still clueless about why he had built the stupid labyrinths in the first place. And I had no idea what had happened to my people or if any of them were still alive. I didn't know anything now I hadn't known before. If anything, I only had more questions.

Frustration quickly transformed into anger. "Damn it!" I shouted, slapping my hand against the rough stone wall. I rested my forehead on the chiseled surface and closed my eyes. "Damn it," I whispered, feeling defeated.

"Well, this is unexpected," Raiden said, followed by a scuffling sound that must have been him setting the boy on the floor.

A silent, humorless laugh shook my chest, and I turned so I could see Raiden, the side of my head still resting against the wall. "No kidding," I said, then explained my theory about the Order finding and completing—and raiding—this labyrinth long ago. "So, this was all pointless," I finished, bitter resentment lacing my words.

Raiden glanced down at the four unconscious people lying on the floor near his feet. "I don't think everyone will see it that way," he said, his voice a low rumble. "Maybe we didn't find what we were looking for, but we saved *them* from a fate worse than death, so..."

"If they ever even wake up," I grumbled.

"And," Raiden continued, the sunshine to my storm clouds, "if the artifacts from the vault are what Hades originally stored here, then we already have the 'knowledge of the ages' and this was just a really long, really weird detour."

I blinked, processing what Raiden had just said. The artifacts from the vault—the doru, the hoplon suit, the regulator, the memory sphere, and the first storage cube—had all been stored in this chamber, once upon a time.

My eyes widened, and my lips parted. "The storage cube..."

With all of our focus channeled into the hunt for this place, I hadn't had a chance to examine the storage cube from the vault further, let alone to make sense of the mass of information stored on the second holodisk from the end of the Rome labyrinth. We hadn't had an iota of downtime, and I hadn't been about to pull the prize artifacts out in public.

I licked my lips. It wouldn't get much more private than this.

I jogged the five steps back to my discarded pack and bent over the bag, opening the main pouch. I shoved my arm inside, searching for the two cubes by feel. Each was approximately six inches by six inches and perfectly smooth.

I found one and pulled it free. Activated by my touch, a silver light illuminated grooves beneath the polished surface. With a hiss, the cube popped open.

But before I could do anything else, Raiden covered the cube with his hand. "Not here," he said, nodding down at our four unexpected burdens. "We need to get them out of here. Hopefully the natives have a healer of some kind."

I bit my lip, staring at the back of his hand like I could see through flesh and bone to the ancient storage cube and the answers it was sure to contain.

"Cora..."

I closed my eyes and bowed my head, knowing Raiden was right. These people's lives mattered more than my desire for answers. Besides, Raiden needed medical attention sooner rather than later.

"Okay," I said and opened my eyes. I raised my head, my stare locking with Raiden's. "Let's get them out of here."

[9]

One step out of the labyrinth, and my boot was nearly impaled by a spear. I froze, the tiny, naked girl cradled in my arms, and scanned the small clearing surrounding the labyrinth's exit and the dense vegetation beyond. It was still night, though there was a hint of lightening to the sky, dimming the stars. Dawn was approaching.

I didn't spot the warrior until he stepped out from his post behind a swath of massive fern leaves. He wore a hide loincloth, an orichalcum-alloy skullcap, and nothing else, save for the black designs tattooed onto his torso and arms and the red band of face paint stretching from temple to temple across his eyes.

The warrior raised his face to the sky and made a sound that reminded me of some of the monkey calls we had heard during our earlier trek through the rainforest. As his call died out, he lowered his chin and marched toward me.

I retreated until my back hit the solid surface of the hologram.

The warrior yanked his spear out of the ground and pointed the business end at me. "Put down the child," he ordered. In English. *Good* English, even if it was heavily accented.

I blinked, stunned. I had watched documentaries about the uncontacted tribes hidden deep within the Amazon Rainforest, and I had taken this warrior and his people for one such tribe. Apparently, I had been wrong.

Ever so slowly, I crouched down and laid the little girl on a bed of moss. I grimaced at the thought of leaving her there. I had seen enough creepy crawlies in my day and a half in the rainforest to scare me away for a lifetime.

Raising my hands in what I hoped was a universal gesture of surrender, I stood and straightened.

But the warrior's attention didn't follow me. Both his stare and his spear were aimed at the head and shoulders of the unconscious woman emerging from the holographic barrier.

"Adonya," the warrior said, burying the head of his spear into the ground and abandoning it as he rushed forward. He grasped the woman by her upper arms and pulled her the rest of the way out into the rainforest, then dropped to his knees and rested her head on his thighs. Ever so gently, he brushed her matted hair away from her face.

"You know her," I said, slowly lowering my arms as I watched his reaction.

"My sister," the warrior said without looking away from the woman's face. His expression was a strange combination of sorrow and wonder. "I thought she was dead; I thought they all were. After Tana and Oryn ran into the labyrinth…" The warrior shook his head, his brow furrowing. When he looked at me, his eyes were filled with questions. "How—how are they alive?" Again, he shook his head. "I do not understand."

I inhaled to respond, but the unconscious man's head emerged from the hologram before I could start.

The warrior gently scooted his sister's body off to the side, settling her next to the little girl. He rushed to the hologram and gripped the man by his underarms, hoisting the dead weight of his body out. "And young Oryn?" The warrior looked at me. "Is he alive as well?"

"Is that the boy?" I asked.

The warrior nodded.

Before I could confirm that the boy was, indeed, alive—if not exactly well—Raiden emerged from the hologram, Oryn cradled in his arms like an oversized ragdoll. Raiden took a single step into the rainforest and froze. But his eyes weren't on me or on the warrior crouching by the three unconscious people on the ground. He was looking past us.

I spun on my heel and watched as a band of these more-than-they-seemed tribal warriors emerged from the surrounding foliage.

There were seven of them, six men and one woman. The woman was short, lean, and her handsome features were gracefully lined by age. All seven newcomers wore loincloths and little more, leaving the intricate designs inked into the skin of their torsos and arms visible. The six men wore the golden skull-caps formed of the orichalcum alloy, but the woman's head was bare, her long, black hair pulled back into an intricate braid that fell down her back.

Only the woman wore anything on the upper half of her body, though clearly not for modesty's sake. A golden pendant dangled between her bared breasts, hanging from a thick gold chain. The pendant was about the size of a silver dollar, and the stone at the center glowed a brilliant peridot. The metal of the pendant wasn't gold, but orichalcum, and the pendant wasn't mere jewelry.

It was a regulator.

The six men stopped, fanning out in the small clearing, and the woman stepped forward. Clearly, she was in charge. She scanned the strange scene before her focus settled on me. She studied me for a long moment, her eyes lingering first on the doru and then on my own regulator, glowing a steady, subtle amber. Finally, her eyes met mine. A hint of that same lime-green glow from her regulator illuminated her irises.

"You have rescued four of our people," she said, bowing her head briefly. "For which we owe you a great debt." The woman straightened her neck, her strange eyes fixed on me. "I am called Ilyana, and I sense you have many questions. I will share what I can after you have had a chance to rest." She turned to the side and extended her arm. "Please, come with us."

Flanked by two of the male warriors, Ilyana led us along a broad, well-traveled path cut through the rainforest. Behind us, the remaining warriors marched along, carrying the labyrinth's unconscious victims. Ahead, the face of a sheer, towering cliff stretched up toward the sky, and a mass of greenery and vines cascaded over the edge high above. So far as I could tell, our current path dead-ended at the wall of rock.

As we neared the apparent end of the road, the two warriors passed Ilyana and approached the face of the cliff, no sign of slowing. And then they stepped through the wall of rock.

I grabbed Raiden's arm, and we halted mid-step, exchanging a look of surprise. Another hologram. I could only imagine what other secrets Ilyana and her people were hiding.

Ilyana stopped a few paces from the wall of rock, glancing back at us over her shoulder. "Come with us, and you shall find out," she said, obviously reading my mind. "Out here, you are hunted. You are in danger," she said. "But with us, you will be safe. The Custodes Veritatis cannot touch you within our city." And with that, she, too, stepped through the illusion.

I looked at Raiden, my hand seeking his. I felt paralyzed by the truth bombs Ilyana had just dropped. She knew about the Custodes Veritatis. She knew they were after us. Even if she had just skimmed that information from our minds, she spoke about the Order with familiarity. This wasn't the first time she had encountered the Custodes Veritatis.

"This is crazy," I breathed, staring at the place where Ilyana had been only a moment ago.

"No shit," Raiden said, his voice gruff. He squeezed my hand, and his lips curved into a faint smile. "I've got your back, no matter what," he said. "It'll be okay, Cora. And, hey—maybe we'll finally find those answers you've been searching for..." Though his words expressed confidence, his eyes were shadowed with uncertainty.

I could hardly blame him; there was a lot to feel uncertain about. Ilyana wore a regulator. She had psychic abilities—like me. And yet, so far as I could tell, she was human. All the other Atlanteans I had seen in Peri's memories had a distinct, not-quite-human quality—too tall, features too sharp, a hint of incandescence to their skin. Rather, all the Atlanteans I had seen in Peri's memories, except for Peri, herself. Except for me. For some reason I didn't yet understand, I looked more human than the others of my kind.

Maybe the same went for Ilyana. After everything that had happened over the past week and a half—after all that had been revealed—I knew better than to assume *anything* anymore. Her people clearly had access to Atlantean tech, so maybe she was Atlantean. Maybe she was more like me than I knew. And maybe she knew where to find Hades. So many maybes...

One thing was certain, though; I wouldn't find out anything standing on this side of the hologram.

I nodded to Raiden, and together, we pushed on, heading for the hologram built into the wall of rock.

The illusion tingled over my skin, and a moment later, we entered a long, straight tunnel. The walls were a concrete-like material—and ancient, based on the pattern of erosion. They were reinforced with periodic posts and beams of pristine stainless steel, cut through by faint golden striations—orichalcum, for strength, I figured. Light bars had been built into the edges of the beams, illuminating the tunnel with a soft silver-white glow.

The passage was narrower near the ceiling than at the floor, which tickled my memory. Or rather, Peri's memory. The tunnel was shaped exactly like the passages aboard the *Tartarus*, the ship that brought Peri and the rest of the Atlanteans to this planet thousands of years ago.

As we followed Ilyana deeper into the tunnel, I leaned closer to Raiden. "This tunnel was built by Atlanteans," I whispered.

Raiden glanced at me, his eyes narrowing, then returned to watching Ilyana ahead of us. "It doesn't look like the labyrinth."

I shook my head. "Atlanteans didn't build that," I told him. "Humans did—at Hades' direction and with his help with the mechanics. But for the overall structure, I think he had to rely on what was, at the time, technologically feasible for humans, construction-wise."

Raiden grunted faintly. "So, what are you saying—you've been here before?"

Again, I shook my head. He was asking if *Peri* had been here before, but so far as I knew, she hadn't. At least, not in any of the memories I had seen. "This tunnel reminds me of the ship that brought them—*us*—here," I said, correcting myself.

Up ahead, the tunnel dropped off, giving way to a series of broad, shallow steps. The edge of each step was illuminated with a glowing strip, just like the beams overhead. At the bottom of the stairway, the tunnel stretched on for another four or five yards, then widened, though I couldn't yet see what lay beyond. I had a hunch we were about to walk into the once-abandoned Beta site. Or maybe it had never been abandoned in the first place?

"Do you want to take over," I thought at Peri. I only had bits

and pieces of her memories, leaving me with a scattershot understanding of her—our—people. I had one foot in two worlds, belonging wholly to neither. But Peri knew everything about this world because this world was *her* world.

There was no response from Peri.

"Peri? Are you there?" I thought at her even harder, earning myself a sharp stab of pain behind my eyeballs for the effort.

I pulled my hand away from Raiden's, raising both of mine to massage my temples with my fingertips. I needed to get some rest, to sleep off whatever remained of the drugs the Order's commandos had shot me up with and hopefully burn off some of the excess energy I had absorbed in the labyrinth.

"You all right?" Raiden asked.

I sighed, lowering my hands. The massage wasn't doing anything besides make me think about the headache even more. "Just tired," I said, glancing at him sidelong as we descended the final few stairs. The temperature was dropping notably as we delved deeper into the earth. "How about you?"

"I'll be fine," Raiden said, his voice a gentle rumble. But the sheen of sweat coating his brow and the pronounced limp marring his gait suggested otherwise.

Eyes narrowing, I raised one hand to press the backs of my fingers against his forehead. "Jesus, Raiden, you're burning up!" I hissed, grabbing his wrist and pulling him to a halt. "The infection must be worse. Why didn't you say anything?"

Raiden's eyes met mine, a feverish fire burning in his gaze. It hadn't been there a few minutes ago. "I'll be fine," he repeated, pulling my hand from his wrist, then releasing it. "Just need some R and R." He continued on his way, limping along and leaving me behind to stare after him.

From this angle, he looked like his usual, sturdy self. Even with the limp. But he was lying to me. He wasn't fine. The antibiotics weren't working, and no amount of resting or recuperating was going to make up for the medicine's shortcomings.

Raiden was running out of time.

I jogged ahead, passing Raiden as I closed in on our mysterious guide. "Ilyana," I called ahead, slowing as I neared her.

Ilyana stopped in the mouth at the end of the tunnel, eyebrows raised.

"My friend needs medical attention," I said, pointing over my shoulder with my thumb. I took two more steps and stopped in front of her. "Do you have a medicine woman or man, or a healer or…" I shrugged. "Or anything like that?"

"No," she said, turning away from me and stepping out onto a broad metal platform that extended the floor beyond the mouth of the tunnel.

My heart sank. If Raiden didn't get the medical attention he needed, and soon, he was going to end up with sepsis. I might not have any medical training, but I had seen enough movies and TV shows to know what blood poisoning looked like. And to know it could turn lethal in a heartbeat.

"We have no need of people with such skills," Ilyana said, glancing at me over her shoulder. "Not here."

"What do you—" But the question died on my tongue as I joined her on the platform.

The platform was positioned about halfway up the wall of an enormous cavern. The cavern's stone walls arched high overhead to form a perfect dome. At the very apex of the ceiling, a burning orb glowed with a blinding light, like a miniature artificial sun. Far below, graceful buildings jutted up from the cavern floor, topped with endless stone spires, looking almost like enormous stalagmites. The sight gave me the impression that the compact underground city hadn't been built, but grown. A band of water encircled the settlement, flowing counterclockwise around the outermost edges of the cavern, and green blanketed the walls to at least a quarter of the way up from the cavern floor.

This was unlike anything I had seen in Peri's memories, and I doubted my certainty that I was looking down at an Atlantean settlement at all.

"What is this place?" I asked, my voice filled with wonder.

"It was called Vytopoli, once upon a time," Ilyana said. "But we call it Akahim."

"So it *is* the Beta site," I murmured, automatically translating the original name from Atlantean to English. The current name, *Akahim*, was no less interesting. It belonged to one of the fabled lost cities mentioned in the *Chronicles of Akakor*, an exaggerated account of a mythical ancient civilization given by a fraudulent indigenous chieftain from Brazil.

I sensed Ilyana's stare on the side of my face. A quick glance her way told me her expression was carefully guarded.

Dozens of questions buzzed around in my mind, but none of those questions were as important as Raiden's life. Tearing my stare from the city below, I turned to face Ilyana, shooting a furtive glance at Raiden as he stepped onto the platform. "Isn't there anyone down there who can help him?"

Ilyana's stare slid past me to Raiden. "I can sense his pain," she said. "His need for healing is great. It is taking all of his willpower just to remain standing." She returned her attention to me. "The asclypos should be able to fix him."

I thought her word choice was strange—*fix him*. Like he wasn't a person at all. Like he was a thing. But the thought was fleeting, and my mind fixated on another word: asclypos. So similar to the name of the ancient Greek god of medicine, Asclepius. Even as I thought of that mythological figure, the part of my brain that understood the Atlantean language knew Ilyana wasn't talking about any being. *Asclypos* wasn't the name of a god; it was a machine, and its sole purpose was to heal.

Ilyana nodded to one of the warriors now standing near a small lever sticking out of the wall to the right of the tunnel mouth. He shifted the lever, angling it downward. With the flip of that switch, the platform shifted beneath our feet, dropping in a smooth, steady motion.

The movement was too much for Raiden's unsteady legs, and he stumbled down to one knee, holding himself partially upright with a fist planted on the swiftly descending metal platform.

"Raiden!" I rushed to him, dropping to my knees in front of him and pressing my hands to either side of his face. "It's going to be okay," I told him. "We're getting you the help you need right now. You're going to be all right. Just hang in there…"

Raiden's eyelids flitted lower, barely staying open. He leaned into me until his head rested on my shoulder and I was supporting the bulk of his weight.

I braced the toes of my boots on the ridged metal floor, countering his weight, and looked at Ilyana. "He can't walk," I told her, my hold on Raiden wavering as, with a metallic *clang*, the platform came to an abrupt halt. "We'll need to carry him."

Ilyana glanced at the two men posted on either side of the platform and gestured toward us with a nod. She raised her fist, palm up, and uncurled her fingers. A horizontal sheet of lime-green energy appeared behind Raiden's head, almost his exact size. She had created a stretcher for him.

"Take our guest to the asclypos," Ilyana commanded.

The warriors quickly lifted Raiden and arranged him on the shimmering green stretcher. The sheet of energy didn't budge under his weight, hovering steadily about three feet above the ground. I watched them propel him off the platform, following a paved path that led to a narrow bridge arching over the stream.

Like the buildings, the bridge looked like it might just be a conveniently placed natural rock formation. Nothing about the arching stretch of stone appeared to have been worked by humans—or by Atlanteans. And yet, the base was too flat, the uneven railing too convenient.

The warriors guided Raiden's stretcher over the bridge, and I took a step toward the edge of the platform to follow.

Ilyana's fingers curled around my arm, just above my elbow, holding me back. "Come," she said, gesturing to the opposite side of the platform. "Your companion will be in the asclypos for some time. Let me show you to a place where you will be able to rest comfortably."

My focus shifted from Ilyana's hand on my arm to her face and then back to Raiden. "I'm not going anywhere without him," I said, pulling my arm free from her grasp.

I took three steps toward the edge of the platform, following the path Raiden's stretcher had taken.

A shimmering lime-green energy barrier flashed into existence in front of me, blocking the way.

"I'm sorry," Ilyana said. "But I'm afraid I must insist you come with me."

Anger coiled my muscles, and I clenched my jaw. "Let me pass," I said, my back to her.

"I cannot," Ilyana said, her voice closer behind me. "Not until we have become better acquainted."

My hands balled into fists. I raised one hand, intending to deactivate the regulator.

"*No!*" Peri's voice gonged throughout my skull, worsening the headache throbbing behind my eyes. My arm froze when my fingertip was barely an inch from the pendant's stone. Peri had taken over.

Now that she was in control, her mind was an open book to me. I could see she feared what might happen if I deactivated the regulator while still supercharged with all the energy from the labyrinth. She hadn't known it was possible to absorb energy like that, and she didn't know what would happen if—when—I unleashed the raw, foreign energy. She imagined a blast akin to a nuclear warhead, leveling this whole underground settlement and burying us under a mountain of stone.

"The Custodes Veritatis raided the labyrinth and stole some extremely valuable artifacts over a century ago," Ilyana said, oblivious to the battle taking place within me. Her hand settled on my shoulder. "And now, here you are, wearing two of those artifacts and carrying another."

Something warm and metal closed around my neck. My hands flew up to the thing encircling my neck as panic caused a surge of adrenaline. Peri—calm, controlled Peri—was suddenly on the verge of losing her shit.

I pulled snippets from her mind, filling in the missing pieces.

A collar. An Amazon collar. A device created back on our home planet, long before Peri's time. A device designed with a single purpose—to give another control over an Amazon's psychic powers.

Peri had been collared once before, thousands of years ago.

The day she died.

"I wish this wasn't necessary," Ilyana said, her hands forming a cage around the sides of my head. "Please try not to resist…"

Her final word was drowned out by a rushing sound, like water pouring over a cliff. Fog closed in all around me until there was nothing but white. Nothing but the raging water.

Until, eventually, there was nothing at all.

[11]

They say in the instant before you die, your life flashes before your eyes. All the moments that gave meaning to your life, that shaped you—every significant interaction, every notable choice, everything that ever mattered to you—flickers through your mind. The good. The bad. And in my case, the pathetic.

I wasn't dying. At least, I didn't think I was dying. But I definitely had the life-flashing-before-my-eyes experience as Ilyana rifled through my memories, searching my past for answers to a question only she knew. I wasn't awake, exactly, but I was present. Aware. Along for the ride.

Peri stood at my side, a silent observer watching Ilyana walk around within my memories. Ilyana had swapped out her mini-malistic primitive garb for a long, white silken tunic, cinched at the waist by a beaded gemstone belt. She would pause a snippet of a memory here or there, replaying it to examine certain bits and pieces of my life further. She didn't seem to be aware of Peri's and my mental projections, like we stood on the observer side of a two-way mirror. So far as I could tell, Ilyana didn't even know about the split consciousness. She only flipped through my own memories, never once pulling up one of Peri's, buried deep beneath my own.

I was a baby in the memories, then a toddler, then a little girl. Ilyana focused on my schooling the most, on my lessons with Emi and with my mom. On the things they taught me. She honed in on forgotten moments from when my mom was writing in her journal or when she was speaking to Emi about me—moments I had been oblivious to. Until now.

Ilyana spent an eternity examining the moment when Emi and I opened the mysterious package from my mom. A little over a week had passed since then—a mere blip of time—yet, I felt ancient in comparison to the naïve, terrified girl in the memory.

"Hades must have done something to these people," Peri said, her hushed voice breaking the silence. "They're human," she added, "and yet, they're more…"

I looked at Peri, my gaze skimming over her face. We both wore the hoplon suit—the exact same hoplon suit—but even dressed the same, there were more differences between us than similarities. She was harder, her spine straighter and her muscles stronger. Her hair, pulled back into a tight bun, accentuated her angular features—*my* features, just maybe a decade down the road. She was confident and tough and capable in ways I had never been and doubted I ever would be.

Standing beside Peri, I felt like a child. A little girl dressed up in mommy's clothes, feet drowning in her shoes.

Peri was the stronger, better version of me. The ideal. She could handle things I couldn't, in ways I couldn't. Like the Order's commandos. Like Davidson. I was just a pale imitation of the original. In our case, they really didn't make them like they used to.

"You're sure they're not Atlantean?" I asked.

"Olympian," Peri corrected. "We come from the planet Olympus. Atlantis was our name for *this* planet." She glanced at me sidelong. "So, technically Ilyana *is* an Atlantean, but she's not one of us."

I narrowed my eyes. "How can you tell?"

Peri frowned, her brow furrowing as she studied the other psychic. "It's hard to explain," she said after a long moment. "It's just a feeling. I wasn't sure until she invaded your mind. Now that I've felt her psychic touch, I know for sure."

"Hmmm…," I said, returning my stare to the woman treating my memories like her own personal Netflix subscription. "You know, I really could've used your help earlier."

Ilyana was now pouring over my mom's journal, slowly examining every page as the version of me in the memory flipped through the book.

"Where were you?" I asked Peri. "Davidson almost killed me."

Peri had had a front-row seat to my every thought and feeling over the past ten days, and the same went for me when she was in the driver's seat. I knew her better than anyone else, and I could only assume it was the same for her. It seemed unavoidable that a certain level of intimacy would develop when two minds shared a body.

But standing here, talking to Peri—I felt awkward. Not like I was talking to a stranger. The opposite. Like I was talking to myself, someone I couldn't lie to. Someone who knew me too well.

"I don't know," Peri said, staring ahead. Out of the corner of my eye, I watched her shake her head. "I was there, but—" She frowned. "I could see and feel everything happening to you, but I couldn't get out. I don't know if it was the tranquilizer, or…" Again, she shook her head.

I glanced at her. "Or?"

"It's getting harder," she said, her eyes meeting mine, just for a moment. "Taking control—and giving it back." She pressed her lips together, forming a thin, flat line, and inhaled deeply through her nose. "I think something's wrong," she said on her exhale. "The headache…"

Dread pooled in my belly. "*What* about the headache?"

Peri raised one hand, rubbing her temple. "It's strange," she said. "I feel like I'm being pushed further and further into the periphery." She took another of those slow deep breaths. "The more I resist, the worse the headache gets." She sighed. "I fear our brain isn't equipped to handle a fractured consciousness."

"Oh," I said, swallowing roughly. Fractured consciousness. That didn't sound good at all. "Well, if that's the problem, what can we do about it?"

"I honestly don't know," Peri said, letting out a humorless laugh. "I could be wrong. I hope I am. This could be nothing— just a hangover from the tranquilizer, or a byproduct of the excess energy stored in our body." After a moment, she added, "Or, it could be what I fear, but I only know of one person who would be able to tell the difference…or who might know how to help."

She was talking about Hades, of course. It always came back to Hades. "What about the asclypos?" I asked.

Peri shook her head. "If the issue is indeed a fractured consciousness, then the asclypos would only help temporarily, treating the damage but not dealing with the root cause."

I blinked, an idea forming. "What if our consciousness *wasn't* fractured?" I asked, holding my hands out in front of me, fingers spread wide. "What if there's a way to, I don't know"—I moved my hands together, my fingers interlocking—"blend our two selves together?"

Peri's eyebrows rose, like she hadn't considered that possibility. I could hardly blame her; while I would leap at the chance to become more like her, I doubted the same could be said for her of me. Talk about a downgrade…

"There's only one person in existence who would even have an idea of how to pull off such a thing," Peri said.

As if on cue, the holographic projection of Hades appeared as Ilyana followed the memory version of me through the labyrinth in Rome.

So much was riding not just on finding Hades, but on finding him *alive*. "But what if Hades is dead?" I said, voicing my worst fear.

Sorrow tightened the skin around Peri's eyes, and she pressed her lips together, nostrils flaring. "Then he's dead." She glanced at me sidelong, the corner of her mouth raising in the slightest, defiant smile. "But then, so was I."

[12]

I woke slowly, feeling rested and rejuvenated. I rolled onto my back, sinking into the soft bed, and stretched my arms out over my head. My toes pointed, and I groaned, my whole body shaking with the strength of the stretch. Peri must have been wrong about the fractured consciousness diagnosis because only the faintest hint of a headache pulsed behind my eyeballs.

My eyes snapped open, and I sat up, sheets pooling around my waist. I scanned my surroundings, momentarily disoriented. I had no idea where I was.

The room was square with pale, polished stone walls. The stone had a pinkish hue that reminded me of quartz. The bed was long and narrow with a wood frame, utilitarian in design, and it took up the entire length of one wall. The sheets were white and incredibly soft, like the finest silk, but heavier. An unbroken bar of dim, golden light shone from the crease between the walls and ceiling all around the room. The only furniture besides the bed was a small, half-moon table set against the opposite wall and the pair of chairs tucked beneath it, all wood and of a similar, simple design to the bedframe. The hoplon suit was folded up on the table, and the doru was propped against the wall nearby, beside my pack.

There was no door.

Panic made my heart stumble, and I scrambled out of the bed, kicking off the sheet tangled around my legs. I was barefoot, and a quick glance down told me I was wearing a light tank top and shorts made of the same, silken fabric as the bed sheets.

"Ilyana!" I shouted, turning around and around, like a door might suddenly appear in the unbroken stone walls. My chest rose and fell with each heaving breath. "ILYANA!"

"You are awake," a woman said from behind me.

I spun around. "Ilyana—"

But the woman standing in a doorway that hadn't been there a moment ago was younger than Ilyana. Younger than me. Little more than a girl, she was short and tan, modestly garbed in a long, white gossamer shift that nearly skimmed the floor. Her features were bold, her nose hawkish, and her gray-green eyes seemed too large for her face. She carried a tray of food, and the pendant hanging on a chain around her neck glowed a vibrant rose pink. A regulator.

I backed up a step, eyes locked on the glowing device.

"Oh no! Please, do not worry," she said, rushing to set her tray on the table before touching a fingertip to the stone in her regulator. A moment later, the bright rose-pink glow faded to a subtle amber. "We mean you no harm, ancient one," she said, bowing her head. "We removed the collar. Please do not be afraid."

I brought a hand up to my neck, feeling for the warm touch of metal I remembered from my arrival. My neck was bare.

"Ilyana feared you were working with *them*," the girl said. "That is why she did what she did. But now we know who you are and why you are here and, well…" The girl reached into a pocket hidden in her skirt. "Ilyana is busy talking with the High Council right now, but she wanted me to give you this," the girl said, holding out her open hand. A holodisk rested on her palm. She set the ancient storage device beside the food tray on the little table. "Ilyana also wanted me to inform you that while you are not a prisoner, it will be safest for everyone—including you—if you remain here until she returns."

I clenched my jaw, fighting the urge to argue.

Fear flitted across the girl's face. "I am sorry, ancient one," she said, her words falling out in a rush. "We are not accustomed to outsiders being here, and Ilyana and the High Council must prepare our people—explain who you are and why you have come." The girl backed up a step. "I, um…I will be outside if you need anything," she said, turning abruptly and stepping toward the doorway.

"Wait," I said, reaching for her vainly.

One foot in the doorway, she looked back at me.

"My friend," I said, lowering my arm. "I need to know—is he okay?"

The girl nodded, a tiny smile curving her lips. "He is sleeping now, but he is well."

"When can I see him?"

"Ilyana has arranged for him to be sent here as soon as he awakens," the girl said. "It may be a while yet. The healing sleep one enters after a session in the asclypos can last days…"

Frustration bubbled within me. If I wasn't a prisoner, then I didn't see why I couldn't visit Raiden, just to see for myself he truly was all right. I inhaled deeply through my nose, exhaling slow and steady, just as I had seen Peri do. And then I nodded.

"What's your name?" I asked the girl as she turned away from me again.

She smiled at me over her shoulder. "Calysto, but everyone calls me Caly." She stepped through the doorway, and a moment later, the opening vanished behind a wall of stone.

Another hologram.

Curious, I crossed the small room in all of five steps and

reached for the holographic stone surface. It was solid, smooth, and warm, and it sent the faintest tingle up through my fingers. I was pretty sure Caly had activated the holographic barrier psychically, which meant I could probably *de*activate it the same way, but that would require risking unleashing all of that wild, raw energy, something Peri had been pretty terrified of letting happen.

I inhaled deeply, blowing out the breath in a huff, and turned away from the hologram. My eyes landed on the tray of food, and my stomach rumbled.

A large, earthenware bowl was filled almost to the brim with a steaming, aromatic broth. Caly must have used some psychic tricks to keep the liquid from splashing over the edge. A stack of golden-brown flatbread was partially wrapped in a cloth napkin and set off to the side of the bowl. There was also an earthenware jug and a matching cup, and not a piece of silverware in sight.

I pulled out the chair and sat, sniffing the steam coming off the broth. It smelled amazing—rich and savory, and just slightly herbaceous. Unable to resist, I lifted the bowl to my lips and took a tentative sip.

The broth was even more delicious than it smelled, and it warmed me to the core. I gulped the rest down in a matter of minutes, then munched on a flatbread while I lifted the jug to fill the cup. A pale golden juice poured out.

I picked up the cup and brought it to my lips, sipping cautiously. It was warm and faintly bitter, a little shocking to the senses when I had been expecting something cool and sweet, like apple juice. It wasn't bad, and once I had pivoted from thinking of it as juice to tea, it was actually quite nice. It reminded me of chamomile tea, but with a floral aftertaste that brought rose petals to mind.

As I ate, my gaze drifted to the holodisk sitting on the table. I set down the cup and picked up the holodisk, flipping the disk over one-handed so it rested flat on my palm.

Activated by my touch, an image flickered in and out of existence above the disk. A hologram. A man, miniaturized and standing over the palm of my hand.

Hades.

He was absolutely still, frozen, until the holographic image stabilized, and he came to life. He looked much the same as he had in the second labyrinth—a little older, more than a little weary, and somehow less sure of himself.

"Peri," he said, a smile curving his lips. It didn't touch his ice-blue eyes. "It worked; you're alive." He spoke in Peri's ancient tongue, and though I could understand him, there was a lag in my brain as the latent knowledge I had gained from Peri kicked in to translate.

"More or less," I said, responding even though I knew this was a recording and Hades couldn't actually hear me.

"I have no way to predict how long will pass from when I record this to when you view the recording. Barring another malfunction, I should still be alive—in cryosleep in the Omega site." He exhaled heavily. "You've never heard of the Omega site, I know. We built it when we first arrived as a failsafe—a cryogenic storage facility and data repository—a last-ditch effort to preserve our civilization should some unforeseen catastrophe destroy our settlements."

I frowned. I knew Peri had trust issues where Hades was concerned. He had deceived her in the past. Now, he was admitting to yet another lie.

"I left a holodisk with the location of the Omega site in the chamber with you and your things. The cube is keyed to your genetic code, so only you can access the location." He looked down, combing his fingers through his shoulder-length blond hair. "If you're watching this recording, then something went wrong, and your transition into this cycle was rougher than planned." He shook his head, then looked up. "I'm sorry for that,

Peri. I should have been there to ease your transition into this new cycle, but…"

Peri's emotions were bleeding into me, and it hurt my heart to see Hades looking so defeated.

Hades sighed. "Circumstances have aligned in such a way to make that an impossibility. I left a holodisk at the end of the original labyrinth containing my logs of everything I've done since your death and explaining what happened to make this such a mess. It wasn't supposed to be like this." He shook his head gently, his breathy laughing containing a note of defeat. "If you found your way here, then you have already visited that labyrinth and have likely already read through my logs."

Biting my lip, I shook my head. That must have been all the text on the other holodisk stored with the geomarker. I hadn't had enough downtime to do more than think about it.

An alarm blared in the background of the holographic recording, and Hades turned to look in the direction of the sound. He cursed, his expression hardening, and he looked back at me. "I am afraid I have run out of time. I must go now if we are ever to have a chance of meeting again. Find the Omega site, Peri. Find me." He reached for something, his arm leaving the holo-gram, but his stare returned to me. "I love you, Peri. If this doesn't work—if I don't make it—hold that truth in your heart. I have done everything within my power to find my way back to you."

Hades pressed his first two fingers to his lips, then held them out toward me. "You're my reason."

The hologram winked out of existence.

"No!" I blurted, reaching for Hades with my other hand. But there was nothing there.

My heart was pounding so hard it seemed to be rocking my entire body. Dread roiled in my belly, making me feel sick to my stomach. I curled my fingers around the holodisk, enclosing it in my fist. My eyes stung like I was on the verge of tears.

This was similar to how I had felt before opening the package from my mom, when I had known in my gut something bad had happened to her. It was how I had felt when Raiden broke the news to me that he was reenlisting. It was how I always felt when I feared for the lives of the most important people in my life, the ones who occupied the largest chunks of my heart.

So why did I feel this way about someone I had never actually met? About Hades? Why was his despairing recording resulting in such a visceral reaction within me? He was the most important person in *Peri's* life. *She* was the one who loved him, not me.

Yet, the thought that he might *not* still be alive, *not* cryogenically frozen somewhere on this planet, terrified me.

My hand trembled as I uncurled my fingers and set the holodisk on the table. Moving robotically, I leaned forward, reaching for my pack. I dragged it away from the wall and closer to me. The doru slid to the side, clattering onto the stone floor. I barely noticed as I unzipped the main pouch of the bag and started pulling items out. The things I searched for were at the very bottom—the two Atlantean storage cubes, one from the Order's vault, the other from the end of the labyrinth in Rome.

I pulled the cubes free and pushed the food tray out of the way with my forearm. By the time I set the cubes on the table, both were open, activated by my touch.

I inhaled deeply and held my breath, then reached into the cube from the Order's vault. It didn't count as stealing if Hades had left the storage cube there for me in the first place.

A single holodisk was stored within the cube. This one held the location of the Omega site. Hades' location.

I pulled the holodisk out of the cube and set it on my palm, waiting for a three-dimensional model of Earth to appear, floating above my hand.

But nothing happened.

Brow furrowing, I bowed my head over my hand, examining the holodisk. It looked exactly the same as the others—a silver-dollar-sized crystal medallion no thicker than a credit card. I brushed a piece of hair off the surface of the holodisk.

The hair didn't budge.

Frowning, I raised the disk up to the light, gently holding it by the edges between my thumb and forefinger.

That wasn't a hair. It was a crack.

My heart plummeted. The Custodes Veritatis must have been trying to open the cube for who knew how long. I could only imagine the methods they had employed in their attempts to open it. Something they had tried must have damaged the disk, obliterating my chances of finding Hades.

Sorrow and frustration merged with fear and loneliness within me. It was no use. Nothing I did mattered because the game was fixed. The board was broken. The path going forward wasn't just blocked, it was demolished. Hades and his stupid, complicated machinations had led me to this place where I was alone in the world. Where I didn't belong—not anywhere, and not with anyone. I had been alone my whole life, and I would be alone until the day I died. It was all pointless, and for the first time in my life, I wished I had never been born at all.

My skin tingled with static electricity, and I could feel the tiny hairs all over my body stand on end. I looked down at my hands and was shocked to see electric-blue and neon-green sparks crackling along the surface of my skin.

My emotions must have excited the energy that had been indelicately crammed into me, and the regulator couldn't hold it all in. I needed to calm down, and I needed to do it *now*.

Panic added to the toxic mix of emotions, and the sparks became tiny streaks of lightning. My hair lifted off my shoulders, floating around my head like I was underwater.

Exhaling slowly, evenly, I set the cracked holodisk on the

table, pushed back the chair, and stood. I sucked in another lungful of air and closed my eyes.

And screamed.

I screamed until my throat was raw and the sound that came out of me was a hoarse whisper. I screamed until I dropped to my knees, panting from the exertion. I screamed until tears streamed down my cheeks, and the only thing I felt was exhaustion.

I slumped forward, shoulders rising and falling with each heavy breath. I was no longer in imminent danger of unleashing a psychic nuke. But, deep down, I knew I had only delayed the inevitable. I would need to find an outlet for the energy, and soon, at a time and place of my choosing.

Before the energy chose for me.

[13]

Sitting in the middle of the bed, I stared at the three holodisks resting atop the sheets. The one on the left contained the location to the second labyrinth, the one in the middle supposedly contained the location to the Omega site—if it wasn't so damaged that the data itself was lost—and the third, on the right, contained an endless stream of Olympian text. Hades' words. His story.

The holodisk on the left was of no use to me anymore. I had gone to the location marked on the holographic model of Earth. I had found my way through the labyrinth. I had completed the task Hades had set before me, and it had gotten me *nowhere*.

Well, that wasn't entirely true. It had led me to the Beta site, a place I didn't know much about because I had yet to be allowed to leave my room. A room that looked and felt a lot like a prison cell, whatever Caly claimed. And, it had led me to a new recording of Hades that directed me toward the holodisk in the middle. The cracked holodisk. One step forward, two steps back. The *only* source containing the location of the Omega site was damaged.

I had one move. One way forward. I needed to find someone technologically proficient enough to fix the damaged holodisk.

A single name came to mind: Fiona. She was the most technologically badass person I knew. And while that might not be saying much, considering I didn't actually know that many people thanks to my twenty-six years of living as a recluse, Fiona really was a genius.

She worked as a researcher in the video game industry because she enjoyed it. The big game companies fought over her time, allowing her to charge top dollar because she was the best. She could find anything online—and I mean *anything*. No firewall could hold Fiona back, no password encryption was uncrackable, and no network was out of her reach. She was fully capable of being a devastating force in the cyber world, if she wanted to be. But she didn't want that. She wanted to be a force for good, to bring joy into people's lives in the form of amazing video games. But mostly she just wanted to play.

I could have reached out to Ilyana. Maybe the tech to fix the holodisk was here in the Beta site. It was an Olympian settlement, after all. But I didn't know these people, and I sure as hell didn't trust them. I wasn't about to hand them Hades' location, especially if he, himself, had hid the location from them. It was too dangerous. In the wrong hands, *he* was too dangerous.

So, my plan was to contact Fiona as soon as I could—she was my best shot at repairing the holodisk—but that wouldn't happen from within the Beta site. Something about Olympian tech rendered all my electronics inert, killing every single battery. That moved reaching out to Fiona to the back burner, right along with finding a way to dispose of the excess mold-derived energy saturating my system. At least the headache seemed to be on its way out. One less thing to worry about…

For now, the middle holodisk was relatively useless to me. I stared at the right-most of the three small, crystalline disks. This was the holodisk Hades had mentioned in the recording, the disk that supposedly explained everything—from why he had created the labyrinths to how I had ended up here, like this.

I picked up the holodisk and set it on my palm. The stream of text appeared almost instantly, projected over my hand like a document on a floating computer screen. The Olympian symbols were incomprehensible, scrolling past faster than my mind could translate them.

I raised my free hand, touching my pointer finger to the holographic screen. The faintest tingle sizzled up my finger, almost imperceptible, and the stream of text froze. I dragged my finger down a few inches, and the text followed.

A tiny smile touched my lips. It was just like navigating a video game menu in VR, except there was nothing virtual about this reality.

I flicked my finger downward repeatedly until the scrolling text stopped and I had presumably reached the beginning of Hades' logs. I hunched my shoulders, letting my posture deteriorate, and focused on the holographic screen. As the symbols became legible, letters became words, and words became sentences. Words written thousands of years ago. Words written by Hades. His words, to me.

I finally made it. Or perhaps it would be more accurate for me to say WE finally made it, as I have been carrying you around with me since leaving the Alpha site. It has been two years since you died—two long, lonely years—and I am tired. I am so tired, Peri. I want nothing more than to escape into cryosleep, but there's still so much to do.

I have ensured the consciousnesses of all those who put their faith in me have been transferred to the Omega site successfully. Nearly three-quarters of our people elected to end their cycles early and enter a state of indefinite incorporeal existence in the Vault of Souls. I persuaded them with pleads and promises, and now the burden of fulfilling those promises threatens to crush me. I cannot help but wonder if those who chose to remain behind and finish out their current cycles—their final cycles—chose the better path. They will die the true death, in time, but they will live however many years are still left in their bodies. That is more than I can say for the others, should I fail.

You must be wondering how any of this came to be. Our fight —your sacrifice—was to prevent this. To prevent the fall of Olympus, or what remained of Olympus. We tried, you and I. And we succeeded in keeping the Tsakali from detecting us. That end would have been definite. This end is softer, gentler. This end still holds the promise of hope for the Olympian race. Of the new beginning we have been working toward for so long.

You see, while you and I were trying to save our people, Poseidon was ensuring their—our—destruction. Or, at least, he thought he was. He destroyed the transference and cloning equipment. I can create a cloned embryo, but that's as far as I can take the process. The incubators are fried. I have tried, so many times, to bring you back. So many failures.

If I had access to a chaos stone, I could power up the gephyra and travel across the universe to the lost colonies to salvage parts and repair the equipment, but that is an impossibility. Not even all the orichalcum spread across this planet could be melted down and super condensed into a chaos stone. The only way to power the gephyra now would be for the anthropos to advance far enough technologically to develop an alternative power source to a chaos stone, if such a thing even exists.

I can help the anthropos—I plan to guide their development —but it will take centuries, if not millennia. There are several promising proto civilizations spread across the continents, but as they stand currently, they are far from ready. Anything worth having is worth waiting for, so I shall wait.

I wish you were here, Peri. I wish I didn't have to do this alone. As I prepare for cryosleep, I cannot help but think how much less daunting this task would seem if you were here by my side. But you're not. That is the reality I must face. I remain hopeful, still, that we shall find a way through this.

This is not how we end. Us. The Olympians. We didn't survive the destruction of Olympus just to erode into nothing.

I will see you again, Peri, my light, my star, my reason. In this life, or in the next.

"Holy shit," I breathed, swiping a tear from my cheek. I couldn't imagine what it was like to be loved the way Hades loved Peri. To love the way she loved him.

Except I could. I had felt it choking me. Suffocating me. Destroying me.

I cleared my throat. I didn't know all the details of what happened at the end of Peri's life, just bits and pieces. I knew there had been something of a rebellion, that the leader had become a tyrant. Poseidon, the mythological god of the sea. Not so mythological, as it turned out. He had become power hungry, craving immortality to the point that he was endangering the Olympian civilization, according to Hades. And I knew the looming threat of some other, outside force had surpassed the danger he posed to the Olympians. The Tsakali, according to Hades' message. Somehow, that had all culminated in Peri's death. And, apparently, the fall of the Olympian settlements here on Earth and a retreat to the Omega site.

This message from Hades was the first of many. And it had taken me what felt like hours to translate. I had access to Peri's knowledge of her native language, but I still had to process it through the neural pathways that existed in my brain. It took time. And energy. Unfortunately, not the psychic kind, of which I had an overabundance. My eyes were growing tired, and my neck ached from sitting hunched over for so long.

As I scrolled to the next message, I lay back on the bed, propping a couple pillows behind my head.

One thousand solar years have passed, yet little progress has been made among the anthropos of this planet. I traveled to every major river valley, but nothing much has changed. I can hear your voice in my head, Peri—give them time, Hades, let them develop naturally. What's the rush?

I know you would be right. Forcing technological advancement upon a people not ready for such power will only bring disaster, not only to this planet, but to the last remnants of our people. The last thing I want is to create another savage, tech hungry race like the Tsakali. We made that mistake once. Never again.

As I read Hades' words, my vision grew blurry, my comprehension hazy. I had to reread the last sentence three times to make sense of its meaning.

Never again.

I blinked, focusing on the words. On the letters.

Never again.

But it didn't do me any good. My eyelids drifted shut, and I didn't have the willpower to lift them again. I was too tired.

I surrendered to sleep, grateful for the reprieve. Reality was exhausting.

[14]

"What's it like out there?" Caly asked, picking at a pull in the bedsheet. She was sitting on the edge of the bed, my uninvited guest keeping me company while I ate.

She had brought me another tray of food almost as soon as I opened my eyes, but this time the bowl held a more substantial vegetable and meat stew. It was unlike anything I had ever tasted —not bad, just different. I wasn't brave enough to ask what the meat was. If I learned it was something like monkey or snake, I wasn't sure I would have been able to continue eating.

"What do you mean—*out there*?" I asked between bites. I set down my spoon in the half empty bowl and looked at the young psychic through narrowed eyes. "Haven't you ever left this place?"

Caly raised her eyes from the bed, her stare meeting mine for a fraction of a second before returning to the pull in the sheet. "Of course, I have," she said, a curious note of defiance in her tone. "I scout the rainforest for trespassers with my troop every seven days."

I raised my eyebrows. "Is that the only time you go above ground?"

She nodded without looking at me.

Once a week, she left this cavern. That was it. She saw the sun—the true sun, not the model glowing high up on the cavern ceiling—once a week. I felt a strange kinship with Caly; her existence was even more sheltered than mine.

"Are there really cities out there, beyond the rainforest, one hundred times the size of Akahim?" Caly looked at me out of the corner of her eye. "Meg claims she saw one when she accompanied her mother on a mission, and she said the buildings were boxy and touched the sky and that the world was filled with Olympians with pale skin and golden hair, just like Hades, and she went on and on about how beautiful it all was." Caly turned her head, looking at me full-on. "She brought back a book with pictures of other places in the world, but I can't tell if it's really real or if it's just pictures." Though Caly didn't ask a direct question, I could see it in her eyes.

I set my spoon down in the bowl and sat back in my chair, processing everything she had just said. "Well," I said, frowning slightly, "your friend—"

"Meg's not my friend," Caly corrected.

"All right..." I raised my eyebrows. "*Meg* is half right. There are huge cities out there, and they are filled with people with all different hair and skin colors, but those people aren't Olympians. They're as human as you and—" I barely caught myself before saying, "me." I wasn't human. "As you and the rest of your people down here."

"But how do you know?" Caly asked.

Brow furrowing, I shook my head. "What do you mean?"

"My m—Ilyana says you're an Olympian," Caly said, and I could've sworn she'd been about to call Ilyana her mom. "But you look just like one of us. How do you know some of those people out there aren't Olympians, too?"

"Well, I—" Unsure how to continue, I pressed my lips together and shook my head.

I didn't have a good reason to give her. I didn't know why I looked more like a human than did the other Olympians from Peri's memories. I would have to ask Peri about it the next time she surfaced. All the other Olympians I had seen in Peri's memories had a distinctive quality that marked them as other—a quality I didn't have. All I knew was Peri believed all of her people to be gone—dead, for all intents and purposes—save for Hades, who may or may not be preserved in cryosleep in some mysterious Olympian fallout bunker he called the Omega site.

"I don't know how, exactly," I told Caly. "I just know there aren't any more Olympians walking around out there."

"Oh," she said quietly. "Sorry. That must be lonely."

I nodded and turned away from her in my chair, shielding myself from her pitying stare. My whole life I had felt isolated, but now I was truly alone. I gave myself a mental shake. If I followed that miserable train of thought, it would lead me into a dark place—a place I wouldn't easily escape from. So, I ignored it, throwing myself whole-heartedly into the task of eating.

I was just polishing off the final flatbread when the hologram barring the room's exit vanished, revealing Ilyana standing in the doorway. She only had eyes for the girl. For Caly, her daughter. It was impossible not to see the resemblance now the seed was planted in my mind—same eyes, same bone structure, same hair. The resemblance was rather striking, masked only by their contrasting demeanors.

"What were your orders, Calysto?" Ilyana asked pointedly.

Chewing as quietly as possible, I looked from mother to daughter.

Caly inhaled deeply, spine straightening and cheeks flushing, and for a moment, I thought she would stand up to her powerful mother. But then she exhaled, her whole body deflating. Her shoulders slumped, and she hung her head, staring at the floor at Ilyana's feet. "Wait outside Cora's room," she said, her voice small. Meek. "Attend to her needs when requested."

Ilyana planted her hands on her hips, her eyebrows rising. "And…?"

Caly huffed out a breath. "And don't be a pest."

I swallowed roughly, trying not to choke on the half-chewed bite, then cleared my throat. "She wasn't bothering me," I said, returning my focus to Ilyana. "Really. It was nice to have the company."

Ilyana stared at me, hard, for far longer than was comfortable. She sniffed, breaking eye contact and looked at her daughter. "Leave us," she said, stepping into the room. "I must speak to our guest privately."

Caly popped up from the edge of the bed and scurried to the doorway.

"And Calysto," Ilyana said, turning partway to catch her daughter's eye. The girl stood in the doorway, frozen by her mother's words. "If anyone comes sniffing around, detain them and alert me—immediately."

Caly gulped and nodded, then stepped out of the room. The hologram returned a moment later, and once again, the wall appeared unbroken.

And here I thought *I* had a strange relationship with my mother. But even with all the secrets and lies, I wouldn't want to trade places with Caly.

Ilyana flicked her fingers toward the hologram, and a thin, shimmering sheet of lime-green spread across the wall, coating the entire perimeter of the room, floor, ceiling, and all. Sighing, Ilyana made her way to the bed and eased down to the mattress, sitting almost exactly where Caly had been just moments ago. Her shoulders slumped, and her expression grew weary, making the resemblance between the two impossible to miss.

"I worry about her," Ilyana said, her voice hushed. "She's too soft. Too innocent. And she is far too curious."

I chewed the inside of my cheek, holding in a retort as I pretended to study the shimmering field of energy coating the floor. Ilyana struck me as the mercurial type, and I didn't want her to lash out at me next simply because I disagreed with her.

I felt a mental tickle and sat up straighter, stare fixing on Ilyana. She was reading my mind.

"You disapprove," Ilyana said matter-of-factly.

I narrowed my eyes at her. Looked like silence wouldn't do me much good when she could pluck the thoughts right out of my head.

"You think I am too hard on her," Ilyana said.

I licked my lips, organizing my thoughts. "I think being soft and innocent and curious are perfectly normal things for a girl her age," I said. Before Ilyana could respond, I added, "And I would appreciate it if you would stay out of my head."

"Impossible," Ilyana said, waving a hand dismissively. "You project your thoughts like an untrained child. I cannot make myself deaf simply to appease your need for privacy."

My mouth fell open.

"It is not your fault," Ilyana continued, holding up a hand to pacify me. "But your mind is open to all with the ability to read it. Your thoughts will not truly be your own until you learn to erect a mental barrier." She took a deep breath. "And until you learn that, I cannot allow you to leave this room."

"What?" I blurted, standing up. "No," I said, shaking my head vehemently. "Out of the question. I need to see Raiden —*now.*"

Ilyana stood as well, both hands raising in placation. "It is for your own safety," she said. "I know you are Cora Blackthorn, but to the rest of my people, you are the powerful Olympian, Persephone. You are strength personified, the one we have been waiting for to lead us out of hiding and into the light." She took a step toward me, stare hardening. "And until you can be that person—at least in the eyes of my people—your presence among them is more dangerous than you could ever know."

I took a step back, stare hardening, and shook my head. "You can't keep me here," I said, fairly sure I was speaking the truth. "If I decide to leave, you won't be able to stop me."

Ilyana raised one eyebrow, lips pursing. "I do not doubt that." The corner of her mouth ticked upward, and her head tilted to the side, just a little. "Remember, I have seen inside your mind—your memories. I know the strength of your power, however untrained it may be. You could obliterate me with barely a thought." She bowed her head, almost in deference. "*But* it is my hope that despite your ability to leave, you will *choose* to stay. At least, for a little while."

My brow furrowed. "I don't understand," I said, shaking my head. "Why would I choose to be a prisoner?"

"A guest," Ilyana said with another of her curious little smiles. She gestured to the chair behind me. "Please, sit, and I will tell you a story. Then, I think, you may come to understand how we can help each other."

Slowly, I lowered myself back down into the chair. "What kind of story?"

"The story of my people and our long history with Hades," Ilyana said, returning to the bed. "The story of how we came to be here, in this place, and why we have remained here for nearly fifteen hundred years." She sat on the edge of the mattress.

I licked my lips, eager to finally get some answers, even if they weren't necessarily the ones I had been searching for.

"And why we have been waiting," Ilyana said, eyes meeting mine. "For you."

[15]

"Over fourteen centuries have passed since Hades visited my people and led us to this underground haven," Ilyana began. "We are called the Zari, and once upon a time, we lived peacefully in the rainforest. Our ancestors built a vast civilization with settlements spanning the length of the great river, but none were as marvelous as our capital, Zaritcha." Ilyana flashed me a knowing smile. "I believe you stumbled upon her ruins a couple days ago."

"Huh," I said, nodding.

"At the time when the Moche ruled the Peruvian coast, blissfully unaware of our presence, our civilization thrived, on the cusp of great technological advancement," Ilyana continued. "Until the twenty-year storm," she said, an ominous note to her voice. "You see, the same catastrophic rainstorm that brought about the destruction of the Moche threatened to do away with my ancestors, as well. Our settlements washed away in the floodwaters until all that remained was great, beautiful Zaritcha. But neither the steel reinforcing our buildings nor our steam engines or electricity could save us from starvation, and—"

"I'm sorry," I interrupted, holding up a hand. "Did you just say *steam engines* and *electricity*?"

A tiny, mysterious smile touched Ilyana's lips, and she nodded.

"But—but," I spluttered. "The steam engine has only been around for, like, three hundred years, and electricity—" I shook my head. "Electricity hasn't even been around for that long."

"According to recorded history," Ilyana said serenely.

"Yeah, but—"

Ilyana steamrolled right over my disbelief. "The Zari are not a part of any written history," she said. "In fact, so far as historians are considered, we never existed at all."

"But—" My voice stalled, words escaping me, and all I could do was shake my head. The ruins I had seen were stone, and remarkably vast and astonishing enough for being hidden all this time in the heart of the Amazon Rainforest, but they weren't exactly *advanced*. At least, not steam engine and electricity advanced.

Once again, I felt that tingle signaling a foreign touch at the edge of my mind.

"Yes, precisely our intent," Ilyana said with a gentle nod. "We began disassembling the city centuries ago, when the Europeans first arrived on this continent, and we stepped up our efforts when the Custodes Veritatis finally showed up. What you see there now are the oldest parts of the city—the ancient foundations."

I stared at Ilyana, at a loss for words. Once again, I wondered how she knew about the Custodes Veritatis. A sneaky little voice whispered in my mind, filling my head with suspicions that she only knew about the Order because she had learned about them while digging through my thoughts and memories.

"Oh please," Ilyana said, somehow making rolling her eyes look dignified. "Think, Cora. How would my people have acquired the holodisk? And how would I—and all of those like me—have attained these psychic gifts? The information I gleaned from your thoughts filled in some gaps, but I had no need of your memories to learn about the Custodes Veritatis. Hades told us about them even before he brought us down here —before he gifted my ancestors with their abilities—and we have been keeping an eye on the Order ever since, both when they venture here, as well as through the eyes of our agents out in the world."

Yet again, I was rendered speechless and reduced to weak headshaking. Ilyana's psychic gifts came from Hades. How was that possible?

"It is a lot to process," she said, "I know." She settled her hands on her knees. "Let me continue—I believe most of your questions will be answered along the way. When I finish, you are welcome to ask any that remain."

All I could do was nod.

Ilyana cleared her throat. "The Zari have long valued curiosity and intellect; ingenuity was required to thrive in the Amazon," Ilyana explained. "Before our relocation down here, all Zari children attended state-run school until their Choosing at the age of sixteen, when they opted to either continue their education, indebting themselves to the state for life, or entered a private apprenticeship. To encourage progress and productiveness, wealth and resources were distributed to each settlement based upon their inhabitants' contributions to the advancement of the Zari people."

"Sounds lovely," I said, unable to hide my sarcasm. I couldn't help but wonder if each settlement sent a couple kids off to fight to the death like glorified gladiators each year, too.

Much to my surprise, Ilyana didn't argue. She tilted her head to the side, acknowledging my skepticism. "It was a brutal way of life, in its own way. I am not justifying the actions of my ancestors, simply trying to paint a picture of the events that led to you and I sitting here, together, and why you are, in your current, unshielded state, safest here in this room," Ilyana said, folding her hands together and resting them on her lap. She was poise personified, and like Peri—like my mom and Emi—she was strong to the core. It was the kind of inner strength I daydreamed about possessing. One day, maybe, but I wasn't about to hold my breath.

If Ilyana picked up on my mini self-pity party, she didn't let on. "Shall I continue?" she asked.

I nodded. "I'll be quiet," I said, raising my hand to my mouth to mime zipping my lips. I tossed away the imaginary zipper and flashed her a close-lipped smile.

The corner of Ilyana's mouth twitched. "Where was I?" She narrowed her eyes. "Oh yes—Hades' arrival." She inhaled deeply. "He came to us during the third year of the storm. It was autumn, and what remained of the Zari people had gathered in Zaritcha, surviving on the last remnants of preserved food. They were starving and wouldn't survive the winter. Hades told us there was a place he could take us—a city hidden underground, just beyond the outskirts of Zaritcha. He told us the city was a wondrous place, filled with technology beyond our wildest imagination and that we would be safe there for as long as we remained, but that there would be a price."

I leaned forward, elbows propped on my thighs, drawn in by the story.

"Hades proposed a bargain," Ilyana said. "A trade. He would bring us to safety, and in return, the Zari would be tied to this place—to Hades and his cause—until his mission was complete and he released us from service. The elders scoffed, accusing Hades of attempting to take advantage of the Zari in their weakened state." Ilyana smirked. "They did not continue to be the elders for much longer…"

My eyes widened, and I fought the urge to ask if she meant that the elders had been killed.

Ilyana nodded. "All thirteen elders were assassinated the

night of their decision, and those who took their place on the High Council unanimously voted to take Hades up on his offer. We followed him down here, and we have been here, serving him, ever since."

Ilyana laughed quietly to herself. "I often wonder what it must have been like for my ancestors when they first came down here. The city had been abandoned for thousands of years and had fallen into extreme disrepair, but with Hades' help and the Zari's innate technological proficiency, my people adapted the existing infrastructure and had the city up and running before winter set in. The cavern provided shelter from the incessant rains and flooding. The canal provided electricity to power the city. The hydroponic fields provided food, allowing us to grow everything we needed on the cavern walls. We were saved."

Ilyana inhaled and exhaled deeply. "Once my ancestors were safe, it was their turn to uphold their end of the bargain. While they built his labyrinth, Hades went about educating a select few of the Zari on the history of his people. He told my ancestors of the war that drove the Olympians from their home world and of their long journey here, to a planet they called Atlantis. He told us of the fall of their settlements here—of Persephone and the part she played in both saving and damning the Olympians. He told us of his failed attempts to resurrect his people—to resurrect Persephone—and of the organization he founded over a millennium prior. Of how far the Custodes Veritatis strayed from their original purpose."

My eyes widened at that revelation. Hades founded the Custodes Veritatis?

If Ilyana sensed my question, she didn't let it derail her story. "Hades gave us so much, but not without a price. Hades knew how time could warp our intentions, and he ensured our commitment to his cause with a single, simple curse." She laughed again, softly, bitterly. "You see, enhancing some of our women with psychic abilities was not the only way Hades tampered with my ancestors' genome. He cursed us with a lethal allergy to sunlight; a curse only Hades, himself, can lift. And for that to happen, we must help *you* find *him*."

My mouth fell open, and I slowly shook my head. I had heard of conditions that caused severe sensitivity to sunlight, but not a lethal reaction. It couldn't be true. It was something out of fiction, a too-real twist on the curse of vampirism. To do such a thing to another person—it was heinous. It was beyond inhumane.

But then, Hades wasn't human.

Ilyana nodded, like she shared my disgust. "Solar urticaria," she said. "The condition is not exclusive to my people, but as we are more or less stuck down here, we have not been able to reel in new blood to diversify our gene pool." She shrugged, sighing as her shoulders dropped. "This is the only place where we are safe, the only place where we can live our lives, fully sheltered from the sun. Each generation waits, biding their time, hoping they will be the ones to finally step out from our eternal night and into the sunlight. Hoping they will be the ones to aid the great Persephone in her mission to find and awaken Hades and finally free our people. Hoping *they* will be the ones to help *you*."

Ilyana's lips curved into a small but genuine smile. "I had almost given up that you would come in my lifetime." Gracefully, she gestured toward me with her right arm. "But here you are, the key to our prison." Her smiled wilted. "And you don't even know who you are."

I sat back, bristling a little. I generally felt inadequate, but I didn't appreciate her rubbing my nose in it.

Ilyana held up a hand. "It is not your fault. George must have died before he had a chance to send a message informing us the child carried by Diana Crane was, in fact, Persephone of the Olympians."

I sat up straighter. "Wait," I said, zipped lips be damned, "are you talking about George Blackthorn?"

"The very same," Ilyana said.

I shook my head, unable to believe what she was suggesting.

For most of my life, I believed George Blackthorn was my grandfather. As I had only recently learned, he was actually the man who took in my mom and Emi when they fled from the Custodes Veritatis. The very elderly man who provided them a cover, who gave them a new, safe life on Orcas Island, hidden away from the rest of the world, only to pass away a few months after their arrival.

I stared at Ilyana, shocked by her implication that George had been in communication with her people.

"He was an agent of ours," she said. "As were his father and grandfather before him. Charles Blackthorn captained the ship that brought a Custodes Veritatis expedition to the mouth of the Amazon River. Curiosity prompted him to charter his own crew to lead him upriver, following the Order's trail. He had an interest in the ancient world, and he had heard rumors of a lost city hidden deep in the heart of the Amazon Rainforest. He suspected this was what the Order was hunting, and he couldn't resist the lure of seeing the lost city with his own eyes." Ilyana's lips twisted into a wry smile. "*Or* the possibility of finding the invaluable treasure such a city was sure to contain—just what he needed to fund his floundering ship-building endeavor."

"Unfortunately for Charles, the Order caught wind of him shortly after he followed them off the river and into the rainforest," Ilyana said. "They attacked his camp at night, just a few miles south of Zaritcha. He fled, wounded but alive, and stumbled upon the ruins. He was badly injured and not likely to survive the night. One of our patrols captured him and brought him down here, where he was healed by the asclypos. An emergency meeting of the High Council was called to discuss these apparently violent explorers, while our psychics examined the wounded captive's mind. In Charles's mind, we discovered that the explorers were none other than the Custodes Veritatis, though they had long since shucked their roots and served a new master, now."

"The pope," I said, filling in the blanks.

I had been certain of the answer, but Ilyana shook her head. "The Primicerius, allied with the Bishop of Rome on the promise to conceal the existence of the Olympians from humankind—and share all research and discoveries—in exchange for nearly unlimited access to Vatican City's resources."

I frowned, chewing on the inside of my cheek. I hadn't expected that revelation, and my thoughts turned briefly to the book tucked away in my pack. The *Liber Veritatis*. According to my mom's journal, it was a compendium of the Order's history, passed down from Primicerius to Primicerius. I would have examined it a lot closer—and a lot sooner—had I known Hades, himself, had founded the Custodes Veritatis. Who knew what secrets were hidden between those covers?

"It will be a fascinating read, I am sure," Ilyana said. "And something I wouldn't mind examining myself..." She bowed her head slightly. "If you allow me."

"Yeah, sure," I said. "Just let me look through it first." I wanted to make sure there weren't any secrets contained within the book that I wanted to remain secret.

Ilyana's stare locked with mine. "I understand completely."

I clenched my jaw. "That's getting really annoying," I told her, my voice tight.

The corner of her mouth lifted, twisting her lips into a smirk. A challenge. "If you don't like it, then stop me."

Annoyed, I narrowed my eyes to the beginnings of a glare.

Ilyana didn't seem the least bit cowed, though her smirk did vanish as she continued her story. "Back to Hades—he spent three years with my people here, building his maze and ensuring we were well established in our new underground home. You see, technical malfunctions in the Omega site guaranteed this was his last chance to set the stage for his people's return. Before he departed, he charged us with three sacred duties: observe, protect, and guide."

"Observe, protect, and guide—" I shook my head. "What does that mean? I mean, I know what it means, but I don't know what it *means*." Again, I shook my head, fully aware I sounded like an idiot.

"Observe the world," Ilyana explained. "Observe the development of human civilization."

My eyes narrowed. It seemed like an impossible task for people who weren't able to leave the safety of their underground city while the sun was up.

"Ah," Ilyana said, responding to my thoughts. "Hades did not share all of his people's technology with us, but he did teach us to use their global observation system, allowing us to monitor the world from our relative captivity," she explained. "While we observed the world from here, we were able to wait in the shadows, being patient, letting the waves of advancement ebb and flow naturally. Once a civilization reached a level of technological proficiency that promised successful gestation of a cloned embryo, the most important task was to lure one who we deemed worthy into the labyrinth."

I scoffed, softly but not inaudibly. It all sounded pretty convoluted to me. Couldn't Hades simply have left my cloned embryo with the Zari and told them to hand me over to this or that civilization when the time was right?

"But who is to say we would still be here?" Ilyana said, once again responding to my unspoken thoughts. "By the time Hades came to us, he had been dropping in and out of cryosleep for more than ten thousand years. For all he knew, it would be another ten thousand years before a human civilization reached the point of technological advancement to resurrect you, and we could have destroyed ourselves in that amount of time. Hades saw the true nature of human civilization—fragile and volatile. By storing your embryo in the labyrinth, Hades was protecting you from the possibility—what he viewed as a probability—the Zari would implode before any human civilization reached the desired level of technological advancement."

"I guess that kind of makes sense," I murmured, even as I wondered if Hades had been suffering from some form of cryogenic cognitive degeneration. At the same time, I thought about how badly I wanted Ilyana to stay out of my head.

Ilyana touched two fingertips to her right temple, closing her eyes for a moment. "That has to be the loudest mental barrier I have ever experienced," she commented. She lowered her hand and opened her eyes, her stare landing on me. "Right idea," she said, "but quite a bit overdone. The barrier does not need to be a mile thick; you just need it to block the view inside. You need only be aware of your desire to shield yourself; you do not need to focus on it—unless someone is actively attempting to break through your mental barriers."

"Oh," I said, heat rising up my neck and warming my cheeks. "Thanks." I cleared my throat. "So, um, what about the other two duties—protect and guide?"

"Ah, yes," Ilyana said. "Protect the labyrinth from all who we deem unworthy. Protect you and the other artifacts. And once you have been reborn, guide you and those who resurrected you along the correct path."

I couldn't help but think they'd slacked a bit on that last duty. The desire to keep Ilyana out of my head was still a conscious thought, but it was no longer in the forefront of my mind.

"Better," Ilyana said. "Much better."

I smiled, giving myself a mental pat on the back. "So, what happened?" I asked, voicing my concealed thought in a more diplomatic way. "How did I end up in the hands of the Custodes Veritatis?"

Ilyana sighed. "It happened in 1925. It was a bad time for us.

We were falling apart—illness had recently swept through our population, claiming the lives of seven of the thirteen members of the High Council, and the chaos that ensued as veritable children vied for the vacated seats nearly destroyed us. Our focus turned inward, and for a few years, we neglected our sacred duties."

Ilyana's stare drifted off to my left, growing distant. "In retrospect, I think your abduction may have saved my people. A small team of explorers discovered the entrance to the labyrinth entirely on their own. The team was led by a man named Percy Fawcett—you may have heard of him, as I believe he has come into some posthumous fame."

I raised my eyebrows. Yeah, I knew of Percy Fawcett, the early twentieth century explorer who had earned a reputation as something of a fanatic as he obsessively searched for what he called the lost city of "Z." He had appeared in several of my video games, and my mom had been weirdly eager to watch the movie made about his ill-fated exploits. I frowned. Maybe her interest hadn't been so weird after all.

"When the thief emerged from the labyrinth," Ilyana said, "the alarms within the city rang so loud they seemed to make the stone itself quiver with Hades' rage." She looked down at her hands, one folded over the other. "Not our proudest moment." She seemed to shake herself out of the trance, and her focus returned to me. "Percy Fawcett and his son slipped through our grasp because we allowed ourselves to be distracted by trivial matters."

I hardly thought a plague sweeping through their small, self-contained city was all that trivial, but I attempted to keep that thought to myself.

Based on Ilyana's lack of a reaction, my attempt was successful. "The Custodes Veritatis arrived later that same year, in great numbers and heavily armed. They were too large of a force for us to fight off in our weakened state, so we hung back in the shadows, holding to our first duty—observe. We watched, unable to interfere as they stripped everything of import from the labyrinth. Their victory was our shame, a just punishment for our weakness."

The self-flagellation was getting to be a little much, and I couldn't keep my mouth shut any longer. "I hardly think Hades would blame you for what happened. You were struggling through a plague—or maybe *the* plague," I said, shoulders creeping up. "I think it's pretty admirable your people were able to pull through, and I'm sure Hades would agree."

Ilyana laughed under her breath, the sound low and somehow sinister. "But you don't know him," she said. She leaned forward, resting her forearms on her knees, her hands still clasped together. "You, Cora Blackthorn, don't know Hades," she reiterated. "According to ancient Greek myths, Hades is the god of the dead, the lord of the underworld."

She stared into my eyes. Into my soul. "But to us, Hades is not a myth. Look around you," she said, sitting up straighter and holding her arms out to either side. "This *is* the underworld, and Hades *is* our god." Fear cast a dark shadow in her eyes. "And we failed him."

[16]

"I must return to the High Council," Ilyana said, standing and dusting off the front of her pristine white tunic. She stepped toward the wall that was sometimes there, sometimes not. "I will send Caly in to help you practice guarding your mind." With a wave of her hand, the hologram completing the wall disappeared and the doorway was once again open.

I stood as Ilyana stepped out of the room. "And then you'll take me to see Raiden," I said, taking a single step toward the doorway. It wasn't a request.

Ilyana turned partway, meeting my eyes for a moment before bowing her head. "Of course. And if he awakens before you are ready, I will bring him to you, personally." She glanced at me sidelong. "Perhaps then you will come to trust me."

I opened my mouth to protest—*no, no, I trust you*—but thought better of it. Empty words that would fall on deaf ears. Ilyana had seen enough of my mind to know my trust had to be earned. The numerous betrayals I had recently experienced aside, spending most of my time in the virtual world made me wary of anyone's intentions.

Pressing my lips together, I nodded.

Ilyana offered me a small smile. "I am glad to see you are feeling better," she said. "If your headache returns and you wish for another session in the asclypos, you need only ask." With that, she bowed her head, then moved into the hallway and out of sight.

I stared at the open doorway, listening to Ilyana speaking softly to someone—Caly, I assumed—but not really hearing what she was saying. I was too distracted by her latest revelation. Rest and recuperation hadn't diminished my headache; their healing machine had. Which meant the headache hadn't just been a product of exhaustion or overexposure to the tranquilizer.

I was forced to accept the very real possibility that Peri and I were facing a literal mental breakdown—like, the physical structures of my brain couldn't support our dual consciousness. My stomach twisted into knots. More than ever, I needed to find Hades.

Caly popped into the room, replacing the hologram with a flick of her fingers. She paused, brow furrowing as she studied me, likely picking up on the swift downward spiral making my mood plummet.

She flashed me a weak grin and crossed the room to perch on the edge of the bed. "Are you all right?"

I chewed on a thumbnail, hugging my middle with my other arm. Now that I was thinking about the headache, the throb behind my eyes seemed more noticeable. "No," I said, numbly shaking my head. "I don't think I'm all right."

Caly bit her lip, hesitating. "Do you want to talk about it?"

Again, I shook my head, focus shifting to the wall behind her. What was the point? What I needed to do was prepare to leave. Raiden and I would be heading out as soon as he had recovered. I rubbed my temple with my fingertips. Maybe I would request another session in the asclypos before we left, but then I needed to get the holodisk to Fiona ASAP.

"I'm supposed to help you with your mental barrier," Caly said. "But if you're not up to it…"

"No," I said, focus returning to her. This was exactly the distraction I needed. "I'm ready. What do I do?"

"You should sit down," Caly said, scooting farther back on the bed and tucking one foot under her leg. "We're going to be here a while…"

If it wasn't for the incessant stream of consciousness pouring out of Caly's mouth, I would have been bored out of my mind. Caly had been talking for hours, or so I guessed. It was impossible to say for sure without access to a clock.

Caly told me about the boy she had a crush on—in great detail—and asked for my opinion as she analyzed what sounded like every interaction she had ever had with him. She told me about Meg, who from the way Caly gushed about her, I gathered was the queen bee of whatever passed for a high school down here. From the sounds of it, this Meg was very good at using her popularity and influence to her advantage. She was a user, plain and simple. The prototypical popular-slash-mean-girl, almost like she had stepped straight out of a teen movie.

Caly also told me about her hopes and dreams of one day seeing a skyscraper and an ocean and the sun. And as she spoke, I couldn't help but feel the weight piling up on my shoulders.

It wasn't just my life on the line, here. If I didn't figure out the location of the Omega site and awaken Hades, Caly would never see the sun. Not ever. Neither would Ilyana nor any of their people. Ever. It was all on me. On me, and on Hades.

Assuming he was even still alive.

I watched Caly's face closely, waiting for any hint that she had picked up on my mounting doubts. But it looked like my mental shields were holding up, because she rambled on about the tales Meg had shared about her mission to Iquitos, upriver in Peru. From what I gathered, access to the global monitoring system was extremely limited, and knowledge of the outside world was handed out on a need-to-know basis. Meg's stories were sacred to Caly.

Caly was just describing a photo of San Francisco—a bird's-eye-view of the Golden Gate Bridge at sunrise—when the hologram in the wall vanished and a young woman appeared in the doorway holding a tray loaded with dishes. She was tall and athletically built, and her dark hair was pulled back in a tight, complicated braid. With her fitted leather bodice and skirt of leather strips, not to mention her general air of badassery, she looked like the modern idea of an Amazon warrior.

Of course, I was careful to think all of this about her *behind* a subtle yet sturdy mental barrier. Or, at least, I hoped it was subtle yet sturdy and not the mental scream I had been projecting at Ilyana earlier.

"Meg!" Caly sprang to her feet. "What are you—I—" Caly rushed forward. "Here, let me help you," she said, finally managing to complete a thought. She relieved Meg of the tray and set it on the table, pushing the old, mostly empty tray back toward the wall.

I leaned to the side to give her more room.

"You missed the evening meal," Meg said, watching Caly rearrange the things on the tray. "I thought you might be hungry."

I frowned, curiosity piqued by Meg's interest in Caly's whereabouts and well-being. Based on admittedly limited information, I had been under the impression that the relationship between Caly and Meg was more one-sided, specifically with Caly envying the crap out of Meg and Meg not giving Caly the light of day. Maybe I had been wrong.

Meg's focus shifted to me, her eyes locking with mine. Her dark stare was intense, filled with a fervor I didn't understand, but then she bowed, folding almost double, and I wondered if I had imagined it. "It is an honor to stand in your presence, ancient one."

My frown deepened. I had the sneaking suspicion Meg hadn't come here to bring Caly food; she had come here to catch a glimpse of me. Looked like my original assessment of the girl had been spot on. She was a user, all right.

"How did you know I was here?" Caly asked, standing beside the table, fidgeting with her hands. Her cheeks were flushed, her eyes bright.

Meg straightened, her stare lingering on me before returning to Caly. "Ilyana asked me to stand in for you on tonight's patrol. She said you had been reassigned, and I figured that meant you were here, attending to our honored guest."

"Oh," Caly said. "Well, thanks, I guess." She gestured to the bed. "Do you want to sit? You can help us. We've been working on—"

"Caly…," I said, drawing out her name in warning. So far as I knew, only Caly and her mom were aware of the strange circumstances surrounding my upbringing. Like the fact that I hadn't been raised as Persephone. Or that I might not be the savior their people had been expecting. Or that I might not be able to save them at all.

Caly looked at me, eyes opened wide and voice muted. She closed her mouth and licked her lips.

"Caly was just filling me in on the Zari's history and customs," I said, fingers crossed behind my back. I really hoped I was pulling off a convincingly confident mental shield. "Thank you for the food, Meg." I smiled, thinking quickly to come up with a way to get rid of her before Caly slipped up again. "It was lovely to meet you," I said, smile locked in place. A clear dismissal, but not rude. I hoped.

Picking up on my unspoken meaning, Meg bowed again,

then turned and slipped out of the room. The hologram of stone reappeared as soon as she was gone.

I blew out a breath, relaxing my posture. "So that's Meg," I said, watching Caly slink back over to the bed. I lifted one of two steaming bowls of broth from the tray and sipped at the earthy, herbaceous liquid.

Caly sat on the edge of the bed, hugging her middle and staring at the floor. "I know what you must be thinking," she said. "I'm not stupid. Meg didn't come here for me; she came here to see you. I was just a convenient excuse. I know she doesn't care about me."

I was quiet for a moment. Interpersonal relationships were far from my strong suit, but I had watched the entirety of Buffy enough times to recognize a *Cordelia* when I saw one. "Then why do you care so much about her?" I asked, genuinely not understanding.

Caly stood suddenly, crossing the room to join me at the table. She pulled the second chair away from the table and plopped down. "I don't know," she said, a faint whine in her voice. "Meg gets the highest marks—in *everything*—and she wins all the contests, and my mother is always commending her in front of others." Caly snagged a flatbread off the tray and started tearing it into bite-size pieces, piling them up beside the second bowl of broth. "Everyone is always looking at Meg."

"You mean, your mom is always looking at Meg," I clarified.

Caly nodded, dipping a piece of flatbread into the broth before popping it into her mouth. She chewed slowly, looking generally miserable.

"But you want your mom to see *you*," I ventured.

Caly shrugged, dipping another piece of flatbread into the broth and eating it. She worked her way through the whole pile, avoiding making eye contact with me until she was finished.

Yawning, I set down my empty bowl and picked up a flatbread. "You know, you're the one who's stationed in here with me," I pointed out. "Not Meg, and not anyone else."

Caly's brow furrowed.

"Ilyana trusts you," I said, spelling out what seemed so obvious to me. "More than she trusts anyone else."

"I—" Caly shook her head, grimacing slightly. "I don't feel so good." She stood and managed a single step toward the hologram blocking the doorway before her knees gave out and she tumbled to the floor.

"Caly!" I screeched, lurching out of my chair and dropping to my knees beside her. I managed to catch her falling body with an arm behind her shoulders just before her head hit the floor. The room spun as I eased her down the rest of the way.

I planted one foot on the floor and tried to stand, but the room seemed to tilt onto its side, and I ended up lying on my shoulder, staring at Caly's profile. Her eyes were closed, her features slack. Her chest rose and fell with each slow, steady breath. She looked like she was asleep, which struck me as odd.

My thoughts felt slippery, and my eyelids drooped.

Why had Caly fallen asleep? And how had she ended up on the floor? How had *I* ended up on the floor? For the life of me, I couldn't remember.

It was my last thought before my eyelids closed and consciousness slipped away.

17

I'm a sleepwalker. And not in some metaphorical, I've-been-asleep-my-whole-life way. At least once a week for as long as I can remember, I have woken up in a completely different place from where I fell asleep. Sometimes I would wake up in my mom's room, sometimes in the woods between Blackthorn Manor and Hill House, where Emi and Raiden lived, and a hundred places in between.

Once, when I was thirteen, I woke as Raiden tackled me to the ground, a woolen blanket wrapped around me like a cocoon. I had been heading for the edge of the bluff. The tide was out, and there was nothing but rocks at the base of the cliff. Three more steps, and I would have fallen to my death. The next day, my mom installed a lock on my bedroom door. On the outside.

Never wake a sleepwalker. It's a common saying, but the reasoning isn't so common. Waking someone who's sleepwalking doesn't hurt the sleepwalker; rather, the sleepwalker might hurt whoever does the waking. Because in the half-dozen seconds between asleep and awake, the sleepwalker experiences a very specific mix of emotions. Confusion. Disorientation. Fear.

The kind of emotions that trigger a surge of adrenaline and, in my case, a fight-or-flight response.

I was usually a flight brand of sleepwalker.

But when I came to, walking through the rainforest in the middle of the night, my wrists tied together in front of me and a rope extending like a leash from the bindings to the unfamiliar woman walking ahead of me, I was all fight. Peri must have been rubbing off on me.

Before my mind was alert enough to process the danger in what I was about to do, I had stopped walking and pressed my fingertip against the regulator hanging from a chain around my neck, tracing it around the stone. The glow faded from subtle amber to a brilliant, otherworldly blue-green. Only when bands of electricity started to dance over the surface of my skin did I realize what I had done.

I had poked a hole in the damn. Now, cracks were forming around the hole, fissures weakening the barrier holding the excess energy stored within me at bay.

My whole body hummed with barely contained energy. I could sense at least a dozen minds surrounding me, but I couldn't concentrate enough to glean any more information from those minds than the fact that they were there. All of my concentration was focused on holding the energy in. If I lost control of it, even for a fraction of a second, it would explode out of me, raw, living energy vaporizing everything it touched.

"Peri," I whispered as tears gathered in my eyes.

But there was no response from my mental roommate. Like before, the drugs used to knock me out must have suppressed her. Even worse, the headache was back at full-force, making it that much more difficult to concentrate.

Staring at me with wide eyes, the Zari woman holding my makeshift leash dropped the rope and stumbled back a few steps.

"What do we do?" another woman asked from directly

behind me, her voice laced with fear. I was surprised to find I recognized the voice. It belonged to Meg.

Slowly, I turned toward her. My loose hair lifted off my shoulders, floating around my head like I was underwater.

I met Meg's eyes, and in the moment of eye contact, I knew what she had done. She had drugged me. Not with her own hand, but she had delivered the tainted food with the intent of knocking me unconscious and kidnapping me, walking me out of their underground city like a glorified puppet.

She was working with a group of rebels within the Zari—all women with psychic gifts, for only they could guard their minds from the rest of the psychics in their midst. They called themselves the Keepers. They were sick of Hades' chains, and they had made a deal with the Custodes Veritatis to exchange me for a supposed cure for their inherited condition. Maybe there really was a cure, but I doubted it.

Meg backed up a step but stumbled. Her loaded pack threw off her balance, and she fell to the ground, landing on her butt.

Now that I had made contact with her mind, I knew everything about her. The excess energy seemed to supercharge my psychic abilities. I didn't even have to try. Her mental barriers crumbled like ancient parchment, and I had instant and complete access to her mind. Her every thought and feeling wasn't just available to me, but known by me.

I had been wrong about Meg. Everyone had been wrong about her. She wasn't strong or brave, and she certainly wasn't manipulative and cruel, like I had assumed. She was afraid. She lived in a constant state of fear, and every single thing she did was born of that fear.

Meg was claustrophobic, with a little fear of being buried alive sprinkled on top.

Fear could be so damn powerful. It could take on a voice and a shape within you, a second, poisonous conscience. It could become the devil on your shoulder, ceaselessly whispering a stream of negativity in your ear.

Meg had long since learned to conceal her fear. To cope with her panic. To hide her weakness, something her mother ingrained in her at an early age. But her fear still controlled her. Just like the fear spawned by my condition had controlled me for most of my life. Meg was a victim of emotional abuse, only the abuser wasn't separate from her. Her abuser lived inside her, eating and breathing right along with her. She could never get away. Never escape.

Meg was just like me. Just like the girl I had been. Never really making a choice. Never acting, only ever reacting out of fear. I didn't want her to die. Not for being afraid. Not for being a victim.

But at the rate my control was slipping, Meg would die—she, along with the rest of the Keepers, would be obliterated by an uncontrolled explosion of energy—and soon. The overflow of energy roiled within me, bubbling out to the surface of my skin. At least it would be a quick death. A blink, and she would be gone. A flash of light, a moment of blinding pain, and she would be free.

A beam of rose-colored light whizzed past my left arm, striking the woman standing behind Meg mid-chest. In an instant, the beam burned a hole through the woman's torso, incinerating her heart, and she collapsed to her knees. Her eyes, wide with shock, met mine. In the instant before her death, her life flashed before my eyes, and I knew her just as well as I now knew Meg.

Her name was Lyvia, and she was Meg's mother. She was the one who had dragged Meg into this mess. She was the one who had actually drugged the food—and the one who had convinced Meg to deliver it. And she hadn't done it out of love; she had done it out of pure selfish desire. She knew about Meg's fear—

she had been punishing her daughter for this perceived weakness her whole life—but this time Lyvia had capitalized on it.

She disgusted me, and I couldn't help but think she deserved the death that awaited her on her next absent heartbeat.

The crack of gunfire broke the connection between my mind and Lyvia's, and dozens of arrows whizzed past me, taking out a few more of my kidnappers. Before Lyvia's mind winked out, I tore my gaze from hers and spun around, searching for the attackers.

There, about thirty feet away, sheltered by thick foliage between a couple of towering trees and illuminated by the haunting glow of the sizzling and snapping energy escaping from my body. My kidnapper's attackers. My would-be rescuers. Raiden with his handgun, and Caly with my doru, both wearing bulging packs on their shoulders. They had come to save me, sent by Ilyana with a full squadron of Zari warriors, not knowing what a grave mistake they were making. Not knowing their good deed would be rewarded with a gruesome, but swift death.

My feet lifted off the ground as the energy pulsed around me, shooting out larger and larger streaks of lightning with each beating of my heart. I was more energy than matter at the moment, and the laws of gravity no longer applied to me.

I clenched my teeth and met Raiden's eyes, chest rising and falling exaggeratedly with each heaving breath. "Get out of here, Raiden!" I screamed, extending my glowing hand toward him. "I can't hold it—" A burst of energy leapt from my palm, lashing out toward Raiden like a solar flare.

Raiden ducked just in time, covering his head with his arms to shelter himself from the ashen debris raining down on him. Caly stood beside him, eyes wide and unblinking.

"Run!" I implored, my voice breaking. "Get out of here! Now!"

Raiden didn't miss a beat. He scooped Caly up like she weighed nothing and tossed her over his shoulder, then took off at a dead sprint down the trail. Other Zari warriors followed suit, but I feared they wouldn't be fast enough to get away.

Every ounce of focus and concentration within me went to holding in the wild energy. I regained some ground, and my feet touched the earth once more. I had bought some time for Raiden and the others to get away. *Some* time, but I couldn't hold on for much longer.

Taking deep, even breaths, I turned around, expecting to find that my captors had fled, as well.

Most had, but not all.

Meg had regained her feet, but she just stood there, unmoving. She was alone. Those of her companions who still could run, had fled, but she hadn't. Couldn't. Once again, fear had her in its grip, and it paralyzed her. Tears streamed from her eyes, streaking down her cheeks, and her whole body shook.

Her thoughts were crystal clear to my supercharged psychic senses. She knew she was going to die, but that wasn't why she was crying. Her tears were born of guilt, of shame. She was sorry. As sorry as anyone had ever been in the history of everything. On top of all that, a single thought streamed through her mind in an endless loop: *wake up, wake up, wake up...*

But this wasn't just a bad dream.

"You should've run," I said through gritted teeth. My heart was breaking for this poor, damaged creature. A tear snuck over the brim of my eyelid and streaked down my cheek. "Why didn't you run?"

"I—" Meg swallowed roughly and shook her head, the motion jerky. "I'm sorry."

"I know," I said, reaching one electrified arm toward her. The blue-green light reflected off the exposed skin of her face and arms. "Close your eyes," I told her. She was about to die; we both knew it, but I didn't want her to see it coming.

Meg's chin trembled and a small sob escaped from her throat. Slowly, reluctantly, she closed her eyes.

I stepped toward her and wrapped my arms around her, holding her tight. She was only the second person I had hugged in as long as I could remember, but it felt like the right thing to do. In the grand scheme of things, she was just a kid. Adults are always telling teenagers that life isn't fair, and Meg was a prime example of that fact. She didn't deserve to be trapped underground her whole life, and she didn't deserve to have such a shit-hole mom, and regardless of what she had done to me, she didn't deserve to die tonight, right here, right now. She didn't deserve any of it, and it wasn't fair. It was complete and utter bullshit.

"It'll be OK," I whispered, inhaling deeply and squeezing Meg as tightly as I could. On my exhale, I relaxed my hold on the wicked energy raging through my body. At that exact moment, Peri emerged from the furthest depths of my mind and ripped the reins out of my hands. The instant she took over, I felt her determination to control the explosion of energy.

In a heartbeat, I was drowning. I was being burned alive. I was caught up in an avalanche, my body being crushed as it was torn apart. I was dead, and alive, and every state in between. I held onto Meg as the world burned around me, consumed by aquamarine fire.

As the last dregs of wild, foreign energy drained out of me, my knees gave out, and I dropped, Meg's body falling with me. I whimpered as my shoulder touched the ground, and then my head struck the soft earth. My skin felt raw, like I had spent too many hours sunbathing, and my vison was eclipsed by an aquamarine void. I could hear a whooshing sound that reminded me of waves crashing against the rocks at the bottom of the bluff.

Was I home? Had I found my way back to Blackthorn Manor?

What felt like a razor sliced across my forehead, over my temple, and behind my ear, the pain jolting through my body. My muscles tensed, making my bones creak.

The sound of crashing waves grew louder. I felt a sharp pressure against my temples, quickly followed by a warm, tingling sensation that slowly spread out, numbing my body and my mind. The pain was gone. The tension, the hurt, the fear, the sorrow…it was all gone. There was only the sound of the waves, and even that was fading now.

I relaxed into the peace, the calm. I let my awareness fade away. Four words drifted through my mind as I sank into the deepest, darkest depths of unconsciousness. Four impossible words, spoken by an impossible voice.

"It will be OK…"

18

"Persephone?" a woman said, her voice hushed.

Another someone touched my temples with gentle fingers.

"Cora?"

My brain throbbed in my skull, and my mind was a tide pool of mismatching thoughts. It took me a moment to figure out the speaker and the toucher were likely the same person.

I groaned, cracking my eyes open and squinting into the darkness. I was on my back, watching fluffy flakes of snow fall from the sky, tinted a soft blue as they reflected back the glow from my regulator. Not snow, I realized. Ash.

"Are you all right?" Meg's face slid into view, illuminated by a dual-tone glow—electric- blue from my regulator and vibrant amethyst from hers.

My brow furrowed. "You're not dead," I said—or tried to say. The words came out as more of a croak.

"Here," Meg said, reaching out and sliding her hand behind my neck. She raised my head and brought the mouth of a water-skin to my lips. "Drink some water. Your throat is sure to be raw after all of that screaming."

Confused, I took in a mouthful of water, sputtering most of it back up before Meg poured a smaller amount into my mouth. I managed to swallow that second mouthful in one gulp. She was right about my throat. The water burned like vodka going down.

I accepted a few more swallows of water, then pushed the waterskin away and propped myself up on my elbows. I cleared my throat, wincing slightly. "How are you still alive?" I asked Meg, barely managing a hoarse whisper.

"You saved me," she said, a small, tight-lipped smile barely visible in the ashen darkness.

I shook my head, then winced. The headache was worse than ever, and my throbbing brain hadn't appreciated the motion. "I don't understand."

"Look around us," Meg said, giving our surroundings an exaggerated scan.

I sat up the rest of the way and looked around. It was hard to see much of anything because of the ash falling from the sky like heavy snowfall. The towering trees were gone, as was the overgrown underbrush. I couldn't even determine if it was day or if it was still night.

"You destroyed everything around us," Meg explained. "But you didn't destroy me. You *saved* me."

I glanced down at myself. The stone in my regulator had reverted from that unnatural aquamarine to its usual electric blue. I was still wearing the loose-fitting, silken tunic and pants, and the ultra-soft fabric seemed to be in perfect condition, save for the half-inch of ash covering the tops of my legs. Like before, with the energy blast that destroyed the Order's commandos, everything I was wearing was unscathed. It was like I was the eye of the storm, a small pocket of safety as I unleashed an electrified hell on the world around me. It was all I could come up with to explain Meg's state of not-deadness.

I raised a hand and massaged my temples with my thumb and fingertips. Worry deadening the ache in my skull. Had Raiden and Caly escaped the energized inferno? An icy fist reached into my chest, closing its cold fingers around my heart and squeezing. Were little pieces of them floating down on me right now?

"How far out does the blast zone reach?" I asked, my voice thick with dread.

"I don't know," Meg said, turning her head to gaze out at the ashen blizzard cloaking the wreckage. "I walked out fifteen paces but didn't want to risk going farther." She glanced at me, her brows drawn together, then returned to staring into the gray-out. "I didn't want to leave you for too long."

Eyes narrowing slightly, I studied Meg's profile. I wasn't connected to her like before, though I could sense the general flavor of her current emotions. Duty. Obligation. Devotion. I couldn't tell more without alerting her to my psychic snooping. And honestly, I wasn't sure I had it in me to really read her mind right now, when my own felt like pulsating jelly.

"I did what I could to alleviate your aches and pains," Meg said, staring out into the fuzzy gray void. "You weren't injured, but your nerve endings were overexcited after the energy flare." She looked at me, finally, a frown turning down the corners of her mouth and furrowing her brow. "I did my best not to invade your privacy, but I couldn't help noticing your brain is—" She broke eye contact, staring down at her hands. "The structure is abnormal."

"How so?" I asked, both incredibly curious and terribly afraid. Ilyana hadn't mentioned any specifics about what she found during her psychic interrogation, only that she had believed me to be in need of a session in the asclypos.

"Adult minds tend to sort of crystalize," Meg explained, "sealing in our personalities and behavioral patterns. But children's brains are more plastic, more malleable. The structure changes easily as they learn and experience new things." She shook her head slowly. "It's like your brain is trying to shift like a child's, but because it's already set in its adult formation, it is fractured, structurally." Her eyes returned to mine. "And the damage is spreading. At the rate I witnessed, I would expect periodic loss of consciousness and short-term memory loss to begin in a few days, increasing in frequency and duration until you're unable to regain consciousness at all."

I swallowed my dread, almost choking on it. Peri had already been fairly certain of our malady—our fractured consciousness was affecting the physiology of my brain—but I had been holding out hope she was wrong. Looked like she had her proof. This made for one hell of a told-you-so.

"Awesome," I grumbled, massaging the base of my skull. Whereas the ache had been contained to the front of my skull before, it now was a full-brain phenomenon.

"You're not surprised," Meg said. Not a question. She sensed the lack of shock roused by her revelation.

I shrugged one shoulder, staring off into the cloud of falling ash. More than anything, I felt disappointment. Here, I had reached a state of relative normalcy—minus the ancient, dead alien consciousness hitching a ride in my mind—allowing me to finally venture out into the world, and I might never get to enjoy it. An outsider might say it was ironic, or even poetic. They might call it a cruel twist of fate. But to me, it was just so very disappointing.

I looked at Meg, about to tell her about Peri and the fractured consciousness—what harm could it do? Except, when I looked at her, I noticed a blister rapidly forming on her cheek. In a matter of seconds, it popped and started oozing blood down the side of her face.

I looked around hastily, until I spotted the tell-tale glow of the sun behind me—just a sliver, barely visible through the thick cloud of ash. "The sun's rising," I said, turning back to Meg. There were blisters on both cheeks now, and on her forehead. "We need to get you to shelter."

Meg's eyes were locked on the deadly glow hovering beyond my shoulder. The color had drained from her cheeks making the crimson blood stand out in stark contrast against her pallid skin.

I tore the waterskin from her grasp and poured the water onto the ground, spreading it around to wet as much of the ash as possible. Working quickly, I scooped up sodden ashes with both hands and slapped the soggy mess onto Meg's cheeks, smearing it around like a spa mud mask. She looked astonished for all of two seconds, then grabbed handfuls of the ashy muck and started covering her arms while I moved on to her legs.

Once she was sufficiently covered in the gray sludge and protected from the sun—for a time, at least—we stood, both scanning the gray expanse stretching out in all directions.

"Any idea of which way to go?" I asked.

Meg shook her head.

"This way it is, then," I said, starting off in the direction I was already facing.

After only a half-dozen steps slogging through the shin-deep ashfall, I started coughing. It was impossible not to inhale the falling ash now that I was moving. I lifted the collar of my tunic so the thin fabric covered my nose and mouth. It didn't stop the flecks of ash from getting stuck in my eyes, but at least I could breathe a little better.

I glanced over my shoulder. With her fitted leather armor, Meg wasn't so lucky. But she was a trooper. She held one hand over her nose and mouth, cupped to shelter her airways.

The ashen wasteland seemed to stretch out into oblivion before us, and the dread spawned by Meg's revelation about my failing neural structure was soon overshadowed by the overwhelming fear that the energy I had released had destroyed far more of the rainforest than I had thought possible. With each passing step, I felt less hopeful that Raiden and Caly had made it far enough away in time.

I shielded my heart against the mounting grief and crippling guilt. Once I let those devastating feelings in, I would be done for. I would collapse into a miserable, sobbing heap. I would be beyond useless—and I couldn't afford that right now. *Meg* couldn't afford that. After everything, I couldn't let her die now.

Not quite ten minutes into our trek—or so I guessed—towering shadows appeared in the not-so-far-off distance. Shadows became half-scorched trees and smoldering underbrush. Thankfully it must have rained recently, or the whole rainforest might have gone up in flames.

After another few steps, the air started to clear, and the rainforest surrounding us looked almost normal, save for seared tree limbs that must have been projected out of the blast zone during the energy explosion.

I dropped the tunic from my face and turned to ask Meg if she had any idea of where we were—and where we might find shelter—only to have her run past me.

"This way!" she called back to me, her pace increasing.

I jogged the first few steps, then settled into a not-so-comfortable run. My arms pumped and my lungs burned after only a few minutes. Clearly Meg was in far better shape than I was. Plus, the threat of being roasted to death by the sun had to be a great motivator.

I was about to tell Meg I needed to slow down when I suddenly recognized where we were. The massive ceiba tree was straight ahead, the opening to the hollow at its base just visible beyond an arching root.

Meg raced ahead, then skidded to a stop mere steps from safety. She raised her hands out in front of her and backed up a step.

I slowed to a jog. "What are you—"

"Cora?" Raiden said, stepping out from the darkness shielding the mouth of the hollow.

Stunned, I stumbled over a shallow tree root. Once I'd regained my footing, I lurched ahead, bounding the rest of the way toward Raiden. I threw myself at him, wrapping my arms around him as tightly as I could. My whole body shook with bottled up sobs as I basked in the relief of finding him alive. I might have sensed his mind if I hadn't been so preoccupied by trying to keep up with Meg, but that didn't matter right now.

I was so caught up in the moment that it took me a solid thirty seconds to notice Caly lurking behind him in the shadows. She held my doru in a steady, two-handed grip, the focus crystal charged a vibrant rose pink.

"Caly?" I said, releasing Raiden and sidestepping around him. I looked from her to Meg and back. She aimed the charged focus crystal at Meg's chest. "What are you doing?"

Caly didn't look at me. Rage burned in her eyes, though it paled in comparison to the sensation roiling from her. I couldn't help but feel a little grateful for the lack of attention spent on me. She spat out a string of harsh-sounding syllables in a language I didn't understand, and my psychic senses automatically sought out her mind for the translation. I slammed into a rock-solid mental wall. This was a Caly unlike I had ever seen. This Caly was truly her mother's daughter.

Meg's shoulders slumped as Caly finished her incomprehensible scolding, and her head hung in defeat.

Caly's attention snapped to me, the rage fading, giving way to warm relief. The corners of her mouth lifted. "We feared the worst," she said, raising the doru and planting the butt end on the ground. "I'm glad to see you survived." The stink eye she sent Meg's way told me loud and clear her relief didn't extend to her one-time idol.

"Are you all right?" Raiden asked, hand gripping my elbow gently.

Glancing his way, I nodded. I wasn't willing to take my attention off Caly for much longer than a glance. Something significant had just happened between her and Meg, and I didn't fully trust her not to turn on Meg and blast a hole in her chest, just as she had done to Lyvia.

"Good," Raiden said, tightening his grip and guiding me into the hollow. "Come on, we've got your stuff. You can clean up and change before we settle in to wait out nightfall."

Caly had already retreated back into the sheltering safety of the hollow, but when I glanced over my shoulder at Meg, I found her in exactly the same place as she'd been, standing in the full force of the morning sunlight. Cracks were appearing in her ashen coating, and crimson streaked the gray all over her body.

I dug my heals into the earth, preventing Raiden from pulling me farther along. "Meg?" My brow furrowed. "Don't just stand there. Come on." I waved her forward. "Get out of the sun."

She folded her arms over her middle and shook her head.

Caly stepped forward, arms crossed over her chest. "She can't follow us," Caly said grimly. "I banished her. She is no longer allowed to have any contact with the Zari for the remainder of her life…however short that may be."

I scoffed and rolled my eyes. "Well," I said, yanking my arm free of Raiden's grasp, "I'm sure she can manage to huddle in the opposite corner of the hollow from you for a few hours without breeching the rules of your banishment." I grabbed Meg's arm, just above the elbow, and pulled her into the sheltering darkness.

When I turned back to Caly, her lips were pressed together in a thin, flat line. "The rules of banishment state that the banished cannot breathe the same air as the Zari," Caly said, raising her eyebrows to emphasize her point.

"Come on, Caly," I said, intending to appeal to the sweet, good-natured girl I had spent so much time with underground.

"She drugged us," Caly snapped. "She was kidnapping you." Caly narrowed her eyes and shook her head. "Why are you defending her?" Her rage had a distinctive, personal note, like that of a woman scorned. Only, this was worse. A love interest hadn't betrayed Caly; she had been betrayed by someone she idolized. Or, someone she *had* idolized.

"I—" Any and every possible explanation stuck in my throat. How could I share the things I knew about Meg, when *I* didn't even have permission to know them? Whatever Meg had done, her reasons weren't mine to tell.

One look at Meg, and I knew she wouldn't utter a single word of defense—or at all—in Caly's presence. I sensed her desire to follow the banishment to the letter of the law, and only her instinctive desire to survive prevented her from running out of the hollow and into the poisonous sunlight to remain compliant.

"It's hard to explain," I finally said. I inhaled deeply, letting the breath out as a sigh. "But even though she probably deserves banishment, I swear to you, she doesn't deserve to die."

My claim ignited a spark of curiosity within Caly, and I sensed her internal struggle to fight past our protective psychic barriers and find out the truth for herself. Caly huffed out a breath. "Fine," she said. "Meg can stay, but just until nightfall. Then I don't ever want to see her traitorous face again."

"Done," I said, nodding once. "She'll leave with us."

Finally, something got through to Meg, and she raised her head, her eyes locking on me.

"Whoa, whoa, whoa," Raiden said, raising his hands in protest. "What do you mean—*leave*? The safest place for us right now is down in that underground city. We need to stay here for the time being."

I offered him a small, sad smile. "We can't stay here."

He raised one eyebrow. "Why not?"

My eyes locked with his. "Because if we stay, I'll die."

19

Raiden sat with his back to the pool in the cavern beneath the hollow as Meg and I stripped down to our birthday suits and waded into the water. Thankfully, most of the pool was shaded by the high cavern walls, protecting Meg and Caly from the sun's toxic touch.

I was really, *really* glad Raiden was turned away because Meg's body was amazing. Athletic and lean, with curves everywhere they should be. Though I was at least seven or eight years her senior, standing beside Meg, I felt like Skipper standing next to Barbie.

Peri wouldn't have felt insecure, which I realized was totally insane because Peri and I *literally* had the same body. This version may not have been as well-honed as her last, but the exact same genetic pattern created it, and it wasn't like I never exercised. I worked out regularly. Or, at least, semi-regularly.

Fine, I rarely "worked out" but I was fairly active. For a gamer.

Peri had a bone-deep sense of confidence and absolute security with herself and her place in the world. She was a psychic warrior in the Order of Amazons. She was the baddest of the badasses, and few warriors—even among the Amazons—could stand against her. How the apple had fallen so far from the tree was beyond me, but it had fallen, rolled, bouncing and bruising, and ended up in an entirely different orchard.

I washed quickly, not lazing about in the pool like I had the last time, and I scraped off as much of the water as I could with my hands before slipping into the hoplon suite. The channels running the length of the suit lit up with a subtle amber glow the instant I picked it up, matching the stone in my activated regulator. The suit slid on easily despite the stickiness of wet skin, and it quickly wicked away the remaining moisture.

I turned my attention to Caly, who was leaning against the cavern wall in the deepest, darkest patch of shade, arms crossed over her chest. Raiden lounged on a boulder nearby, prepping some MREs for an impromptu picnic. Unlike Raiden, who was giving Meg and me some privacy, Caly's glare never left Meg.

"Fiona seems like our best bet to fix the holodisk," I said, returning to a subject we had touched on only briefly before retreating to the cavern. "Unless you suddenly remember some secret holodisk repair machine you guys have stashed away down there, Caly…"

Caly finally tore her glare away from Meg and met my eyes. "There's nothing like that," she said, lowering her arms. She pushed away from the wall and started pacing, pausing every few steps to kick a stray pebble or scraggly shrub. "At least, not that we know about." She put a little more force behind her next kick, beheading a delicate white flower. "Hades didn't exactly share all the Olympian tech with us. There're entire buildings we don't enter because their purpose is a mystery."

I nodded lazily as Caly's words confirmed my understanding of the situation. I looked at Raiden. "So, we go to Ireland, then."

Fiona was as tech-savvy as any MIT graduate or NASA engineer. She was a one-time child prodigy who had grown into a jaded young woman, utterly disinterested in the world around her. The real world bored her, so she spent her ample free time in virtual reality. Plus, I trusted Fiona. She wasn't just my only choice. She was the right person for the job, period.

I made my way over to Raiden and the cluster of stool-size boulders situated near the far side of the pool. He had already prepped four MREs, and the warmed entrées were propped up against our packs. He absentmindedly rubbed the side of his bad knee as he stared across the pool at the holographic entrance to the labyrinth. He was right here, within arm's reach of me, but his mind was a million miles away.

I studied him for a moment, then surveyed the offerings and promptly reached for the chili mac. It was my favorite of the MRE entrées I had tried so far, which wasn't really saying much, but at least it was edible.

I settled on the boulder to the right of Raiden. "Is your knee bugging you?" I asked him.

He blinked, looked at me, then glanced down at his knee like he hadn't even realized he was rubbing it. Maybe he hadn't. He shook his head. "It feels normal," he said, then laughed under his breath. "Which is weird because I got used to the ache." The way he said it made me think he missed the pain.

"Well, there's your silver lining," I said, scooping a bite of chili mac into my mouth.

Raiden raised one eyebrow.

I swallowed and cleared my throat, returning the spoon to the food pouch. "You get blood poisoning in the middle of the Amazon Rainforest, almost die, and end up not just healed of the infection, but healed *everywhere*. No more bad knee." I tilted my head to the side, bringing the loaded spoon up to my mouth. I paused before taking the bite. "Silver lining," I said, eyebrows raised, then stuck the loaded spoon into my mouth.

Raiden grunted and returned to staring up at the entrance to the labyrinth. "As soon as we put some distance between us and this place, I'll try the satphone," he said. "Let our moms know where we're headed. Hopefully they can meet us there."

I nodded as I chewed, not fooled by the subject change.

Losing the constant ache in his knee was clearly bugging Raiden, and I had a sneaking suspicion it had something to do with the memory I had seen of the military disaster that had turned Raiden from a team member to a lone survivor in the blink of an eye. While I easily could have deactivated my regulator and plucked the exact reason from his mind, I didn't need to have been raised among the psychically gifted to know doing so would be poor etiquette. Besides, my intentions would be broadcasted loud and clear when the channels running the length of the hoplon suit changed from amber to electric blue.

"And we'll need help getting transport to Ireland," Raiden continued, oblivious to my armchair analysis of his wounded psyche. "Diana's bound to have some connections down here."

I stuck the spoon into the congealing chili mac, set the half-eaten pouch on my lap, and licked my lips. "Um, yeah, about that..."

Raiden looked at me, his expression blank.

I shifted my attention across the pool, watching Meg finger-comb her long, dark hair. "Meg's not just *leaving the rainforest* with us," I said, the words falling out in a rush. "I want to bring her to Ireland." Reluctantly, I returned my attention to Raiden, breath held as I waited for his reaction.

Bringing Meg meant waiting for nightfall. It meant travel would be much more difficult, and we would have to be very strategic to keep her safe. But, in a roundabout way, she was in this mess because of me. All the Zari were—thanks to Hades— and that knowledge was a heavy weight on my conscience. I would do everything I could to help the Zari once I reached the Omega site, but that felt like a far distant future, dependent on too many unknowns and what-ifs. But I could help Meg, here and now, and I *would* help her.

Raiden stared at me for a solid five seconds, his expression unchanging. He inhaled and exhaled deeply through his nose, his head bobbing the slightest nod. "I figured you were going to say that."

I blew out a breath. Both surprised and relieved by his reaction.

"But if she slows us down too much," Raiden said, a sharp edge lining his words, "we're leaving her behind."

I clenched my jaw, holding in a retort. Raiden knew full well he couldn't do a damn thing to make me follow orders. Not physically, at least. He was bigger, but I was better.

"I won't let you sacrifice your life for hers," Raiden said, eyes turning glassy. "I can't lose you, Cora. I just…" His voice broke. "I can't."

I gulped, my heart aching. I would do almost anything to ease his pain. "All right," I said, slipping one hand behind my back, my fingers crossed. "If she slows us down too much, we'll leave her behind."

Uncrossing my fingers, I picked up the spoon and took another bite of luke-warm chili mac. I would do *almost* anything.

But not that.

[20]

"Are you absolutely sure about this?" Caly asked me, hands on her hips as she eyed Meg.

The other Zari young woman stood near the mouth of the hollow with her hands clasped together, her head bowed slightly, and her eyes downcast. It was dusk, and the bright, verdant colors seemed to drain out of the rainforest with the fading sunlight.

"Yes, Caly," I said. "I'm sure. She's coming with us."

"I don't like it," Caly said, her eyes narrowing on Meg.

With a growl of frustration—the first real emotion I had seen from Meg since the banishment—Meg yanked her regulator off over her head and thrust her arm out toward me, the glowing amber pendant dangling from its golden chain.

Caly's mouth fell open, her eyes widening in surprise. Her shock at Meg's seemingly random action was so severe that she broke the laws and spoke directly to the banished girl. "Are you sure?" Caly asked Meg, her brow furrowing.

Meg nodded once, raising her eyes to meet Caly's, just for a moment.

Raiden and I exchanged a confused look, and he frowned as I shrugged.

When Caly turned her attention to me, her eyes were bright. "Take Meg's regulator, Cora."

Hesitantly, I did as she directed. Clearly something important was happening, but as before with the banishment, I had no clue what that something was.

"Now deactivate your regulator," Caly told me. "And, whatever you do, don't let go."

Again, I did as she directed, running the tip of my pointer finger around the stone set in my regulator until the glow changed from subtle amber to brilliant, electric blue. The chain grasped in my hand started to hum with psychic energy, the vibrations increasing until they sent an uncomfortable tingling sensation through my hand and up my arm. The metal heated, stinging my palm. The burning was almost unbearable, and I had to fight the urge to open my hand and drop the other regulator.

Until, suddenly, it stopped. A point of bright blue appeared in the heart of Meg's regulator, slowly bleeding out through the amber like ink in water. After a few seconds, the stone was an exact match to the one in the regulator worn around my neck.

I glanced at Caly sidelong. "What just happened?"

"You just synced Meg's regulator with your own. You created a bond between the two regulators, and that bond will carry over to you and Meg when you are both wearing them. Your regulator is now master to hers," Caly said, her voice grave. "As *you* will be master to *her*."

My lips parted, and I shook my head. "Uh no," I said, fighting an even stronger urge to drop the regulator, now. "Hard no. I'm nobody's master." A hysteria-tinged laugh escaped from my chest. "I'm hardly even *my own* master." I shook the regulator at Caly. "Undo it. I don't want it," I said, then repeated myself, emphasizing each word. "I do not want it."

"What is done cannot be undone," Caly said, raising her chin stubbornly. "And even if it could be changed, I wouldn't do it."

Hurt and shame rolled off Meg in waves. She did nothing to guard her mind, and I could sense the reason for her reaction without even searching for it. She had offered me her soul, and I had shunned her offering. Her emotions bled into me, overpowering my own.

Turning to face Meg, I swallowed roughly, tears welling in my eyes. "I—" I cleared my throat, swiping a tear from my cheek. "I'm sorry. I didn't mean—" I shook my head. "It's just that I don't believe in, you know, *slavery*." I closed the distance between us and held the regulator out to her. "But if this is what you want, then I accept." I waited for her eyes to meet mine, then flashed her a half-assed smile. It was the best I could manage at the moment. "Just don't expect me to start ordering you around."

Meg sniffed and nodded, raising both hands to wipe her tear-streaked cheeks before reaching for the regulator. The instant I let go, vibrant amethyst streaks cut through the electric blue, reminding me of the color variations in an iris. In a heartbeat, Meg's mind was laid open before me, and I was suddenly seeing double—both through her eyes and through mine. It was like a tether had formed between us, removing all barriers between our minds. Her memories of the past, her thoughts about the present, and her hopes and fears for the future were available to me with the merest thought. And because we were so deeply connected, I knew she was experiencing the same thing, only in reverse.

I closed my eyes, concentrating on blocking out the flood of information flowing into me. I focused on the tether connecting us and clamped down on it, locking it in a psychic vice. I tightened that vice as much as I could until only a trickle passed through.

I sensed Meg's general emotional state—shock and sympathy—and I had an idea of her surface thoughts. I knew her shock was in response to learning about my complicated coexistence with Peri, though Meg wasn't connected to Peri's consciousness like she was to mine, and her sympathy stemmed from learning about the patheticness that was my existence up until I received the package from my mom a little over a week ago.

When I opened my eyes, my stare locked with Meg's. Tears streaked her cheeks, and she reached for me with her free hand, gripping my upper arm tightly. "I had no idea," she said, sniffling softly. "I'm so sorry, Cora."

I shrugged one shoulder, my stare slipping to the far wall of the hollow.

Meg gave my arm one last squeeze, then let go, wiping the fresh tears from her cheeks.

"We should go," Raiden said, stepping closer to the mouth of the hollow and squinting into the darkness beyond. The sliver of moon and starlight cast the surrounding foliage in a ghostly gray light, and a chorus of chirps and croaks had replaced the lush daytime sounds. Raiden checked his oversized watch, tapping the watch face a few times, then sighed.

At the sound of movement to my right, I turned to watch Caly approach. She stopped just out of arm's reach.

"Can you give us a moment?" she asked me softly. There was no hint of hostility in her expression, only an unexpected gentleness.

I nodded once and stepped away, moving to join Raiden at the mouth of the hollow. I stood beside him, the butt of the doru planted on the hard-packed earth. The electric-blue glow emanating from my suit and weapon cast the rainforest beyond in an otherworldly light.

"We're going to move fast," Raiden said, his voice a low rumble. "If she can't keep up…"

I glanced at him sidelong, certain that skepticism was written all over my face. "She's in better shape than either of us," I said. "And she has a lot more experience trekking through this rainforest than we do." I patted his arm. "Don't worry so much." The corner of my mouth tensed, forming a wry smile. "You'll get wrinkles."

Raiden's eyes crinkled at the corners.

At a rush of emotion from Meg—surprise mixed with hope—I focused on our connection. Caly had just told her she thought Meg had done a noble thing, binding herself to me, and that she didn't believe Meg deserved banishment.

"I'll voice my opinion after the High Council views my memories of what happened," Caly said, offering Meg a small smile. "Regardless of what they decide, your banishment no longer holds any weight to me."

Meg's joy flooded into me, making my heart swell with love for Caly. Tears of pure happiness formed in my eyes.

A small sob escaped from Meg, and she threw her arms around Caly's narrow shoulders. "Thank you," Meg whispered, before loosening her hold and backing away a step. "I won't forget this." She started toward the mouth of the hollow to join Raiden and me but paused and turned back to Caly. "I see you, Calysto," she told the other young psychic. "You are far stronger than you think. One day, you will see that, too." Meg bowed her head, then straightened and turned away from Caly, coming to stand at my side.

"Ready to go?" Raiden said, peering out into the dark rainforest.

I glanced over my shoulder, eyes locking with Caly's. *"Thank you,"* I mouthed.

Caly bowed her head, and when she straightened again, she stood a little taller, her shoulders squared and her spine a little straighter. There was no doubt in my mind that her mom would be proud of her.

"Good luck," Caly said, her voice resonant in the darkness.

[21]

"Got a signal!" Raiden said, stopping abruptly. Even though his voice was raised, the soft roar of the downpour muffled his words. Apparently, there's a reason they call it a *rain*forest.

The soles of my boots skidded in the slippery mud as I came to a halt behind him. We had been steadily marching onward for so long, driven by our unrelenting trail leader, Meg, that it felt strange to stand still. My ponytail was plastered down the back of my neck, soaked through by the endless deluge pouring down from the sky, but at least the hoplon suit kept the rest of me warm and dry.

Raiden turned to face me, flashing me a broad grin as he punched numbers into the satphone. His chest heaved with each breath, both from the exertion and from excitement, and every few seconds, he shivered. He wasn't so lucky to be wearing a temperature- and moisture-controlling bodysuit, and the non-stop rain had saturated his clothes and left him chilled to the bone. My regulator was still deactivated, the stone as well as the hoplon suit and doru glowing that tell-tale electric blue, and I could sense his discomfort. It was fairly extreme, though the desperation of our situation was a sufficient distraction.

Meg, on the other hand, wasn't the least bit bothered by her sodden state. This was her home turf—since starting her training as a small child, she had spent hundreds, maybe even thousands of nights walking this rainforest. In her experience, it rained more often than not. And when it rained, it poured.

Meg continued on for a few more steps until she sensed through our clamped bond that I had stopped. She turned and retraced her path until she was peeking over Raiden's shoulder at the screen of the satphone. I expected to sense curiosity from her, but she recognized the device. Tamped down as our bond was, I couldn't pick up on the reason why she recognized the phone. At least, not without being obvious about the fact that I was snooping.

Raiden brought the satphone up to his ear, his stare sliding past me to some distant point in the rainforest as he focused on listening rather seeing.

"The High Council uses satphones to contact our agents out in the world," Meg explained. She must have sensed my surface thoughts.

I shifted my attention to her, thinking of what Ilyana had told me about George Blackthorn, my not-grandfather, and his connection to the Zari. So, it looked like there were more people out there like him, functioning as the Zari's eyes and ears in a world they couldn't inhabit.

"Every few days—in the safety of darkness, of course—we escort a couple of the members of the High Council out beyond the boundaries of the dampener," Meg continued. "They make their calls and discuss the new information on the way back to Akahim." A tiny, wry smile curved her lips. "I'm sure you can imagine how excited the High Council was when their agents in the Custodes Veritatis told them about you showing up in Rome…"

Nodding to myself, I thought back to the events in Rome. It felt like a lifetime ago. The Zari High Council must have been floored to learn that Persephone hadn't been lost, after all. She was right here, inside me.

"Mom," Raiden said, the single word yanking my attention back to him. "Why did it take you so long to answer?" he asked. "Where are you? Is everything OK?"

I could just barely hear Emi's voice, muffled and unintelligible to my ears.

Eyes narrowing, I focused on Raiden's mind, tiptoeing past the thin barrier Caly had taught him to erect, preventing the psychically gifted from picking up his every thought and feeling. Like tuning to a radio signal, Emi's voice slowly became clear to my psychic ears.

"...and you know I can't tell you where we are."

Raiden grunted. "We're on the move, and we need transport. I thought Diana might have some connections."

"I'm sure she does," Emi said. There was a muffled scuffling sound, and then my mom's voice replaced Emi's. *"From where to where?"* she asked. *"But no locations or coordinates,"* she added in a rush.

"Uh..." Raiden's stare locked with mine, a hint of panic lighting his eyes as he tried and failed to think of a way to covertly communicate our travel plans.

As the seconds ticked by without more of a response from Raiden, my mom made an exasperated sound. *"Put Cora on the phone."*

Thinking fast, I accepted the phone when Raiden offered it to me and brought it to my ear. "Hi Mom."

"Hi Cora-bora." This was only the second time I had heard her voice since thinking she might be dead, and it flooded my body with relief. I allowed myself a long moment to bask in the warm sensation, then forced myself to focus on the task at hand.

How could I describe the locations of where we were and where we needed to go in a way my mom would understand, but that nobody else would? My thoughts floundered as I considered my options.

Suddenly, it clicked—souvenirs. My mom *almost* never sent me packages while she was away on expeditions, but she always brought a souvenir home for me.

"You know the thing I like to lounge on when it's sunny?" I said, attempting to subtly refer to the hammock strung up between two trees near the edge of the bluff. My mom had brought it back from Brazil three or four years ago, specifically when she'd flown in and out of Manaus, Raiden's chosen point of departure for this next leg of our grand adventure.

"Yes," my mom said after a quiet moment, "I know what you're talking about."

My lips curved into a pleased smile. "The place where you got it—that's where we need to get *from*."

"All right, I'm following," my mom said.

Now, how to convey Ireland in a subtle way? So far as I knew, she hadn't gone on any expeditions to the Emerald Isle. Mentioning Fiona would be too obvious. I quirked my mouth to the side as I thought.

It took a little longer, but eventually it came to me. "Angel," I blurted. Angel, the soul-cursed vampire who was Buffy's love interest during the first three seasons of the greatest show *ever* was from Ireland. It was where he had been born, and where he had been *re*born as a vampire. My mom used to watch *Buffy* with me. It was our weekly ritual when she was home; when she was away, I would record any new episodes and save them for when she returned.

My mom was quiet for a long moment. "You're going to have to give me more than that, sweetheart."

I tapped my foot in the sloppy earth, the toe of my boot making a soft slapping sound. "You know—grr…argh," I said, quoting the bit that followed the credits of every episode.

"Ohhh," she said, and I could practically hear her smiling.

"Got it," she said. "But you could still be talking about a few different places…"

"Birthplace," I said, hoping desperately that I wasn't being too obvious.

"I see," she said. "Are you going there to see who I think you're going to see?" She was referring to Fiona, the only person she knew that I knew in Ireland.

I grinned. "Exactly."

"All right," my mom said. "I can get you there. Find locker number…" She drew out the "r" sound, like she was waiting for something. "Locker 314 in the central bus station in your departure city," she told me. "You know the combo to the lock. There will be further instructions inside."

"OK, thanks," I said, then glanced at Meg. She would need some heavy-duty sun protection if she was going to make it halfway across the world alive. "Can you make sure there's a burka or a nun's habit in the locker, too?"

"Sure…" I could hear the desire to ask why in my mom's voice, but my mom knew as well as I did that the less information we exchanged over this unsecure line, the better.

"And Mom?"

"Yeah, sweetie?"

"The faster we can get there, the better."

My mom was quiet for a long moment. "What's wrong?"

Out of nowhere, tears flooded my eyes, and I was suddenly very grateful for the camouflage provided by the cold, rainy night. "It's a long story," I said, sighing. "Can you guys meet us at *you know where*?"

"Yes, of course," she said.

"OK, good," I said. "I'll explain everything then."

"All right…" My mom didn't sound happy with the arrangement. "Be careful, Cora," she said, stealing my half of our usual goodbye.

My chin trembled, and I sniffed back a sob. "Always."

22

"Thank you," I said, flashing a closed-mouth smile as I accepted the brightly patterned blanket from Davi, the riverboat operator's grandson.

Even if he didn't understand my words, he caught their meaning well enough, grinning and bobbing his head enthusiastically.

Davi was a sweet kid of around fourteen or fifteen years, and he had fallen head-over-heels in love with Meg the second we stepped foot on his grandfather's riverboat. He had been more than happy to dig through their storage bins in search of a blanket for his lady love.

I carried the blanket to the stern of the rudimentary craft, where Meg was huddled in the sliver of shade the boat's canopy provided from the rising sun. "Here," I said, shaking the blanket out and draping it over Meg's shoulders.

She adjusted the blanket, raising it over her head to shield her face, too. Her relief was palpable through the bond we shared, and now that she was protected from the sun's poisonous rays, she allowed herself to relax a little.

"Do you need anything else?" I asked, hands resting on my

hips. It wasn't like she could do much while hiding under the blanket.

Meg shook her head and flashed me a tight smile. "No. Thank you, though."

"OK, well, just shout if you need anything." I waited for her to nod before turning away from her and making my way up to the bow of the riverboat, leaving Meg under the watchful eye of her admirer.

Raiden stood at the snub-nosed bow with the boat's owner and operator, Jojo. The rain had waned from a downpour to a drizzle about an hour before we reached Jojo's village. At least the overcast sky provided some protection from the sun, but it wasn't nearly enough for Meg's well-being.

I touched Raiden's arm, exchanging a tense look with him. In his head, he was already sifting through arguments for why we should leave Meg behind. I didn't even need to push past his mental barrier to know that; it was written all over his face.

"She not well?" Jojo asked, glancing over his shoulder at Meg. His broken English was so heavily accented, it took me a moment to puzzle out the meaning of his words.

I shook my head. "Not exactly."

Jojo narrowed his eyes and called back to his grandson, speaking in his native tongue. Jojo's mind was unguarded, and I sensed the meaning of his words. He viewed Meg as a danger, and he wanted Davi to keep his distance from her.

The boy trudged up toward the bow, plopping down on the bench lining the left side of the boat and splitting his attention between glaring at his grandfather and staring longingly back at Meg.

"You trouble," Jojo said. "You pay double—triple to keep blanket."

I clenched my jaw, but nodded, agreeing to the sudden price hike. After all, he was right. We were trouble—more trouble than he could ever guess. I did not, however, look at Raiden, though I felt his eyes boring into the side of my face. He wanted to dump Meg as soon as possible.

I speared him with my sharpest side eye and shook my head, once to the left, once to the right.

Raiden huffed out a breath and crossed his arms over his chest, his stare shifting from me to the river winding out before us, a thousand miles of arguments and excuses in his eyes.

"How much longer until we reach Manaus?" I asked Jojo. We had been on the boat for a couple of hours, but I had no internal map when it came to traveling the Amazon River.

"Midnight," Jojo said, then frowned. He didn't like the prospect of having us on his boat for such a long time, and he was playing with the idea of demanding even more money from us.

I considered calling him on his unvoiced extortion but thought better of it. Based on his provincial existence, my reading of his thoughts would probably make him think I was some sort of witch. Fear would only breed hostility, and we needed Jojo and his riverboat.

I crossed my arms over my chest, mirroring Raiden's tough-guy pose, and kept my mouth shut. Knowing how Jojo would see me if he was aware of my psychic abilities—as a monster—bothered me more than I would have expected. I couldn't help but wonder how the rest of the world would see me. What if they knew I wasn't just a psychic, but an *alien* psychic? Would that be worse? Was the Custodes Veritatis right to hide the existence of my people from the world?

Hating that train of thought, I turned and trudged back to the stern of the riverboat where our packs were propped against some well-used crates. I crouched in front of my pack and dug through the main pocket in search of the storage cubes, mentally cursing myself for yet again stowing them near the bottom of the bag.

Two-thirds of the contents of my pack was on the deck by the time I found the cubes. I pulled them out and set them beside me on the deck, then went about stuffing everything back into the bag.

Finally, I propped my re-packed bag against a crate and leaned against the pack, the two ancient storage cubes in hand. I quickly plucked out the holodisk containing Hades' logs, watched the holographic writing appear over my palm, and scrolled to the point where I had left off.

I skimmed the lines of Olympian writing, seeking the last words I remembered reading.

Never again...

―――

"Hey, Cora," Raiden said, nudging my shoulder.

"Huh?" Blinking, I tore my stare from the holographic screen and focused on Raiden. His face was lined with concern. "What?" I asked, brow furrowing. My head throbbed, and I rubbed my temples with my thumb and forefinger.

I glanced at the blanket-cloaked lump that was Meg. At some point during my perusal of Hades' ancient logs, she had stretched out on the bench, covering her entire body with the blanket. Through our bond, I sensed she was asleep.

I returned my attention to Raiden. "What's wrong?"

His eyes narrowed, his gaze scrutinizing. "Just making sure you're OK," he said, dropping to one knee in front of me. "You were pretty zoned out," he added. "I had to say your name three times."

Tensing one side of my mouth, I shrugged. "Sorry," I said, returning the holodisk to the open storage cube and pushing the cube shut. "Maybe it's all in my head, but I feel like it's harder to understand Olympian now than it was before. I have to concentrate on each word to understand its meaning." I sighed and shook my head. "It makes my brain hurt even more." I scrubbed my hands over my face, taking a moment to massage my eye sockets with my palms.

As soon as my focus returned to Raiden's face, I knew I shouldn't have mentioned my headache. The worry lines on his forehead had deepened, and I sensed fear emanating from him, even through his flimsy mental barrier. He was terrified of losing me.

Funny enough, I was afraid of that exact same thing. The language becoming more difficult to translate was frightening enough, but making matters worse, I hadn't heard a peep from Peri for quite some time. The last time I had felt her presence was right before the energy explosion, when she had wrested control at the last second, intent on minimizing the damage. Maybe she had managed to dampen the explosion a bit, but I feared she might have unintentionally sped up the physical degradation caused by our fractured consciousness.

"I'm sorry, Raiden," I said, extending my arms over my head and arching my back in a much-needed stretch. "I meant that figuratively," I lied, then sank back into my pack-turned-backrest. "Bad joke…"

Raiden let out a noncommittal grunt, but the fear wafting off him faded to a barely perceptible level. It was still there, only it no longer made my heart hurt from sympathy pains.

On foot and knee, Raiden shuffled over to his pack a few feet away. He unzipped the front pocket and drew out two protein bars. "Hungry?" he asked, holding one out to me.

I nodded and accepted the protein bar, the package crinkling in my hand.

Raiden pulled a full water bottle out of a side pouch and turned around, resting against his pack beside me, his arm brushing against mine. He stretched his legs out in front of him and twisted the lid off his water bottle, raising it to his lips for a couple of swigs. He lowered the water bottle and wiped his mouth with the back of his hand, then cleared his throat.

"So," he said, "did you learn anything useful from that thing?" He glanced at the storage cube containing the holodisk of Hades' logs.

I bobbed my head back and forth, not quite sure myself. "Yes and no," I said, leaning my head back to stare up at the stretch of clouds visible beyond the edge of the riverboat's canopy. I could just make out the spot where the sun brightened the sky, directly overhead. It was the middle of the day, which meant I had been lost to Hades' increasingly pessimistic ramblings for hours.

"I don't have any more of an idea where the Omega site is, if that's what you mean," I told Raiden. "But I feel like I have a much better understanding of Hades and what drove him to create the labyrinths…and to curse the Zari."

"Oh yeah?" Raiden said, words garbled by a mouthful of protein bar.

"Yeah." I raised my head, already feeling the first signs of a crick forming in my neck and stared down at my own protein bar. "Every thousand years he would wake from cryosleep and venture out into the world to check the progress of human civilization." I thought back to all I had read—seven millennia of hope gradually turned to disappointment. "At first, he would get excited about each new civilization, viewing it as the one that would eventually push mankind far enough along the progress meter to help him save his people." *Our people,* I silently corrected myself.

Raiden swallowed the bite he was chewing and looked at me sidelong. "Save them, how? I thought all the Olympians were dead." After a moment, Raiden added, "Except for you, of course…and maybe Hades."

I nodded as he spoke. "Yeah, so did I," I said. "But as it turns out, Hades stored thousands of Olympian consciousnesses in the Omega site—in a chamber he calls the 'Vault of Souls'."

I fiddled with the corner of the protein bar's wrapper as I recalled the crystalline orb that had once held Peri's glittering blue consciousness and imagined the Vault of Souls to be like a massive library filled with row after row of shelves packed full of such orbs. In reality, it was probably a lot more sci-fi and spacey than that. Less *Harry Potter*, more *Alien*.

"He was biding his time," I continued. "Still is, hopefully— waiting until humans develop the tech to create an energy source strong enough to power the gephyra." I glanced at Raiden. "That's an Olympian machine that creates a gateway joining two distant points across the universe, kind of like a stargate."

I knew Raiden would understand the reference. He had never been into sci-fi shows and movies—not like I was—but he hadn't hated the *Stargate* franchise. I supposed the military element must have been strong enough to hold his interest.

"Once Hades could get the gephyra up and running," I continued, "he planned to check out a few of the abandoned Olympian colonies on other planets and scavenge parts to repair some damaged equipment here on Earth—stuff he needed to transfer those stored consciousnesses into new bodies."

"You mean, clones?" Raiden said, crumpling his empty protein bar wrapper until it was hidden in his fist. "Like with Persephone…and you?"

I tore off one corner of the protein bar wrapper and set it down beside me on the boat's deck. "Hades didn't—doesn't— want to clone our people," I said cautiously. Hesitantly. "That was just for me…to bring me back." I poked my nail into the corner of the protein bar, making a crescent-shaped indentation. "You know, so I could help him deal with the bigger issue of saving our people." I avoided looking at Raiden, not wanting him to pick up on the half-truth. I wasn't too keen on letting it spill that Peri and Hades had actually been in love—or that Peri's feelings for Hades seemed to be bleeding over into me.

"I'm not sure it counts as 'saving' something if it's already gone," Raiden murmured.

I sighed, shoulders slumping. "Fine, you're right, he wants to resurrect them," I said with a woo woo finger wave. "Bring them back from the dead. It's probably how he ended up as the ancient Greek god of the dead in the first place."

We were quiet for a long moment.

"You know what I can't quite figure out?" Raiden said.

I turned my head to look at him, eyebrows raised.

"If he's not planning on cloning the rest of his people—"

"My people," I interjected.

"Yeah, yeah," Raiden said, waving a hand dismissively. "If he's not planning on cloning them, then how is he going to bring them back?" Raiden narrowed his eyes in thought. "I mean, they'll need bodies…"

I swallowed purposely, my saliva suddenly feeling too thick and tacky. I had really been hoping Raiden wouldn't ask that question.

I inhaled deeply, held my breath for a few seconds, then let it out slowly. "The original plan," I finally said, "was to imprint Olympian consciousness on human minds. Not like how Peri is in here"—I tapped the side of my head—"sharing the real estate." I took another deep breath. "A complete overwrite, like a recording over something on a VHS tape."

"Hold up," Raiden said. "Like, body-snatching?"

I raised one shoulder in a half-hearted shrug. "Kind of, yeah," I admitted. "That was the *original* plan, over twelve thousand years ago. According to Hades, the transference equipment was irreparably damaged during the civil war that brought the downfall of their settlements here on Atlantis." I shook my head. "I mean Earth. Now, Hades is interested in working with mankind to find a way to bring our people back. He realized long ago that once humanity progressed to the point they would be able to help him, they weren't likely to be open to sacrificing members of their species to save an alien race."

"I wouldn't be so sure," Raiden grumbled. At my frown, he explained, "If Hades bartered with the promise of sharing that fancy tech of his—especially the gephyra—almost any government would leap at the chance to make the trade." There was no missing the sharp edge to Raiden's tone. "All Hades wants is a few thousand warm bodies." Raiden laughed bitterly. "That's the cheapest commodity around."

My brow furrowed, and I shook my head. I couldn't believe that of mankind. I *wouldn't* believe it.

"I love how pure your heart is," Raiden said, raising a hand and gently skimming his knuckles over my cheek. "But it's not all roses out there." His hand fell away, and his stare drifted past me. "The world is a dark place. A cold place. It just takes one person to not give a damn about the rest of us, and it's all over."

I set the protein bar on the deck, directly on top of the torn-off corner of the wrapper. Raiden's mood had soured my appetite. I wasn't hungry anymore.

In my heart, I hoped he was wrong about humanity, but my gut told me he wasn't. I had spent my whole life dreaming of being able to step out into the world. It had always seemed like such a glorious place, filled with endless wonders. And with people who made it that way.

Admittedly, I had had a self-imposed prolonged adolescence, but that was over now. I was finally entering adulthood. The place where dreams wither and die.

23

I squeezed my eyes shut, blocking out the holographic screen projecting Hades' seemingly endless stream of writing. The sun had already set, and the rainforest on either bank of the river was being leached of color as twilight faded to night. The holographic words glowed brighter and brighter as the surrounding light faded.

I inhaled deeply, filling my nose with the exotic river smells. Hades' mood had actually seemed to improve in the latest log entry, with humanity entering what he called a golden age of development. He had mentioned two promising civilizations in fairly close proximity—what I assumed to be ancient Egypt and ancient Mesopotamia based on his descriptions—and another in a valley bordered by a vast and towering mountain range, which I figured had to be the Indus Valley bordered on the northeast by the Himalayas.

I estimated Hades had recorded this latest log entry around the year 2,000 BC, give or take a couple centuries. Without a quick internet search, I couldn't be more specific, but it sounded like he was describing the Middle Kingdom of ancient Egypt, a time of growth and prosperity for the region. The great pyramids of the Old Kingdom were already in existence and were considered historical monuments to the people of the time, and Hades had mentioned a newer pyramid was under construction.

Hades had compared the technological boom spanning those civilizations as reminding him of the ancient golden age on Olympus, a time of burgeoning cultures that had merged to bring about the dawn of the global Olympian civilization. My heart was breaking for the guy because I had already read the book on the history of Earth. I knew what happened in a few chapters—the ultimate plot twist. Spoiler alert: the dark ages were coming.

Sure, dynastic China would rise during that time, bringing about a whole slew of technological advancements, and new civilizations would be booming in parts of the Americas. But there would be no grand, global civilization culminating from the three civilizations Hades had been making googly eyes at. Not even the technological nudge or civic guidance he claimed to have provided each of the three civilizations would lead to his desired outcome.

In fact, the Egyptian Middle Kingdom was doomed to fall to the mysterious Hyksos, an as-yet unidentified people hailing from Eastern Asia. Wouldn't it be ironic if Hades' intra-civilization meddling had inadvertently led to the end of this golden period?

There was only one way to find out. Besides, I still had hours to kill before we reached Manaus and could start the next leg of the journey.

I opened my eyes and stared at the holographic screen projecting up from the holodisk on my palm. My arm had tired ages ago, and I had long since rested Raiden's pack on its side and was using it as an armrest. It took my sluggish, pained brain several long seconds to find the place where I had left off, at a break between log entries.

. . .

Well, I was wrong. Any similarities between the civilizations of Atlantis and the ancient golden age of Olympus were all in my head. Perhaps the outcome would have been different if I hadn't interfered. Perhaps the only way forward is to allow for a natural progression of civic, spiritual, intellectual, and technological advancement. Or perhaps I should have gone about it differently. Regardless, I no longer believe the people of Kemet are the key to our solution.

I do, however, see potential in a new civilization forming across the sea from this land. They appear to have made great strides in a very short time, since emerging from a relative dark age. My plan is to spend some time with them before re-entering cryosleep. I can imagine what you are thinking, Peri. I can practically hear your voice whispering through my mind: Leave them be. Don't force it. It didn't work last time, so why make the same mistake twice?

Except, I think this time will be different. I know, as the old saying goes—repeating actions and expecting a different reaction is a sure sign of madness. If that is the case this time, then I shall consider my lesson learned. No more meddling. This, I swear to you.

I'm all packed and ready to head out. I shall let you know how it goes when I return. As always, Peri, my heart is with you.

"Holy crap," I murmured, emerging from the pseudo-trance induced by deep diving into Hades' logs. This latest entry was epic, containing two massive implications.

First off, I had a good idea of the general location of the Omega site. Just like that.

I wasn't sure if Hades had slipped up, or if he had purposely left this clue. Either way, reading between the lines led me to believe the Omega site—and Hades, himself—was located somewhere in Egypt. In one line, he had referred to Egypt by her ancient name, *Kemet.* But then, in the next line, he referred to Egypt as *this place.* It was a massive leap in the right direction, but not nearly enough to negate the need to repair the cracked holodisk. It did, however, lead into the next implication.

Hades was headed to ancient Greece. Looking at the time period in question, some time in the window of 1000 to 800 BC, he had to be talking about the ancient Greeks. At that time, they had been in a transitional phase, emerging from a dark age, just as Hades had mentioned, and entering a period now known as Archaic Greece.

I was eager to read his next log entry, despite knowing the pain concentrating on translating his words would bring to my already aching brain. I stretched out my neck to either side, then refocused on the holographic screen.

I have returned, obviously, and you will not believe what I discovered across the sea! They know of me—or, rather, of us! The people of Kemet must have relayed the legend of my visit a thousand years ago. Their beliefs about me have been grossly warped by time, but it is astonishing, no less. They believe Olympus to be some mythical mountain that functions as the home of the gods, and I, Hades, haven fallen into the role of their god of the dead. Of course, once I learned this, I had to assume a pseudonym, lest the people come to believe I was there to reap their souls.

. . .

They had legends about you, too, Peri. You are believed to be my wife, stolen away from your mother's side and taken to the underworld to rule alongside me half of the year. You are the source of their seasons, bringing about growth and warmth when you reemerge to the surface, while your absence six months later heralds the harsher, colder season. It truly boggles the mind.

I know I should not say it—the Greeks would tell me I am tempting the gods by uttering such words—but I think this is going to be it. I believe these people are the key. I spent years with them, developing their language and guiding them toward a path of prosperity and enlightenment. I helped them form a group consisting of their most brilliant and forward-thinking members, with the intent that they will continue to guide the civilization toward the desired advanced state of development. I believe this is where I failed with the people of Kemet. I set them on a path, then abandoned them. But my Guardians of the Truth will step in when necessary, preventing any missteps or backward slides.

Honestly, Peri, with their innate curiosity about the world, I could see the Greeks reaching the necessary level of technological advancement well before I next emerge from cryosleep in one thousand years. But I shall give them time. No need to be careless and exhaust the cryogenerator. After all, as you know all too well, I am nothing if not incredibly patient.

It is impossible not to hope that the next time I awaken, I will find myself in a world capable of resurrecting our people—and of resurrecting you. My heart is with you, Peri, as always.

• • •

Exhausted, I blinked gritty eyelids and numbly returned the holodisk to the storage cube. As Hades' hopefulness increased, so did my own dread.

So far, there had been no mention of labyrinths or convoluted schemes to bring about my return in Hades' absence. Something must have gone wrong shortly after this last entry. Could it possibly have been the same something that had cut his recording short on the holodisk the Zari had given me? He built the first labyrinth in ancient Roman times, and if his cryosleep schedule continued as it had been for the previous ten millennia, whatever had forced him to change his plans would be happening soon.

"Hey," Raiden said, crouching in front of me, forearms resting on his thighs. "You're taking a break. Good." He flashed me a quick, close-mouthed smile. "Perfect timing."

My brow furrowed as my head tilted to the side. "Why?"

Raiden stretched out an arm, gesturing to whatever lay beyond the left side of the riverboat. "Welcome back to Manaus."

[24]

"Thanks for the ride, Jojo," I said as Raiden counted out cash to pay our ferryman.

The snubbed-nose bow of the riverboat rested on a small, sloped patch of grassy riverbank, wedged between a hodgepodge of docks and anchored barges littering this stretch of the river. Off to the left of our landing place, a large open-air structure at least as long as a football field stretched inland from the riverbank. It looked like a covered marketplace, with shuttered stalls bordering a broad central avenue. A few cars sat in the parking spots in front of the stalls, but most were empty.

I sensed Jojo's guilt about his impromptu price hike. His unprotected mind took little effort to read. He wasn't about to turn down the money, but he felt bad, nonetheless, his unsettled feelings compounded only by the thought of dropping us off on the outskirts of Manaus in the middle of the night. This city was the most dangerous place he had ever been, and while he desperately wanted us off his boat, he didn't wish us harm.

Sensing an opportunity ripe for the picking, I set my hand atop Raiden's, pausing his money-counting. "How far is it to the central bus terminal?" I asked Jojo.

We were clearly in an industrial area, and I doubted the bus terminal was anywhere nearby. The last thing I wanted to do was walk through nearly all of Manaus—the most dangerous place Jojo had ever been—in the middle of the night, even with Raiden and Meg, two of the most formidable people I had ever met.

Raiden looked from me to Jojo and back, surprised by the question.

Jojo eyed the back of my hand, like his stare could burn a hole through it to reach the money. "Fifteen kilometers, maybe twenty," he said, his stare snapping up to meet mine.

I nodded once as he confirmed my suspicion. The terminal wasn't remotely close. "We'll pay double if you help us find a car to take us to the bus terminal."

Jojo hesitated, but only for a moment. Double his already elevated price—the money was too good to turn down, and helping us get off the street promised to ease his guilt. He nodded and held out his hand, palm up.

I removed my hand from Raiden's and watched him pay Jojo the original amount. "We'll give you the rest when you finish the job," Raiden said in a no-nonsense tone as he pocketed the rest of the money.

Jojo turned and rattled off a few quick orders to Davi, then hopped off the boat and scurried up the grassy bank toward the slumbering marketplace, quickly slipping out of sight. He was pretty limber for a guy his age.

I stood with Raiden and Meg near the stern, watching in silence while Davi poked around the boat, doing this or that. Within a few minutes, Jojo popped back into view, waving for us to join him.

I exchanged a glance with Raiden, then peeked over my shoulder at Meg. She wore the blanket draped around herself like a robe, covering her flashier Zari armor. I, too, had camouflaged my less conventional hoplon suit by covering it with cargo pants and a long-sleeve T-shirt, and even with my regulator deactivated, the electric-blue glow was only faintly visible through the fabric.

"Well, shall we?" I said, eyebrows raised.

Meg nodded, flashing me a tight smile that did little to mask the tension in her face. She had accompanied her mother's team to Iquitos, a smaller city in the Peruvian part of the Amazon, closer to the Beta site, but upriver, making the travel time longer. That trip had been equal parts overwhelming and wondrous, and Meg was both nervous and excited about experiencing another, larger city. But mostly nervous.

Another, smaller part of her was filled with an unexpected yearning to have her mother by her side. Her emotional reaction to losing her mother had been strange. I had picked up on the barest traces of anger and sorrow, but more than anything, she felt relief. Now, however, the sorrow raged unexpectedly.

Raiden gripped the boat's railing and jumped over, landing on the riverbank with a squelching *thump*. His boots slipped in the squishy ground, and he almost lost his footing. "Careful," he warned. "It's slippery."

"Noted," I said, turning my attention back to Meg as she brushed past me to disembark. "Meg," I said as I grabbed her arm, just above the elbow. The contact increased the flow of thoughts and feelings passing between us, and my heart swelled with grief, tears welling in my eyes. "I'm so sorry," I said, knowing the words meant next to nothing.

"Don't be," Meg said as the sorrow flowing through the bond waned, giving way to a flood of gratitude. Her eyes were glassy, but her stare was hard. "Mother wasn't kind, not to anyone—least of all to me. But she was there. She was always there, using her slippery words to twist my thoughts, and it feels weird to be moving through the world without her." Meg covered my hand with her own, giving my fingers a squeeze. "Give me time," she said. "I just have to grow accustomed to being free of her."

I stared into her eyes for a long moment. Because of the bond we shared, I knew her words were honest. I let go of her arm and squeezed my eyes shut, wiping away the lingering tears.

Meg hopped over the boat's railing, landing on a less-slick grassy patch of the riverbank.

I wasn't feeling nearly as agile or sure-footed as either of them, especially not with the bulky pack resting on my shoulders. Ever so carefully, I stepped over the railing and perched on the outer edge of the boat's deck on my heels. I planted the butt of the doru on a grassy portion of the riverbank, prodding the ground to make sure it was firm, and then I carefully stepped down.

The three of us climbed up the slope, and within minutes, we were zipping away from the Amazon River in a cab, Jojo watching us go, his pocket filled with money and his conscience free of guilt.

I sat sandwiched between Raiden and Meg, my mind awhirl with guesses about what we would find in the locker at the bus terminal. I was a bundle of raw nerves, my fears and worries piling up until they threatened to barricade me in. Once I knew our next steps and the path to Ireland was laid out before us, then I would be able to relax. Maybe then the headache would let up a little. Not go away—that wouldn't happen until we tracked down Hades and he untangled the mess of comingling consciousnesses overloading my brain.

If he even could.

My hand sought Raiden's, and I rested my aching head on his shoulder. Both he and Meg were busy staring out the window, watching the streets of Manaus pass by as we sped through the city. Manaus at night seemed like an entirely different place from what Raiden and I had seen of the city during the day, when we had passed through here to stock up on supplies for our ill-fated rainforest trek. But my attention was all on what might come next, there was nothing left to appreciate the sights and sounds of this exotic place.

What a pity that I had been dreaming of exploring the world for so long, and now that I was out here, I couldn't even enjoy it. No living in the moment for me. All I could think about was tomorrow, and the next day, and the day after that. And wonder how many tomorrows I had left, and if I would survive this *adventure* long enough to make it home to my beloved Orcas Island.

I loved *The Wizard of Oz*, but I had always hated the part at the end of the movie when Dorothy says she's not going to leave home "ever, ever again!" For the first time in my life, I could relate. There truly was no place like home, and I feared I would never see mine again.

━━

I sit on a piece of driftwood on a sandy beach, waves crashing rhythmically before me and stars shining down on me from the clear night sky. A breeze caresses my skin, cool, but not cold, It never gets old—this world and all the wonders it holds.

I hear footsteps behind me, and when I sense the mental signature of the one who approaches, my heart beats faster. I close my eyes, wondering if it was a mistake to take this mission. I probably should have backed out once I discovered Hades would be joining us. Every time I think about him, my emotions get all twisted and my thoughts tangle into a knot until I can't tell up from down, let alone right from wrong. I've managed to keep my distance during the long weeks abroad, so far, but it hasn't changed anything about anything, least of all about us.

As Hades steps over the long piece of driftwood on which I sit, I activate my regulator, needing that additional barrier between my mind and his. Between his heart and mine.

"I don't want to intrude," Hades says, standing in front of the driftwood. It's obvious he is waiting for an invitation to sit.

I struggle with a response. My heart wants him to stay, but my head is screaming for me to run away. I peer up at him, then glance at the length of driftwood. "Be my guest," I tell him, my stare returning to the vast ocean before me, but my attention locked on the man settling in beside me.

"Beautiful, isn't it?" he says, leaning forward to rest his elbows on his knees, unintentionally copying my position. It's so strange seeing him out here, away from his labs and lab minions. Out here, it's easier to forget he's royalty. It's easier to see him as a man. It's easier to get into trouble.

I nod and sit up straighter, fidgeting with the retracted doru resting across my lap.

"What if we didn't have to go back?" he asks.

My brow furrows, and I look at him.

"What if we stayed out here?" he continues. "Just you and me and all the beauty and wonder this world has to offer..."

My heart beats faster, and my stomach does a little flip flop that reminds me of when the Tartarus would enter faster-than-light travel. It's a dream, what he's proposing. An impossible dream. "Demeter would kill us."

Hades scoffs and shakes his head. "My dear old sister has far more bark than bite."

Now it's my turn to scoff. He might have grown up with Demeter back on Olympus, but I am the one who trains with her relentlessly, day in and day out. I am the one who serves her and follows her orders. I am the one she plucked from the ranks of the genetically engineered plebeians and raised to the highest honor among our people—a full-powered Amazon warrior—and the one she could take everything from, if she so wished. She might only be able to bark at Hades, but she could bite me. Hard.

"Think about it, Peri," Hades says, angling his body toward me. His ice-blue eyes are filled with a fervent light, and I realize he's being serious. "We could sneak away and live among the anthropos. We could study them and learn to be a part of their society. We could be free to live our lives as we wish."

I stare at him for long seconds, my heart hammering in my chest. Finally, I clear my throat to respond. "You're a prince of Olympus," I say, my eyes narrowing. "You are *free."*

Hades laughs under his breath and shakes his head, finally breaking eye contact. It's both a relief and a disappointment to be free of the intensity of his stare. "Power doesn't equal freedom," he says, peering out at the horizon. "You, of all people, should understand that."

His words strike a chord within me, and for a while, I simply look at him, studying his strong profile. I used to think there was a cruelty to his features, but now there is nothing about his looks that doesn't please my eyes. It's easy to accept the stern façade he wears, a mask hiding the man few people ever have the privilege of truly meeting. I forget that sometimes, even after the moments we've shared. Hades makes it easy to forget. He's so good at playing his part.

"I would be afraid," I tell him, averting my gaze to the sand at my feet as his face turns toward me. "To stay out here," I add. "To run away."

Hades sighs. "Because of my sister…"

Partially, yes, but it's more than that, and I shake my head, still staring down at the sand. "The Alpha site is my home," I say, my voice quiet, small, ashamed. Besides the Tartarus, it's all I've ever known, and I wouldn't even know how to start a life without that place. Without our people.

Hades reaches for my hand, curling the fingers of both of his hands around mine before I have the chance to pull away. It would be easy to disengage, had I wanted to. But I don't want to.

I look at him, my eyes locking with his.

Hades scoots closer on the driftwood until his knee touches mine. "Home doesn't have to be a place," he says. "Home can be a person." His grip on my hand tightens. "I could be your home."

. . .

I started awake when the car braked suddenly, my heart thudding and head pounding. I had dozed off, and Peri had taken advantage of my unconscious state by feeding me one of her memories in a dream. It was insanely reassuring to connect with her. To know she was still in there, still with me.

But it was impossible not to notice that each time she reached across the fissures in our fractured mind to either make contact with me or to take over my body, the headache worsened. Same went for me breaching that barrier to access her knowledge of her ancient language. *Any* contact at all between us exacerbated our condition. Much as I hated to admit it, it was probably best to limit any cross-consciousness contact to absolute necessity: translating Hades' logs was a must, but nothing else until we found Hades and fixed the problem. Unless a life-and-death situation popped up. Again.

"We'll figure this out," Meg said, patting my knee as Raiden reached across me, a wad of money in hand to pay the driver. Apparently, we had arrived.

Meg opened the door on her side of the car and slipped out, and I slid along the seat to follow her while Raiden finished up with the driver. We walked around the back of the car and waited for the driver to pop the trunk.

The Manaus bus terminal was a boxy, white building with sky-blue trim and periodic patches of graffiti. Dozens of homeless people sat or lay scattered along the sidewalk in front of the building, filling the air with the residual stench of unwashed bodies.

Meg leaned in closer to me. "How is it they have no homes?" she asked, her brow furrowed. Homelessness didn't exist among her people, making it an entirely foreign concept to her.

"Capitalism," I said, knowing the word would give her a focus to search my mind for the explanation.

The crease between her eyebrows deepened as she pulled the information from my mind. "It is like this everywhere?"

I shrugged. "Most places."

Meg shook her head. "But, *why*?"

I frowned. The trunk of the car finally popped open, saving me from having to formulate an answer.

I was already hoisting my bag onto my shoulders by the time Raiden joined us, grumbling about the steep rate the driver was charging to wait for us, on the likely chance that we would need him to take us somewhere else after this. I tucked the retracted doru between my pack and my back, thinking a glowing staff was likely to draw too much unwanted attention.

Once Raiden had his pack situated on his shoulders, he scanned the accumulated homeless people huddling under the overhang at the front of the bus terminal. His hard scowl was a warning to each and every one of them not to mess with us.

"Easy tiger," I said, brushing his arm with my fingertips. I was trying to lighten the mood, as well as ease my own anxiety. I still wasn't remotely comfortable being around more than a few people at a time, and there were dozens here, despite the early morning hour. Or maybe because of it. In my limited experience, a lifetime of isolation tended to bring out one's inner agoraphobe.

Each uneasy for our own reasons, the three of us stepped up onto the curb and made our way into the bus terminal. It was dimly lit, and the smell of unwashed bodies was thicker once we passed through the doors. We paused just inside the entrance and searched the cavernous space for some indication of where the lockers might be.

A half-dozen people sat slumped in the seats arranged in rows in the center of the large room. The concrete floors were sticky and littered with a smattering of plastic bottles, food wrappers, and crumpled paper.

"There," Raiden said, pointing to a tiny blue sign on the wall in the far corner displaying a white padlock and an arrow. A dark, narrow hallway stretched out beyond the corner, leading out of sight.

We crossed the space, circling around the back of the seating area, and made our way to the hallway. I glanced over my shoulder, giving the central space one last scan, thinking someone would be crazy to lock up anything of value here. A tiny seed of fear settled in my gut, sprouting worry and doubt. What if whatever my mom had stowed in the locker had already been stolen? Would she risk being so careless?

I raised a hand to rub the back of my neck, though it only seemed to draw attention to the impenetrable tension tightening my muscles, an unwelcome by product of the constant and steadily worsening ache in my skull.

A wall of sky-blue lockers filled the back half of the hallway on one side, the other offering two dingey doors displaying small man and woman signs. The smell of human waste seeping out into the hallway was enough to keep me far, far away from those doors. Even if I had had to go, I would have held it. Better to pop a squat in an alleyway than marinate in that filth, even for a minute or two.

"Here," Raiden said, pointing to a banged-up locker door.

The blue paint was peeling away from the metal in some places, scratched off into lewd images and illegible words in others. There was no number on the locker, only a pair of small screw holes in the door where the number plate had once been. But a quick glance at the lockers to either side confirmed that this was the one. The padlock was of the combo variety, as my mom had implied.

"Diana said you would know the combination, right?" Raiden said, shifting his attention from the locker to me.

My eyes met his, just long enough for me to flash him a quick smile, and then I stepped closer to the locker and reached for the padlock. I spun the dial around clockwise a few times, then slowed as I neared the first number: two. I inhaled deeply and held my breath, spinning the dial counterclockwise ten notches to the twelve, then slowly inched it clockwise to the nine and gently tugged down.

The lock gave, and I blew out a relieved breath. "Darwin's birthday," I said, grinning at Raiden over my shoulder. "She uses it for everything."

I quickly maneuvered the padlock free and opened the locker door. I could feel Raiden and Meg crowding in behind me to get a better look inside. My fears were instantly assuaged as I took in the contents of the locker. A canvas tote bag filled the majority of the space, and a small manila envelope had been propped up against the bag, with my name scrawled across the front in blocky capital letters.

I plucked the envelope out of the locker, then looked at Meg, nodding back to the bag that remained inside locker. "That's probably for you," I told her. "Go ahead and get changed."

While she did that, I turned to Raiden, exchanging a hopeful look before bending the prongs holding the flap of the envelope shut. I lifted the flap and peeked inside, then turned the envelope upside down and dumped the single notecard within onto my open hand. Two lines had been scrawled onto the card in that same, blocky handwriting that adorned the envelope.

-2.979340, -59.899481
  03:26

"Coordinates," Raiden said.

I nodded. "And a time, from the looks of it."

So, we had our meetup information. It was just after one in the morning, which meant we had a little over two hours to get there…wherever *there* was.

Seeming to read my mind, for once, Raiden slipped his pack

off and quickly fished his pocket atlas of Brazil out of the bag. He flipped back and forth between a couple of pages before settling on one. "Looks like a random point in the rainforest, a couple miles northeast of Manaus." Raiden's eyes narrowed. "My guess is it's a remote airstrip."

I nodded slowly, thinking his guess made sense. "All right, let's head back to the car," I said, hoping the hike through the rainforest wouldn't be too long or arduous.

I turned around to check on Meg and found a nun standing in her place. I raised my eyebrows, impressed that she had figured out how to put the moderately complicated getup on.

Meg adjusted the head covering, tucking in the tail end of her braid. "I saw some women wearing these in Iquitos," she explained. "They were viewed with respect by the other denizens of the city." The corner of her mouth lifted in a sly smile. "This will be a good disguise."

I returned her smile, and some of the tension eased from my body. One less thing to worry about.

"Ready?" Raiden said, pack returned to his shoulders and eyebrows raised.

I exchanged a glance with Meg, deactivated my regulator—better safe than sorry—and then I nodded. "Ready."

[25]

Our driver sped through the streets of Manaus, encouraged by Raiden's promise to include a hefty bonus if he dropped us at our destination in under twenty minutes. Raiden had picked out a spot at the end of a road that, according to his map, was as close as a car could get to the coordinates on the notecard. The driver had tried to bargain the time limit up to thirty minutes, but Raiden hadn't budged, tapping his watch and raising his eyebrows to indicate that the countdown had already begun.

Pavement gave way to dirt and the road narrowed as we entered the wooded outskirts of the city. We only stopped once en route, the car skidding to a halt for a trio of goats to saunter across the road, our driver cursing in Portuguese. The next time the car stopped, the timer on Raiden's watch had 27 seconds left.

The driver turned in his seat, his eyes lingering on the face of Raiden's watch before snapping up to Raiden's face. "We are here."

"And on time, to boot," Raiden said, pulling the pre-counted cash out of his front pocket and reaching between the front seats to hand the wad of colorful bills to the driver. But when the driver made to take the money, I grabbed Raiden's wrist and pulled his hand out of reach, having picked up on a shocking train of thought in the driver's mind.

Motivated by greed, the driver had just made the decision to drive off—with our things—the second we were out of his car. He figured that anyone willing to fork up so much cash for a single ride out to the middle of nowhere had even more money and other valuables stashed in their bags. He had no idea just how valuable…

It wasn't that the driver was a bad guy. If my newfound psychic abilities had taught me anything, it was that there was no such thing as good and evil. No such thing as black and white. The whole world was gray. Even Henry, the Primicerius of the Custodes Veritatis and all-around villain had semi-honorable reasons for doing the things he did. The real struggle plaguing the world wasn't between good and evil, it was between the ends and the means. The so-called bad guys just happened to lean toward the ends-justifying-the-means school of thought. People like our driver, and like Jojo, recognized an opportunity when it presented itself. That was all we were to him—a means to an end. A quick way to get ahead in a place that wasn't full of many such opportunities.

"Pop the trunk," I told the driver. "We'll get our things, and *then* you can have your money."

Meg pushed her door open and stepped out of the car, and I scooted across the bench seat to follow her out. Raiden hung back inside the cab, money held hostage in his fist while we pulled our bags from the trunk.

Once I had my pack situated on my shoulders, my doru in hand, extended to its full, gloriously glowing length, and Raiden's pack was resting on the grass bordering the road, I knocked on the back windshield.

Raiden glanced my way.

"Ready," I mouthed, making a wrap-it-up gesture with my hand.

Raiden nodded, then turned back to the driver. He handed him the money and opened his door, crouching forward to exit the car.

"Raiden!" I called out in warning. Too late.

Raiden barely had both feet on the hard-packed dirt road when the driver slammed his foot down on the gas pedal. The car peeled out, and Raiden tumbled to the ground, grunting as he landed on his hands and knees. For a moment, I feared he had reinjured his knee or aggravated his bullet wound, but then I remembered those injuries were a thing of the past.

"Nice place," Raiden said, standing and dusting off the front of his cargo pants. "*Real* nice people."

A nervous laugh climbed up my throat and tumbled out of my mouth. I slapped my hand over my mouth, but the laughter found its way out through my nose in the form of an unladylike snort. It didn't help my ever-present headache, but for a moment at least, I forgot about the pain.

Raiden paused in the middle of dusting off his cargo pants to shoot me an unamused look. "Yuk it up, Chuckles," he said, a half-smile cracking his stern façade as he straightened, brushing off his hands. He twisted his wrist to see his watch, then pointed off into the thick rainforest lining the side of the road. "We go that-a way. Ready?" he asked, glancing from me to Meg and back.

I peered into the dense wall of underbrush filling nearly every nook and cranny between the tall trees. The last thing I wanted was to start trekking through the Amazon Rainforest again, even if it was only for a single mile, but it was hardly like I had a choice. "Ready as I'll ever be," I said dryly.

Raiden pulled his trusty machete, and picking a seemingly random place, marched toward the woods and started hacking, while Meg slipped out of her cumbersome getup. She wouldn't need it out here, not while it was still night.

My mildly raised spirits plummeted with each successive

hack of Raiden's machete. At this rate, we would never make it to the coordinates in time. And then my brain shifted into a functional gear, and I realized that the tool we needed to burn a path through the rainforest was in my hand.

"Raiden," I said, making my way toward him, but keeping out of range of the machete's backswing.

He swung the machete. "Just a few"—he swung the machete again—"more"—he drew the machete back—"swings."

I caught his wrist before his next hack. "Hold up for a sec," I told him. My lips curved into a sly smile. "I got this."

He lowered the machete, gesturing to the dense wall of greenery as if to say, "Be my guest."

Tucking the butt end of the doru under my arm, I widened my stance and aimed the focus crystal at the unsuspecting foliage. With a thought, I channeled psychic energy into the doru, charging the focus crystal. The electric-blue glow brightened steadily. Until, suddenly, I released it.

A burst of blinding blue energy slammed into the dense vegetation, cutting through the rainforest like a hot knife through butter. In a blink, a tunnel appeared in the woods, rimmed by singed, smoking foliage. It went on for a hundred yards or so, dead-ending in a cluster of smoldering vines, leaves, and branches.

Raiden whistled, long and slow. "Yeah," he said, frowning as he assessed my work, "I'd say you got this."

"Let's go," Meg said, jogging past us and heading into the brand-new tunnel, the canvas tote bag slung over her shoulder. "Time is short," she called back to us.

I exchanged a look with Raiden. "How short, exactly?"

Raiden glanced at his watch. "We've got just under an hour," he said, his voice grim. Which meant all we had to do was beat a slug's pace of one mile per hour, and we would be good. Easier said than done.

"Well, all right, then," I said, turning to run after Meg, the cumbersome pack making my gait awkward. I could hear Raiden's heavier steps close behind me.

We slowed as we closed in on Meg at the end of the tunnel. I shifted the doru, adjusting the angle slightly to the east at Raiden's direction, and blasted a new path through the dense rainforest. I did it eighteen more times, and I was about to request a short breather when the twentieth tunnel ended in a circle of inky darkness rather than a wall of smoldering foliage. We had reached a clearing.

Meg stopped a few paces from the clearing and waited for us to catch up. Raiden reached her first, slowly inching forward until he was nearly flush with the opening at the end of our smoldering tunnel.

"There's a man out there," Meg said as I slowed from a stumbling jog to a dragging walk.

My chest heaved with each breath, and I pinched my waist with one hand in a vain attempt to ease the stitch in my side. I was exhausted, running on adrenaline fumes. I had been so focused on our current goal—and on the basic task of putting one foot in front of the other—that I hadn't been paying attention to anything my psychic senses were picking up.

Through the bond I shared with Meg, I skimmed all the pertinent information in an instant. A man named Hal Johanson was standing near a small private jet. He was a mercenary pilot, and he was waiting for us. For me. He owed my mom a favor, and he was prepared to do whatever it took to complete the task and return to blissful, debtless living.

I nodded to myself as I processed the information. "Good," I said softly. "All good."

I quickly relayed the situation to Raiden, and ten minutes after we stumbled into the clearing, we were speeding down the dirt runway in Hal's plane, the nose of the craft angling upward as we lifted into the air.

The plane was older, but not old, the interior laid out for

leisure and comfort rather than packing in passengers. I sat across from Raiden in an armchair-style recliner, a collapsible table separating us. Meg had already stretched out on the sofa on the opposite side of the plane, the blanket from the riverboat covering her from head to toe.

I had made all sorts of grand plans to continue translating Hades' logs, and once that was finished, move on to reading through the *Liber Veritatis*. I was more curious than ever to dive into the pages of the Order's once-lost book of secrets, especially hearing Hades describe how and why he had set up the Custodes Veritatis in the first place.

But as I stared out the small window, searching the darkness for some sign of the dense rainforest below, the adrenaline crash hit me hard. My eyelids drooped; I didn't even try to fight it. I slouched in my seat, reclining the seatback as far as it would go. Maybe sleep would bring some much-needed relief to my aching head.

Besides, I would be confined to this tin can for another eighteen hours. I could afford a good night's sleep and still have plenty of time to translate Hades' final few entries on the holodisk *and* dig in to the *Liber Veritatis*.

I yawned, jaw cracking, and shifted in my seat to get more comfortable before surrendering to sleep.

[26]

"No...," I breathed, sliding the writing on the holographic screen
up and then down as I searched for the place where I had left off.
"No, no, no, no..." I hunched forward in my seat, resting the
hand holding the holodisk on my lap as I scanned line after line
of incomprehensible text. I tangled my fingers in my hair and
tugged, the sharp pain countering the throbbing ache in my skull.

"Cora?" Raiden said, returning to his seat after a visit to the
cockpit.

Both he and Meg had been absent when I woke. From the
sounds of someone being sick in the bathroom at the back of the
plane, flying wasn't agreeing with Meg's stomach. I could sense
her queasiness through our bond, strong enough to unsettle my
own stomach.

Raiden sat on the edge of his seat, his knees angled toward
me. The table had been collapsed, and the only thing that separated us now was the concern wafting off him in waves. "What's
wrong?" he asked.

"It doesn't make any sense," I said, my scrolling growing
more and more frantic. My chest tightened, my throat constrict-
ing. Tears of frustration burned in my eyes. "Why doesn't it

make any sense?" I asked nobody in particular, my voice a little too high pitched.

I leaned forward even more, reaching into my open pack with my free hand. After a several-second search, I found my mom's journal and pulled it out of the bag, setting it on my lap. My fingers trembled as I unwound the leather cord one-handed and opened the book, flipping through the pages to the end where I had been recording my translation of Hades' log entries. When I reached the last page of writing, I froze.

The handwriting wasn't mine. Everything save for the last two lines was clearly a translation of Hades' logs, but *I* hadn't written the translation. Those last two lines stood out, written in all caps, the final three words underlined.

I'VE DONE ALL I CAN. OUR FATE IS IN YOUR HANDS NOW. GOOD LUCK, CORA.

I tore my stare from the page and sought Raiden's eyes. "What happened while I was asleep?"

"Uh..." Raiden licked his lips and cleared his throat. He averted his gaze, his focus dropping to the journal open on my lap. "About that..."

The bathroom door folded open, and Meg stepped out. "It was Persephone," she said, drawing both my and Raiden's attention her way. Her voice sounded a little too weak, and her face looked a little too pale.

Using the seatbacks for support, Meg made her way up the aisle toward us. She knelt in the space between my and Raiden's knees and raised her hands, gently pressing her fingertips against my temples.

"Close your eyes," she whispered. "That should make this a little less disorienting."

I stared at Meg for a moment, but sensing she had something important to share—something she couldn't share through our tamped-down bond—I did as she instructed and shut my eyelids.

For a moment, there was only darkness. Until, suddenly, I was seeing the interior of the plane again, only I wasn't seeing it through my eyes. I was seeing it through Meg's.

I stare out the window. The horizon is just starting to brighten, and I can already feel the tingle of the sun's touch on my skin. Sighing, I slide the window shade down. Raiden and I have already lowered the rest of the shades in preparation for sunrise.

A tickle in my mind draws my attention to the other side of the plane. Cora is waking up. Except, she feels different. Not filled with uncertainty and self-doubt; she is confident and determined. Powerful. I'm intimidated just by the feel of her.

Because this isn't Cora at all. This is Persephone.

I've known she is in there, but this is my first time sensing her presence—her inner strength—and it's intense. No wonder Hades was drawn to her.

Raiden is asleep across from her, completely unaware of the transformation.

Nervous, I watch Persephone out of the corner of my eye. She leans forward, reaching into Cora's pack. She pulls out one of the storage cubes and Cora's leather journal, quickly removing a holodisk from the cube and returning the cube to the bag. She scrolls through the holographic records for a moment, searching for something, but then she stops and begins writing.

I focus on the bond linking us together. I can sense her purpose: to complete the translation for Cora. She is focused and determined, but beneath all of her strength and confidence, she's afraid, just like Cora. As I search for the source of her fear, her head snaps up, and her stare locks with mine.

I freeze, physically, mentally. I'm a block of ice under her frigid stare.

"I need to concentrate," she says, her English strangely accented, even to my ears. Her voice sounds different from Cora's, and not just the accent. It's deeper, stronger. "And you're not helping…"

My cheeks heat, and I break eye contact with her, staring down at my hands instead. "Sorry," I murmur.

I focus on other things in an attempt to avoid the urge to poke around in her mind. I think about my mom, but that brings me back to the incident in the rainforest and her death—and to Cora—so I move on. I think about Ireland and what we'll find there. Raiden shared some of what he knows of the land earlier, while Cora was asleep, and I'm eager to see a place as green as my home, but in an entirely different way.

After a while, my thoughts turn to my uneasy stomach, but focusing on that only makes the queasiness worse, and I rush to the bathroom. I remain in the bathroom, taking long, deep breaths, until the nausea passes, and my body has stopped shaking. I take one last deep breath, then stand and open the door.

I can feel Persephone's gaze the second I reemerge from the bathroom. Once again, I freeze under her cool scrutiny.

"Come here, child," she says, glancing at the couch near her armchair.

Hesitantly, I make my way up the aisle and sit, facing Persephone. Her presence is even more intense and intimidating up close.

"I need you to pass on a message to Cora," she says, then raises her eyebrows. "Can you do that for me?"

I gulp, then nod.

The hint of a smile touches her lips. "Good."

Persephone leans forward, resting her elbows on her knees. And then she begins.

"Greetings, Cora," she says. Again, she smiles, and this time

it actually touches her eyes. "I tried to reach you in your dreams, but the distance between us is too great now, and I fear attempting to cross it will damage our brain irrevocably. I took a calculated risk taking over like this. It's bound to worsen the damage and shorten our window to find Hades, but I believe it to be worth the risk."

She pauses, inhaling and exhaling deeply through her nose, and I get the sense that she's formulating her next words. "You see, the true source of an Amazon warrior's power is not psychic energy, but knowledge. We have access to information unavailable to others. We know the thoughts and feelings of those around us. We understand their motivations, and we know their actions before they're even executed. This allows us to move through the world a step ahead...to have a sense of what will happen before it does."

Persephone presses her lips together, the corners lifting in the smallest of smiles. "Hades is a complicated man, and he has only become more complicated since I died. Solitude has not been kind to him, and his desperation to revive something of his old familiar world grows with each passing millennium. You need to understand this—to understand him—because I won't be there to help you."

She looks down at her hands, threading her fingers together deliberately. "This will be our last communication," she says, lifting her gaze to meet mine. "You have the strength and cunning within you to see this through to the end. I know you can do this Cora—I know you can save us both—and I would consider it an honor to live out the rest of my life merged with you."

Again, her lips curve into a faint smile, and tears well in her eyes. She sniffs, wiping at the corners of her eyes with the pad of her thumb. "But, if it comes down to a choice between the two of us—if Hades can only save one of us—I choose you, Cora. I have lived countless lives, but yours has only just begun."

She sniffs again, then clears her throat. "I'll leave a note for Hades in the back of the journal, but..." She separates her hands, gripping her knees. "You may need to use his love for me against him. Let your will to survive guide you. You can do this. I know you can."

The warmth leaves her eyes, and her expression hardens. "Share this memory with Cora when she awakens." It takes hearing Cora's name for me to realize Persephone is no longer talking to Cora; she's talking to me. "And if—when—you find Hades, give him this," she says tearing a sheet of paper covered in Olympian writing out of Cora's mom's journal.

"That is all," Persephone says, her gaze dropping to the floor. "You may go."

Meg removed her fingertips from my temples, and the shift in perspectives disoriented me. It took me a moment to make sense of what just happened. I *was* Meg, and I'd *been* talking to myself —or rather, to Peri. The switch wasn't something my brain could handle easily, so I squeezed my eyes shut and dry-scrubbed my face with my hands like I could wash away the memory of being Meg and somehow reset my sense of self. I already had a loose grip on my identity these days, and this hadn't helped matters.

"Sorry," Meg said, standing and retreating to the couch nearby. I could sense her movement, even if I couldn't see it. Guilt and apprehension flowed through our bond from her to me, confusing my sense of self further. I couldn't tell where her emotions ended and mine began.

I shuttered my mind as best I could and focused on the throbbing pain pulsing like a second heartbeat in my skull. That was mine. That belonged to me—to my brain. My physical body. Not Meg's, and not Peri's. Mine. Physical sensation was all I had left. The only thing that was mine alone. I gripped it tight, letting it anchor me to reality.

Across from me, Raiden was a shining beacon of concern, the sheer strength of his emotions chiseling cracks through my mental barrier. The regulator was active, and the amber stone should have been deadening my psychic senses. Should have been. Wasn't.

I took long, deep breaths, reinforcing the barrier and centering myself on *me*. Once I felt certain the raging river of fear flowing through my veins was mine, and mine alone, I lowered my hands and opened my eyes.

"Cora?" Raiden's voice was soft, tenuous.

I closed my eyes, just for a moment, ensuring my mind was still locked up tight. There was still the faint trickle of guilt from Meg, but I couldn't do anything about that. "I'm fine," I told Raiden, opening my eyes and meeting his.

He was leaning forward, toward me, his hands grasping his knees in a white-knuckled grip. His warm, brown eyes were glassy with unshed tears. No psychic powers were required to see that he was terrified—for me.

I covered his hands with mine, wedging my fingertips between his fingers and his knees until some of the tension left him, and he seemed to relax a little. His hands were ice cold. I curled my fingers around his, squeezing like I could imbue them with some of my warmth, and flashed him a tight, closed-mouth smile. "I'm fine, Raiden," I said again, hoping to reassure him. "Promise."

Raiden turned his hands over, his fingers engulfing my whole hand. "I can't lose you, Cora," he said, the pad of his thumb tracing a path over the back of my hand. "I can't—" His voice broke, and he bowed his body over our joined hands, hiding his face from me. His shoulders shook with the force of his silent sobs.

My breath hitched in my throat, and tears welled in my eyes. Raiden was the strongest person I knew. He was the guy who had managed to laugh right after getting shot in the leg, the guy who constantly battled crippling survivors' guilt and a pretty serious case of PTSD, but still wanted to be a part of the world, the guy who did what was right, instead of what was easy. And he was crumbling, right in front of me.

Reaching out with my free hand, I ran my fingers through his hair, the short, loose curls tickling my skin. I scooted to the edge of my seat and slid off to kneel on the floor in front of him, hugging his head against my chest.

"It's going to be okay," I whispered. "It's all going to be okay."

I'd never been less sure of anything in my life.

But if there was one thing I *was* sure of, it was that I couldn't do this without Raiden. I needed him clear-headed and bringing his A game. And if that required a little good-natured fibbing, so be it. Right now, he didn't need truth. He needed belief. Faith. Boundless, reasonless, evidence-less faith. In God, or in *the* gods, or in the universe, or in Peri, or in Hades. In himself, maybe, or possibly even in me.

I hugged Raiden tighter against me, tears leaking between my lashes and gliding down my cheeks.

For once, my mom was wrong. Truth wouldn't be the light guiding us through the darkness. The darkness was too heavy, too deep. We would need something stronger to guide our way. We needed to have a little faith.

Maybe faith would guide us to ruin. Maybe that was the only outcome. Maybe it always had been. But right now, standing still meant certain death. Forward momentum—one foot in front of the other—then, at least, we had a chance.

If faith kept us moving forward, it was enough.

[27]

A somber cloud drowned out all good humor and conversation for the rest of the twenty-hour flight to the private airfield where we would be landing in Northern Ireland. Raiden spent the long hours sitting across from me, halfheartedly flipping through the issues of *Time Magazine* stashed in the plane's built-in magazine rack.

I was glad my regulator was activated, subduing my psychic gifts, because I wasn't sure I would've been able to handle juggling both his fears and worries along with my own. Thankfully, Meg fell asleep shortly after sharing her memory of her interaction with Peri, leaving my mind, for once, quiet.

For a solid hour after viewing Meg's memory, I alternated between skimming through the *Liber Veritatis*, shooting furtive glances at my mom's journal, the corner just peeking out from the top of my pack, and staring at the cover of the issue of *Time Magazine* topping the discarded stack on the floor beside Raiden's seat. The magazine's headline read: *Can the Atlantea Project save us?* The subheadline proclaimed that CERN, the European Organization for Nuclear Research located in Switzerland, was on the cusp of achieving a true, renewable energy source, thanks to a meteor recently recovered from the Bering Sea.

I was hesitant to read Peri's translation of Hades' final logs. My gut told me I wouldn't find much reassurance there, not after her cryptic final message wishing me a dismal "bonne chance".

Unfortunately, my attention lay elsewhere, and I hadn't been able to glean much from the *Liber Veritatis* beyond its general layout. It was broken into sections based on each Primicerius over the millennia, and the earlier sections appeared to be not only translated into Latin, but highly abridged. An introduction explained that each time a Primicerius retired—read: died—the contents of the book were reproduced in a new volume, including plenty of blank pages in which the new Primicerius could record his experience as the leader of the Custodes Veritatis.

From my rough skim, it appeared that most of the earlier entries had been reduced to a scant summary, including only the details deemed important during each successive reproduction to make room for later entries. I couldn't help but wonder where the earlier editions were stored and how different their contents must look from that of the book in my hands. How much had been lost in translation? As the Order's motivations and purposes changed, the contents of their sole historical record must have changed as well—and drastically, I could only assume.

But as I settled in to read the initial entry in depth, the details escaped me. I couldn't focus on the words printed on these pages, not when Hades' words were burning a hole through the cover of my mom's journal, begging for my attention.

With a sigh, I returned the *Liber Veritatis* to my pack and exchanged it for my mom's journal. I would have to read the remainder of Hades' logs eventually. Might as well do it now, when no one was chasing after me or shooting tranquilizer darts at me.

I leafed through the pages until I found the place where my

slanted handwriting transitioned to Peri's bolder script. Even her handwriting made mine look weak in comparison. But all self-deprecating thoughts fled as I read the first line of Hades' next entry.

Something is wrong.

I licked my lips, tucking my foot under my leg and curling up with the leather-bound book, eager to find out what Hades meant.

The cryogenerator caused a power surge in the mainframe's core when initiating the restoration process. I must spend some time on repairs before re-entering cryosleep—another surge in the core could damage the mainframe and compromise the entire Omega site. If the core fails, then the Eberus will lose power, and the preserved embryos of our people will perish. Their last chance at life will be destroyed.

I can move some embryos into individual cryopods, but I only have several dozen pods and neither the time, equipment, nor manpower to procure the materials to create more. My current plan is to transfer you into a cryopod, as well as Despoina and some of your other spearsisters, but I dread having to pick and choose which of the rest of our people deserve such preferential treatment, should those embryos prove necessary. I am not my brother, and unlike Poseidon, I do not believe some of us are innately more deserving.

· · ·

I shall think on the solution while I repair the core. I will return soon to update you on the situation.

Peri had started each entry on a new page, and I flipped the page, eager to find out what happened next. I suspected that fairly soon I would understand why Hades had resorted to his ridiculously complicated labyrinth scheme and how I—and Peri—had ended up in our current predicament.

I continued reading.

I finally have the core in a stable condition. This isn't a worst-case scenario, but it's not good. My repairs are more of a patch than an actual fix, and they won't last forever. I think I can get a few more cryosleep cycles in, but without a chaos stone to generate a new power core, my repair options are limited and temporary, at best. It always comes back to the need for a chaos stone, doesn't it?

As a precaution, I may lengthen the length of my cryosleep cycles from one to two thousand years. That should buy the people of Atlantis some more time to reach the necessary level of technological proficiency. As they stand now, they have made substantial progress, and though I am uneasy about their penchant for religious turmoil, I remain steadfast in my belief that they are the answer to our power problem.

You see, my fledgling civilization has given way to a greater empire. They call themselves the Romans, and their thirst for power is both admirable and frightening. They are on the cusp of imminent change, but it remains to be seen whether that change will be great or terrible—will they seek scientific enlightenment, or will their blind faith in the comfort and safety of tradition lead them back into the darkness? It could go either way.

They seem to crave the sense of security and control offered by religion, much more so than the ancient peoples of Olympus ever did, and I am forced to recognize that, similar as they may be, the humans are not the same as us.

Soon, I will depart to sow more seeds and do what I can to push the people of this planet toward the path of enlightenment. I shall update you once more upon my return, before I re-enter cryosleep. Know that you are with me, in my heart, wherever I go.

I shifted in my seat, hunching over the journal, curious to read more of Hades' account of the ancient people of Earth. The possibility that he was still alive out there, frozen in cryosleep, created a link to ancient times, making it feel like the things he was describing were happening now, rather than thousands of years ago.

I turned the page, reading on eagerly.

I have finally returned. Two years have passed, and I am more hopeful than when I left that when I next wake, the time will come for us to be reunited.

I spent quite a bit longer with the Romans than I initially intended. They have made even greater progress than I thought—

their understanding of mathematics and astronomy is truly astounding. Just one more great leap forward in understanding, and they will be on track to reach the point of technological advancement required to aid me in my quest to save our people.

Already, many of their great thinkers are shucking the chains of religious belief and studying the world around them with eyes unburdened by faith. Many others are joining these great thinkers, learning from them in institutes built for the sole purpose of spreading knowledge. Mark my words, Peri—a great revolution of thinking is coming.

I have decided to shorten this bought of cryosleep rather than lengthen it. I feel we are close. So very close. I do not wish to miss the window of opportunity. I am not, however, blind to the dangers of such an era. Pushback from traditional ways of thinking is always strongest when a group teeters on the cusp of great enlightenment. I would be remiss to ignore my fears that the coming revolution may not be as peaceful as I would hope.

That social volatility, along with the failing power core, has convinced me it will be best, in the long run, to err on the side of caution. Should the worst happen and I die the true death before the people of this planet are ready to assist in the Olympian resurrection, I have set up a failsafe—a labyrinth to test the worthiness of any who enter and to guide any who reach its heart along a path that will lead back here, to the Omega site and to what remains of our people. Even if the Eberus fails and the majority of the preserved embryos die, those in cryopods will be safe, as will all of the consciousness orbs in the Vault of

Souls. There will still be a path toward the resurrection, only it will be up to you to forge that path.

You, Peri, are an integral element of this backup plan, though I hope it will not come to this. The labyrinth is located near the Roman capital, and I have left your consciousness orb as well as the cryopod containing your preserved embryo in the central chamber, along with everything you would need to be successful. The humans need only to follow the instructions I have inscribed on the walls, and you will be resurrected. The method is imprecise and far from desirable, and there is a chance for genetic contamination as well as unpredictable altered genetic expression—it is a true last resort. However, should I expire, this is the only way forward for our people, and for you.

An icy seed of dread settled in my belly as I was forced to acknowledge the ever-increasing likelihood that Hades *had* died, thus resulting in my undesirable method of resurrection. If that was the case, then Peri and I were officially up shit creek, not a paddle in sight.

I continued to read, trepidation increasing with every line.

Once you have been resurrected, Peri, you can guide the humans here, to me—if I still live—and to what remains of our people. I do not think it likely this will happen. I hope it will not, but if your resurrection does occur in such an unfortunate way, know I am sorry to leave you with such a monumental task. I would leave this to another, but you are the only one I trust with the future of our people. Truly, I am sorry.

.   .   .

May the next time I wake prove this all to be unnecessary. As always, Peri, my heart is with you. Until we meet again...

I gulped, Hades' words making me increasingly disconcerted. I flipped through the pages following this latest entry. Just two entries left. Clearly, Hades had survived his next bout of cryosleep, but then what? I inhaled deeply. Only one way to find out...

We've got a problem, Peri—or rather, we've got multiple problems. The power core is failing, and the auto-wake sequence was initiated a century early.

I stopped reading for a moment, mentally calculating when this entry had been recorded. According to his last entry, he was supposed to slumber for another five hundred years. I placed his previous two entries at a century or two after year zero, what with the religious turmoil he mentioned, attributing that to the rise of Christianity, which meant he had likely recorded these latest disconcerting thoughts sometime between the years 500 and 700 AD, the time of the early Medieval Period in Europe.

Not for the first time, I felt an immense surge of sympathy for Hades. He was a man alone. A man apart. A man lost among aliens, just trying to survive.

I took a deep breath, swallowing my sorrow, and read on.

I honestly don't know what I'm going to do. Re-entering cryosleep will put the Eberus at risk, and while the loss of that, alone, would not spell the end of Olympus, it would make that sad outcome all the more likely.

. . .

To make matters worse, the Romans have failed me. The great enlightenment I foresaw was obliterated and the humans of the continent formerly occupied by the Roman Empire have plunged into an unprecedented dark age. The regression is unlike anything I have seen before. I cannot help but wonder if this is all hopeless. Perhaps we were wrong to set our sights on this world. These people are much more willful than are the Olympians, making their civilizations dangerously volatile.

I don't know what to do, Peri. Do I just give up? Do I accept the futility of the situation? Do I abandon all hope of ever seeing you again?

If only you were here to advise me. And yet, here I am, all alone.

I turned the page, expecting Hades' morose monologue to continue. But it didn't. The next page marked the start of a new entry. The final entry.

Perhaps now, I would discover what happened to Hades. Perhaps now, I would finally find out if all hope was truly lost.

I must apologize for my last entry, Peri. The darkness that has overcome my chosen people seems to have momentarily infected me, but my outlook on the future has regained some of its former, hopeful light. Regardless, even I must admit this is likely to be my final entry.

. . .

I managed to rewire the mainframe to run off the backup power core, but that weaker core was never meant to power the Omega site at full functionality for more than a few years. I have shut down all systems save for base infrastructure, life support, and the cryoengine. The cryogenerator's auto-wake sequence is now keyed to trigger the next time motion is detected within the entry corridor. If that ever happens.

Ah, you see, here I am, sliding back into the darkness. This pessimism is insidious, spreading throughout my mind and infecting my thoughts before I even realize what is happening, but I shall do my best to hold those dark thoughts at bay.

It all rests on your shoulders now, Peri. I have given up on the Romans and the peoples of the surrounding lands, and I was forced to move you to a second labyrinth built on a distant continent. It pains me to know you are so far from me as I prepare for indefinite cryosleep. But let us not focus on such sad truths.

I must tell you about that which has rekindled the small flame of hope I shall carry with me into the long, impending slumber. I happened upon a surprisingly advanced civilization in the heart of an enormous rainforest on the far side of Atlantis—the most promising and advanced civilization I have encountered on this planet. Unfortunately, years of poor weather had pushed the civilization to the brink of collapse, and by the time I reached them, their end was inevitable. They could not be useful in the way I would have liked, but they could still be of use.

· · ·

I chose to save them and move them into the Beta site, at the same time enlisting their help in constructing a second labyrinth, of which they are now the caretakers. The move will no doubt stunt the development of their civilization, but perhaps stagnations is all that is needed for those in such an important role. They will remain the same, while the civilizations all around them transform. They will hold steady, while others rise and fall. They will watch the world around them, but be not of it, for their role is far more significant. They will usher in a new dawn and bring about the return of our people.

I must believe this will be the outcome, though when I look back upon the tangled path I have laid out before you, I fear there is no chance for success. So many things could happen to foil such a convoluted plan. The chance for failure far outweighs the chance for success, and in my heart, I am resigned to the grim inevitability—that you will never be revived, and that my body will die when the backup core fails and the cryogenerator loses power.

I don't know why I'm recording this, when the likelihood of you ever reading it is so low. Perhaps I just needed to say goodbye. I am truly sorry, Peri. I have failed you. I have failed our people. Your sacrifice was all for nothing, and of this, I am eternally ashamed.

Farewell, Persephone. I shall think only of you as I drift into cryosleep, and I shall cherish the potential of what we almost shared. I shall, until my final moments, hold you in my heart. I love you, always.

. . .

Tears stained my cheeks as I reread Hades' final words. His pain was palpable, and his sorrow bridged the chasm of centuries separating us.

But at the same time, hope rekindled in my heart. Hades hadn't given up. He hadn't simply lain down to die. He had returned to cryosleep, which meant there was a still a chance that when I found the Omega site, I would find him, too. And he would be alive. He would be able to save me.

If we made it in time.

"Aisling," a petite blonde woman said, thrusting her hand out as she strode away from a compact black sedan parked near the bottom of the steps leading down from the plane. She wore jeans and a white T-shirt under her black leather coat, and the butt of a pistol was just visible every other step. Her palm slapped against mine mere moments after I set foot on the asphalt of the private runway, and she shook my hand brusquely, her grip firm. "Aisling Ó Béara, miss, at your service." Her words were spoken with the same lilting accent I was used to hearing from Fiona.

"Nice to meet you," I said. "I'm Cora."

"I know who you are, miss," Aisling said, releasing my hand and offering it to Raiden and Meg in turn. She didn't bat an eye at the apparent nun in her midst. "Your mother sent me."

I deactivated the regulator as subtly as I could and skimmed the surface thoughts and memories from her mind, double-checking that she spoke the truth. Satisfied she was, I reactivated the regulator a few seconds later. I also picked up on a military background as well as her years of history working alongside my mom on her private expeditions.

Sensing Raiden's questioning stare, I met his eyes and nodded, just once, letting him know her story checked out.

Aisling popped the trunk so we could stow our bags, then ushered us into the car. She reminded me of Raiden with the way she constantly scanned our surroundings, searching for enemies lurking in the shadows.

Soon enough, we were safe in the car, Raiden in the front passenger seat, Meg and me in the back. We wound through the Irish countryside, the green rolling hills grayed out by the starlight.

"Wait, where are we going?" I asked as Aisling pulled the car onto a long, winding riverfront drive that, so far as I could tell, only led to one place—a castle sitting on a bluff jutting out into the North Atlantic Ocean. That lone structure stood out against a brilliant backdrop of glittering stars in the clear night sky.

Aisling took her right hand off the stick shift to gesture to the castle ahead. "Imeall Castle," she said, "home to one Fiona Ó Faoláin." After a moment, she added, "Imeall means 'edge', as the castle was once believed to be perched on the edge of the world."

My mouth fell open, not because of the name of the castle, but because the castle in question was Fiona's *home*.

I had known Fiona for a decade, at least. And in those ten plus years, not once had she mentioned living in an honest-to-God castle. The thing was the epitome of a medieval castle, with weathered gray stone and notched battlements. It was roughly square, with massive round towers bulging out at each corner and a huge arched entrance with an iron-reinforced gate. The only thing missing was a moat.

"This place makes Blackthorn Manor look like a quaint cottage," Raiden murmured, glancing back at me around the headrest of the front passenger seat.

Meg was as in awe as the rest of us—save for Aisling—but then, awe had been Meg's general state of being since leaving the familiarity of the Amazon Rainforest. Almost everything was new to her.

When we were about fifty yards out, the formidable gate blocking the castle entrance started to rise. The final stretch of the road gave way to an ancient looking stone bridge crossing a short but deep crevasse.

I leaned forward as the car decelerated. A woman ducked under the rising gate and stepped out onto the bridge, and my eyes widened at the sight of her. She was tall and slim, her dark hair pulled back in a low ponytail and her features shadowed in the dim starlight.

My mom.

My heart was suddenly hammering. My throat constricted, and my eyes stung with the threat of tears. Emi joined my mom, and the tears were no longer threatening to escape. The flood-gates had opened, and tears streamed down my cheeks.

The car was still rolling when I pushed the door open and jumped out, making a beeline for my mom. I hadn't seen her in over a month. For a while there, I had thought I might never see her again.

My mom rushed forward to meet me, stopping a few steps away. Old habits.

I slammed into her with an audible *oomph*. My arms clamped around her back, and I pressed my cheek against her bony shoul-der, unable to stifle the sobs building in my chest.

She only hesitated for a moment before wrapping her arms around my shoulders and squeezing me tight.

The last time I hugged my mom, I was five years old, and her touch had felt like needles stabbing into my skin. But not this time. I clung to her, hugging her for the first time in twenty years, and it felt amazing.

"It's all right, sweetheart," my mom said, one hand rubbing up and down my back as she made soft, soothing noises. "It's OK."

Emi gave my forearm a quick squeeze before heading past us, no doubt to greet Raiden.

"Welcome to my castle, *bitches*!" That high-pitched voice with its almost sing-song lilt was unmistakable. I may never have met Fiona in person, but I *had* spoken with her nearly every day for the past ten years, and I would have known her voice anywhere.

She bounded into the open gateway, posing with her arms thrust out to either side like she had just performed a trick. She dazzled us all with her spirit fingers for a few seconds, then marched past the place where my mom and I were huddled together, heading for the others nearer to the car. She winked at me as she passed.

I couldn't hold in the laugh that bubbled up from my chest. And in all reality, I didn't want to.

Online, Fiona was a character. Truly larger than life—but then, so many people took on bigger, bolder personalities in the virtual world. It was easy to be *more* when there were no real consequences or repercussions. I had always figured that was the case with Fiona, too, and that when I met her in real life, she would be the Fiona I knew, just a slightly subdued version. And yet, that didn't seem to be the case. If anything, *real* reality amped up Fiona's personality, as impossible as such a thing seemed.

My mom pulled back, not releasing me but putting just enough room between our upper bodies that she could see me. "Oh, Cora-bora," she said, eyes tracing the no doubt puffy lines of my tear-streaked face. "I'm so sorry." She inhaled deeply, releasing the breath in a sigh. "I should've told you." She shook her head. "I should've—"

"Hey," I said, interrupting her with a whole-body shake. "It's OK," I said, and I was a little surprised by the conviction in my own voice.

A couple weeks ago, when all this started, I was more upset

with my mom than I had ever been before. I had been angry and disappointed and hurt. More than anything, I had wanted to track her down so I could demand some answers. An explanation *why*.

But the more I thought about it, the more I understood. Everything my mom had done, she had done out of love—at first out of her love for my people, and then out of her love for me. Yeah, sure, I still wished she had told me the truth about my origins earlier than, oh say, two weeks ago. But rehashing the past seemed like such a waste of time now that it was looking like my time might be running out. I wasn't willing to waste whatever time I had left with my mom arguing about things that couldn't be changed. It was water over the dam, or under the bridge, or swept out to sea, or whatever. It didn't matter. The water was gone, but we were still here. *That* was what mattered.

Unaware of my wandering thoughts, my mom touched the stone in the regulator hanging from the golden chain around my neck. "So, it really does help?" she asked, gaze leaving the pendant and rising to meet my eyes.

I nodded, sniffing as my lips curved into a smile. I released my mom and swiped the tears from my cheeks with both hands. "Works like a charm," I told her, but my smile wilted as I considered how to tell her about the issues that had cropped up since her disappearance. "But now we've got a new problem…"

Concern shadowed my mom's eyes as I explained about Peri and the fractured consciousness mess. As difficult as it was to share my ailment with my mom, I didn't sugarcoat the truth. She needed to understand the direness of the situation. I watched her face as her mind worked through the implications, as horror, guilt, and grief transformed her features. For a moment there, I thought the grief might bury her, but a new emotion lit her eyes, pulling her through.

"Can I—" My mom hesitated, quickly wiping away the tears staining her cheeks. She cleared her throat, looking slightly bashful. "Would it be possible to speak with her—with Persephone?"

I shook my head, flashing my mom an apologetic smile, not the least bit surprised by her request. This was *my mom* after all. "Not until after we find the Omega site and fix whatever is going on in here," I said, tapping the side of my head with two fingertips.

My mom nodded, more to herself than to me. "We'll figure this out," she said, gripping my shoulders as she put on a brave face. The concern was still there, lingering in her eyes, but she had her mission—an action to focus on—which had always been her preferred coping mechanism.

My mom's focus slid past me to the group making their way across the bridge. I sensed their approach through my bond with Meg.

"And this must be our nun?" my mom said, amusement softening her voice.

Again, I nodded, sniffing one more time and wiping the final stray tears from under my eyes before turning to face the others.

Fiona skipped ahead, jumping to a stop in front of me. "Greetings, traveler," she said, pressing her hands together in front of her chest and bowing deeply.

Small but mighty. That was Fiona's self-proclaimed motto, and the description certainly fit the bill. She was a smidge shorter than Emi, putting her at a whopping five feet, two inches, but she had the kind of presence that drew eyes to her. Her hair color was indeterminate; the long locks twisted up in a top knot were a shocking neon orange where illuminated by the artificial light spilling through the gateway behind me. In every photo I had seen of Fiona over the years, her hair was a different color. Her skin was the flawless ivory of one who either rarely ventured out into the sunlight or was fanatical about sunscreen use. Her features were generally unremarkable, save for her eyes which were a clear emerald green.

Fiona straightened and lowered her hands, giving me a good

view of the graphic on her oversized hoodie. A skeletal leg with an arrow shooting through the knee.

The reference to our mutual favorite NPC line from *Skyrim* made me grin. "Let me guess," I said, eyes meeting hers, "you used to be an adventurer?"

Fiona made a clicking noise in one cheek and shook her head in mock disappointment. "Damn arrows to the knee…"

I chuckled, and she grinned. Not a second later, her arms were around me, locking my own arms against my sides. I returned the embrace awkwardly, only able to use the lower half of my arms.

"You scared me, you dummy," she said, her voice a low murmur. She released me suddenly, then punched me in the shoulder, and not gently.

"Ow!" I exclaimed, rubbing my shoulder. "What was that for?"

Fiona shook out her hand, her own face slightly pained. "For making me think you were dead," she said, glaring. But her anger vanished between one heartbeat and the next, and her grin returned. "I feel better now."

"Awesome," I said, my voice dry. I glanced at the others, standing around us. "I take it you've met everyone?"

"You betcha," Fiona said, nodding in Raiden's direction and waggling her eyebrows. "Hubba hubba," she mouthed.

I choked on a laugh, cheeks heating instantly, and redirected my attention to my mom. "Um, Mom," I said, gesturing to Meg.

The Zari warrior woman had shucked her nun's habit and was now standing on a bridge in Ireland in her full Xena-esque glory. The only thing marring her look was the hiking pack on her shoulders.

"This is Meg," I told my mom. The introduction felt woefully inadequate, but how was I supposed to describe the psychic bond I shared with Meg without launching into a full-on two-hour lecture about the history of the Zari people?

"Meg, this is my mom, Diana," I added, more for social acceptability than necessity—Meg knew exactly who my mom was, thanks to our connection.

My mom stepped forward, extending her hand toward Meg.

Meg hesitated only for a moment until she picked the appropriate response from my mind and clasped my mom's hand.

My mom froze mid-pump of Meg's hand and turned to look at me, eyes widened in surprise. She had spotted Meg's regulator. I didn't need to be actively reading her mind to see the questions forming in her head.

"She's human," I said quickly, glancing from my mom to Meg and back. I figured asking if she was an alien like me would have been her first question. And then I added, "It's a long story."

My mom's eyes searched mine for a solid five seconds as she vacillated between accepting my deferment of her burgeoning interrogation and demanding to know more right now. Again, no mind-reading necessary. I just knew her that well.

"I look forward to hearing it," my mom finally said. She turned back to Meg, finished the handshake with a final pump, and offered the clearly out-of-place young woman a warm smile. "A pleasure to meet you, dear."

I choked on a laugh, masking it with a cough. Only my mom would take a good, long look at this veritable warrior princess and call her "dear."

"Let's get inside before someone catches a chill," Emi suggested, and our small group slowly ambled toward the gateway, my mom hanging back to speak with Aisling.

Fiona linked her arm through mine and leaned in close. "Tell me you've tapped that," she whispered, pointing to Raiden with her chin. He walked ahead of us, his head angled toward his mom as the two conversed in hushed voices.

My eyes bulged and my cheeks burned, my blush returning with a vengeance. "I, um…" I cleared my throat, mind frantically searching for a subject change. "Tell *me* how it is that you have a castle," I blurted. "What are you, like, royalty or something?" Her gamertag *was* IceQu33n, and I wondered if there was some actual significance to the name.

Fiona froze mid-step. With our linked arms, that meant my forward motion stopped, as well.

I looked at her, surprised by the reaction.

Fiona bit her lip. "I, ah…I bought it," she said, then added, "the castle, I mean. I bought the castle. Last year."

"Oh." My eyebrows drew together. "OK." I couldn't hide the sting of knowing she had hid this from me. I mean, I would think buying a castle would come up at some point during the daily conversations with my best friend, but apparently I was wrong.

"I'm sorry, Cora," Fiona said in a rush. "Of course I wanted to tell you when I was castle shopping, but then I would've had to admit to lying to you about my job and I was afraid of how you would react and, well, it just seemed easier not to say anything." Her shoulders slowly bunched up as she spoke, finally slumping after she finished.

I shook my head, unsure how to respond. "What do you mean you lied about your job?"

Fiona sighed, her petite frame seeming to deflate. "I'm not a video game researcher," she said. "I'm a game *developer*."

"OK…" I wasn't sure where she was going with this.

"For Rockville," she added.

My mouth fell open. Rockville Softworks made *all* the best games. In fact, their upcoming release was probably my all-time most anticipated game. Ever. *Allworld Online* promised to revolutionize the gaming experience by gamifying thousands of popular TV, movie, and book franchises in a boundless VR universe. I was ready to slay all day in *Buffyland* and spend a few months getting to know Mr. Darcy *really* well.

"Fio…" I swallowed roughly. "Are you working on *Allworld*—"

"Yes!" she blurted. "I'm the lead developer on the project." Her gaze dropped to the ground, and she looked like she might be sick. "I wanted to tell you, Cora, I really did, but I signed an NDA, and you never know who's listening online, and…" She sighed. "I just—I'm sorry."

"Wow," I said, processing what I had just learned. Instead of being upset, I felt electrified. Adrenaline flowed through my veins, making my whole body feel like it was humming. "Wow," I repeated.

I knew Fiona was a genuine genius, and I had long since thought her talents were put to waste, but this was amazing news. The best news I had heard since all this craziness started.

"So, you're like the best coder out there," I said, more of a question than a statement, despite the lack of inflection at the end.

Fiona shrugged. "GCHQ knocks on my door every few months to see if I'm interested in joining up, but working for the government just sounds like a real buzzkill." Finally, she lifted her gaze, her eyes once again meeting mine. "Besides, I figure I can do as much good bringing people joy and entertainment as I can providing intelligence for the government, so…"

"Uh huh," I said, barely hearing her words. I was too revved up on the amazing implications of her recent revelation. "Fio," I said, jiggling her arm excitedly, "I forgive you, but I need your help with something."

She raised her eyebrows, clearly surprised by my reaction.

"There's this disk," I started, pausing to lick my lips. I was so excited that I was bouncing on the balls of my feet. "It's damaged, and I need to extract the data."

"Oh, yeah, sure. No prob," she said with a wave of her hand. "What kind of disk? SD? CD? Floppy?"

My responding smile was filled with apologies. "Alien."

[29]

Emotional roller coaster? More like an emotional rocket ship. Talk about going from the lowest low to the highest high. For a while there on the plane, I had been fairly sure my end was seriously nigh. But now, surrounded by all of my loved ones—and knowing from Peri's translation of Hades' final log entries that there was a real chance Hades was still alive in the Omega site— I felt some of the weight lift off my shoulders, and hope put a spring in my step.

When I first thought of bringing the damaged holodisk to Fiona, the plan was a pure hail Mary. A shot in the dark. A legitimate crapshoot, like the whole save-Cora mission was riding on a wing and a prayer.

But the enthusiasm with which Fiona attacked her study of the holodisk gave me hope that maybe the odds weren't stacked quite so high. Maybe the success rate was more in the range of improbability than in the realm of impossibility. Fiona made me feel like we had a real, fighting chance. Like our actions could actually impact the outcome. Like we were in control of our fate, at least to some degree.

The headache was still there—and worse than ever—but it

didn't bother me as much as it had a few hours ago. It felt less like the harbinger of my doom and more like the symptom of a pesky illness that would go away just as soon as we found the cure.

Just as soon as we found Hades.

Fiona's study was located in the round chamber at the top of the northeast tower of Imeall Castle—because it made her feel like Merlin, at least, that's what she said. The ceiling was glass, to allow natural light in during the day and to enable climate-controlled stargazing at night, with built-in automatic shades for when Fiona desired a glare-free environment. The perimeter of the circular room was divided into three clearly delineated sections, with a work station in the center so meticulously organized it looked like it could be featured in a Martha Stewart special on techno-crafting.

Fiona's gaming station took up one section around the outer edge of the room, with a huge TV, an oversized recliner, and just about every video game console ever invented. Two narrow bookcases stood like columns on either side of the TV, displaying a video game collection that made even me jealous. A giant fishbowl sat on a side table beside the chair, a goldfish named Shrek swimming lazily around his own little castle. Fiona's multi-monitor monster of a computer was set up in another space, and the final area was taken up by tall bookcases stuffed full of technological manuals and coding texts, most either spiral-bound or stored in three-ring binders.

I wandered around the study for a solid twenty minutes while Fiona prepped her workspace to run a bunch of diagnostics and tests on the holodisks. I had given her the functional but no longer useful disk marking the location of the South America labyrinth for reference.

"You're welcome to wait, Cora," Fiona said, "but this could take a while…"

I spun around from my examination of binder spines

displaying hand-written titles that made absolutely no sense to me to find Fiona watching me through a pair of magnifying glasses.

She flipped up the lenses, making her look slightly less like a mad scientist. "I say this out of love," she said, raising her hands defensively, "you look like shit."

My shoulders slumped.

"Your room is all made up for you," she added. "You might as well use this time to rest up while you can. It sounds like once I extract the info, you'll be on your way..."

Rubbing the back of my neck, I nodded slowly. We had already eaten, and everyone was up to date on the situation. My mom and Emi had retired to the grandiose library, my mom scouring maps of Egypt in search of potential locations of the Omega site, while Emi binge read the *Liber Veritatis*. Meg was there, too, surfing the internet on one of Fiona's many spare laptops, absorbing everything she could about the world beyond her Amazon kingdom. And last I had seen him, Raiden had been in the castle's ridiculous and totally unnecessary armory prepping our weapons and gear for the trip we would be making as soon as Fiona cracked the code. We already had all the necessary falsified documentation to get us from Belfast to Cairo.

Everything that could be done either had been done or was in progress. There was nothing left for me to do, except stay alive. Which, I realized, was probably more likely to happen if I started taking better care of myself by doing crazy things like, oh say, sleeping.

"Yeah," I said, stretching my neck first one way, then the other. "That's probably a good idea." Unless whatever physical changes were happening inside my skull were akin to a concussion, in which case resting—and sleeping—was a terrible idea.

I frowned, thinking it couldn't hurt to double check with Emi on the way to my room. She and Meg had discussed at length what was going on inside my head. If Emi thought it was all right for me to sleep, then I would sleep.

I made my way to the door of the study, pausing in the open doorway to look back at Fiona. "You'll let me know—"

"As soon as I find anything," she finished for me, not looking up.

I watched her studious examination of the holodisk for a few more seconds, but I figured my lurking probably wasn't helping with her concentration, so I turned away and started down the spiral staircase. Once I reached the base of the tower, I headed into the long hallway that followed the castle's northern wall, leading to the living areas.

On one side of the passage, the stone wall was solid and unbroken all the way to the bend at the very end of the hallway. On the other side, trios of arched windows broke up the gray stone, the small panes of glass set in an intricate pattern. The windows overlooked the starlight courtyard, the silvery light the only illumination in the dark hallway, save for the warm artificial light seeping into the hallway from the chandelier in the great hall.

When I reached the end of the passage, I peeked around the corner to see if anyone was in the great hall. The elongated dining table was empty, long since cleared of the dishes from our middle-of-the-night feast, and only some candles in silver candlestick holders and a crystal vase of fresh flowers remained. I had counted at least a half-dozen staffers since arriving here, and I could only imagine how much effort it took to keep a castle like this not just maintained, but livable.

I headed through the doorway at the end of the hall and started up another winding staircase. I climbed until I reached a doorway about three stories up, leading to the corridor above the great hall. The hallway beyond was long and windowless, but doors broke up the endless stretch of gray stone on the left side, slightly musty floor-to-ceiling tapestries on the right.

I wrinkled my nose as I made my way to the first door on the left. Warm light spilled under the crack at the bottom of the large, arched door, flickering slightly. I smiled to myself. My mom always did love to work by firelight. She claimed natural light revealed secrets in her beloved ancient documents that artificial bulbs never could.

Placing both palms flat against the heavy wood door, I pushed just enough to inch the door open a crack.

"…and you're certain this is the exact location of the Beta site?" My mom said, her voice slightly muffled. Knowing her, she was probably talking into a book or bent over a map.

"Yes," Meg said, "I'm certain."

"Hmmm…," my mom murmured, making a noise I had heard her make a thousand times while contemplating this or that historical puzzle. "There must be some identifiable link—some other variable we can use to narrow down the potential Olympian sites," she thought aloud. "We could create a cross section using the map of tech dead zones and…I don't know. *Something* else. There *must* be some other variable…"

My smile returned, and I shook my head. Sure, my mom and I had our differences, and I hated that she had spent so much of my life away on this or that adventure, but knowing the sole purpose for all of those trips had been to help me was a balm to the old, open wound. Finally, I felt like I was actually healing.

I poked my head into the library, peeking around the edge of the door until I spotted my mom bent over a table covered in dozens of maps near the intricately carved fireplace. She was in her element, surrounded by towering bookcases packed full of books, from antique leather tomes to year-old paperbacks and everything in between.

Meg knelt on the floor near my mom's chair, examining a map pulled up on the laptop's screen. Emi sat curled up in an armchair a little farther from the fireplace, a Tiffany floor lamp lighting the pages as she devoured the *Liber Veritatis*.

"Goodnight," I called softly into the room.

The attention of all three women snapped to me.

I raised a hand in a half-hearted wave. "Wake me if you discover anything," I said, though it came out more as a question.

"Sleep well, Cora," Emi said, smiling at me before returning to her book.

Meg bowed her head in my direction. Through our bond, I could sense that Raiden had already bid them goodnight, as well.

My mom stood and made her way to me, weaving around armchairs and end tables. When she reached me, she rested her hand on my arm, rubbing up and down a few times. "How are you feeling, sweetie?" The concern in her eyes was equally comforting and troubling.

I shrugged one shoulder. "I've been better," I admitted, issuing the understatement of the century.

My mom laughed without smiling. "We'll figure this out," she said, squeezing my arm as she leaned in, pressing her lips to my cheek.

Unused to such casual close contact, I froze, entire body stiffening. A second later, I closed my eyes, relaxing as my mom pulled me into a side hug through the half-open doorway.

"Get some rest, sweetie," my mom said, holding me tight.

I nodded against her neck, soaking in her familiar, herbal scent. She had smelled the same for as long as I could remember.

"I love you *so much*, Cora," she said, her voice growing thick with emotion. "I won't let *anything* happen to you," she added. "Not anything."

Again, I nodded. It was all I could do without betraying how close I was to crying.

My mom pulled back, her gaze skimming over my face as she smoothed down my hair and tucked a flyaway strand behind my ear. "You're the best thing that ever happened to me," she said, a tiny smile curving her lips and tears glistening in her eyes.

"I couldn't possibly be prouder of the woman you've become." She squeezed my shoulder one last time. "Sleep tight, Cora-bora," she said, before turning away and heading back to the fire and her waiting maps.

I eased the door shut and sniffed, swiping under first one eye, then another to clear the threatening tears. My mom was rarely so open and expressive, and it was like she had infected me with her desire to share her feelings. I suddenly felt the need to do the same.

I needed to talk to Raiden. There was something I wanted to get off my chest before I laid down to rest. After all, I might not have too many more chances to let him know just how much he meant to me.

I turned away from the library door and hurried down the hall. I rounded the corner at the end, bypassing the doorway to yet another of the castle's four towers and headed down the corridor leading to the guest rooms. Or, at least, to the *livable* guest rooms. Only four of the castle's bedchambers had been renovated and updated with modern conveniences, including the lord's—or *lady's*—chambers.

Over dinner, Fiona had shared that she'd been dragging her feet on restoring the guest rooms on the floor beneath this one because she didn't want to accidentally displace any resident ghosts. Well, her actual words were, "I don't want to mess with the *wu*," but I had read between the lines.

I passed the door to the room I was sharing with Meg and headed for the next one down. Raiden had his own room, and my mom and Emi were sharing the third. I knocked on the solid wood door to Raiden's room, three quick raps with my knuckles.

I heard movement on the other side. Raiden was moving slowly. I had probably woken him.

My heart was suddenly hammering in my chest, and I swallowed roughly, taking a step back from the door. If I hurried, there was still time for me to rush to my room. To run away. To hide.

I gritted my teeth and clenched my fists, arms held straight down at my sides. "No more running," I said under my breath.

The door opened, and I took a reflexive step backward.

Raiden stood in the open doorway, his torso bare and his sweats riding low. His dark hair was mussed, and his eyes were slightly unfocused, confirming my suspicion that he had been asleep. "Cora?" he said, a crease forming between his eyebrows. "Are you okay?"

I gulped, wringing my hands, if for no other reason than because I didn't know what else to do with them. "I, um…" My focus dropped to the floor, and I swallowed roughly. The eager emotional bravado of moments ago had fizzled away, scared off by fear. But still, I refused to run away.

So, I did the only thing I could think of doing that didn't involve fleeing. I threw myself at Raiden, hooking my arms around his neck and diving for his lips.

My teeth cracked against his, and he hissed in pain, pushing me away with a solid grip on my waist.

I reared back, one hand covering my mouth. "Oh my God," I said in a rush. My cheeks were on fire, and my front tooth throbbed, though the pain was nothing compared to the wound to my pride. "I'm so sorry!" I buried my face in my hands and spun on my heel, intending to flee down the hallway to my room.

"Cora, wait." Raiden caught me by the elbow, halting my escape.

I peered down at his hand, one of mine still covering my face, my chest heaving with each overexcited breath.

"Don't go," Raiden said, his voice rough with sleep. "Please."

Ever so slowly, I dragged my gaze up from his hand along the line of his sculpted arm and tattooed shoulder to his face.

There was no judgment in his eyes. Only warmth. Only desire. Only love.

My mortification melted under his stare. The way he looked at me, I felt strong and beautiful. I felt loved, absolutely and completely. There was no space for shame in his stare. No space for hesitancy or for fear.

Raiden pulled me into his room and shut the door. Embers burned in the fireplace, lighting the bedroom with a dim, fluttering glow. The pulse in his neck raced, and his chest rose and fell with each too-fast breath. I wasn't the only one who was nervous.

I leaned back against the door, feeling like I needed the support.

Raiden's gaze slid down the length of my body, the slow progression over my T-shirt and cargo pants exciting me further. When his eyes returned to mine, he stepped closer, his fingers sliding under the hem of my T-shirt. His fingertips glided up over my hips, and his thumbs teased the sensitive flesh on either side of my belly button, awakening a whole charm of butterflies within me.

He lifted the hem of my T-shirt over my chest, and I raised my arms to allow him to pull the shirt off over my head. His lips were on mine as he unclasped my bra, and suddenly my bare chest was pressed against his. The sensation was intense and intimate, and so much more than I ever thought I would get to experience in my stunted excuse for a life.

As the kiss deepened, Raiden swept me off my feet—figuratively *and* literally—and soon he was laying me on the bed and unfastening my pants. All the stop signs in my head had been obliterated, replaced by endless green lights.

"Raiden, I—" I inhaled a shaky breath. My pants were off, and his hands were sliding up my thighs, heading for my underwear, and I was having a hard time thinking straight. "I love you," I told him, finally.

Raiden froze, his knees between my legs, his eyes locked with mine. A heartbeat later, his lips were crushed against mine, and his hands were everywhere they needed to be.

But before anything momentous could happen, he broke the kiss, rising up on sturdy arms, breathing hard. He cocked his head to the side, his eyebrows drawing together. "Do you hear that?"

I blinked, feeling more than a little dazed, then narrowed my eyes and focused on listening. I could hear a knocking sound, like someone was knocking on a door, except it sounded faint, distant.

Raiden rolled off to the side, and I sat up, instinctively pulling the corner of the quilt over my bare chest. I ran a finger around the stone in the regulator, deactivating and reactivating the device in a fraction of a second, just long enough to sense the source of the knocking.

"It's Fio," I told Raiden. "She's knocking on the door to *my* room." My lips curved into a hopeful smile. Had she pulled the data from the holodisk already?

Raiden was already off the bed and pulling on his sweat-pants. I scooted to the edge of the mattress and frantically searched for the rest of my clothes, but all I could find were my pants and a sock. I snatched Raiden's T-shirt off the arm of the chair near the fireplace and pulled it on over my head. It reached mid-thigh. Good enough.

I rushed to the door, heart pounding with excitement.

"Fio," I said, stepping out into the hallway.

She was already hustling toward me, an old-school cordless phone held with the mouthpiece pressed against her chest. "Oh my God," she whispered, scanning me from the toes up. "Were you just—" Her expression blanked, and she plastered on the fakest smile I had ever seen. "Hi Raiden!" She stopped a few steps away and thrust the phone out toward me. "It's for you, Cora."

I frowned, exchanging a look with Raiden. Why would someone be calling me, here? My stomach twisted into knots, not liking the implications, and I licked my lips. "Who is it?"

"Some guy," Fiona said with a shrug, shaking the phone at me. "Sounds like he could be a Skarsgård."

I didn't want to take the phone, like it was the hottest hot potato in the world. Hand shaking, I forced myself to reach for the phone. I inhaled deeply and brought the receiver to my ear. "Hello?"

"Hello, ancient one." The faintly accented voice sent shivers down my spine. It was the last voice I wanted to hear—the voice of Henry Magnusson, the Primicerius of the Custodes Veritatis and number one pain in my ass. "I'm so glad I finally found you."

How nice for you to have everyone you love under one roof. And how convenient for me…

As I changed into the hoplon suit, aware of Raiden's and Fiona's watchful gazes—both had followed me into the bedroom I was sharing with Meg—Henry's words replayed in my head, over and over again. And as his words replayed, rage simmered in my veins.

You hold their fate in your hands, ancient one—amnesty, or death.

I fastened the closures on the boots, then pulled on the gloves, smoothing them over my forearms. I flexed my fingers, hands shaking.

Join the Custodes Veritatis. Stand by my side and declare your loyalty to our cause, and your loved ones will be safe.

I bent over, finger combing my hair to the crown of my head and twisting it into a tight bun. I secured the bun using the hair tie on my wrist, then straightened and stared at my reflection in the diamond-paned window. I looked fractured, the image of myself broken up by the strips of metal framing each tiny pane of glass. It was an accurate portrayal of how I felt. Fractured.

Or continue to work against me, and I will unleash the fires of heaven upon you and everyone you love.

It was an impossible choice. I couldn't help Henry. I couldn't hand Hades and whatever remained of my people over to the Custodes Veritatis. But I couldn't refuse; to do so would forfeit the lives of everyone I loved. Much as I wanted to flip Henry the bird, figuratively, I couldn't. I wouldn't.

I had decided what I would do the second Henry ended the call. There was a third choice. *My* choice.

I was going to kill Henry Magnusson. I was going to kill the crazy bastard and end this madness, once and for all. Whatever happened to me, at least my loved ones would be safe. And the Olympians would still have a chance; once Fiona repaired the holodisk, my mom could lead an expedition to the Omega site, revive Hades, usher in the return of the Olympians, and all would be well. They could finish this without me.

I turned around, heading for the bedroom door.

Raiden stepped in front of me, blocking my way. He crossed his arms over his chest and raised one eyebrow, challenging me to step around him. "Tell me what's going on."

I opened my mouth, but when no words formed, I shook my head. I hadn't been able to explain right after the phone call, and I still couldn't tell him. He wouldn't let me go. Not like he could stop me, but he would do everything in his power to try. He would make me hurt him. And to save his life, I *would* hurt him.

Fiona stood from her perch on the foot of the bed, arms hugging her middle. "It was him, wasn't it—the leader of the Order?"

"I have to go," I said, eyes pleading with Raiden to understand. I was doing this for him. For all of them. One day, he would understand.

The sound of pounding footsteps heralded Meg's arrival before she barreled into the room. "You can't do it!" she exclaimed.

"Do *what*?" Raiden said, looking from me to Meg and back.

My mom and Emi appeared in the doorway a moment later, watching from either side of Meg.

I clenched my jaw, chest heaving as I glared at Meg. She had no right to do this. No right to stop me.

"She's going to get herself killed!" Meg told Raiden, gesturing frantically with her arms. Her focus returned to me. "And you're going to get me killed, too. That's part of the deal—this bond we share," she said. "If you die, *I* die."

"I'm not the one who's going to die today," I snapped, not remotely certain of any such thing. I just knew I wouldn't be the *only one* to die today.

Meg guffawed. "Think about it, Cora," she said in a rush. "They aren't going to just let you walk out of there after you kill him."

My fingers itched to deactivate my regulator, but the second I did that, Meg's psychic powers would be unleashed, as well. Maybe I had more raw power, but she was a trained, deadly weapon, and without Peri's help, I doubted I would be able to beat her. I curled my fingers into fists instead. "Then I'll kill them all," I grated out.

"Cora!" my mom gasped, and Emi covered her mouth with a hand, tears shimmering in her eyes.

"You're not a killer, Cora," Raiden said, deep voice calm and cool despite the wild light in his eyes.

"Oh yeah?" I said, nostrils flaring and eyes burning. "How many people have you watched me kill in the last few days, huh?" I inhaled and exhaled shakily. First there were the goons on the boat, then the commandos in the jungle, and then however many of the Zari didn't make it out of the blast zone in time. "Because I've lost count," I hissed.

"That was in the heat of the moment, kill or be killed," Raiden said. "It's not the same as cold, calculated murder."

I gulped, his words seeping in through the cracks in the icy shell surrounding my heart. "He's going to kill you guys," I said, my voice seeming to echo inside me, like I was hollow. A tear snuck over the brim of my eyes and slid down my cheek. "If I don't come work for him, he's going to kill you—all of you."

"No, sweetheart," my mom said, brushing past Meg as she stepped into the room. She stopped on Raiden's right, her expression hard. "He's going to *try* to kill us." Her lips curved into a grim smile. "That doesn't mean we have to let him."

"But it's never going to end," I said, pitch rising and voice trembling. "He's never going to give up. He's never going to just let us *be*."

My mom stepped closer, reaching out with one hand to cup the side of my face. "Nothing in life worth having comes easy." She smiled again, softer this time. "*Act*, Cora, don't *re*act. Don't give Henry this power over you. Don't let him destroy you." She moved her hand from my face to my chest, pressing her palm over my heart. "Don't let him destroy this." She shook her head, her eyes searching mine. "I promise you, he's not worth it."

I swallowed roughly.

"Fight, Cora," my mom said, eyes pleading. "Fight with us. Fight for something that matters…for your people. For the Olympians, and for the humans. Fight for each of us, standing with you in this room." She gripped my upper arms with both hands. "You're not in this alone. We're with you, no matter what." She gave me a little shake. "So *be* with *us*." Her chin trembled. "Please, sweetie…"

My shoulders started to shake with barely contained sobs. A gut-wrenching noise clawed its way up my throat and burst out of my mouth. I collapsed against my mom, my whole body shaking with the force of the breakdown. I squeezed my eyes shut and pressed my face against her shoulder, hiding from the others. "I—I'm sorry," I whispered.

My mom rubbed my back, her hand making slow, methodical circles. "Shhh," she murmured. "Shhh…" She cleared her throat. "I'm almost afraid to ask, but I know Henry too well. How much time did he give you to decide?"

I inhaled shakily, sniffing to clear my now stuffy nose. "An hour."

[31]

"We have to go, Fio," I said, my voice low and urgent. I placed my palms on her worktable and leaned closer to her, the piping in the gloves of the hoplon suit glowing with an electric-blue light. "Now!"

The others were all down in the courtyard, loading the car with our bags. Fiona had quite the selection of getaway cars, but we had settled on using her largest vehicle, a refurbished old VW bus. Hardly the fastest or the most inconspicuous vehicle she owned, it was the only one that would fit all of us and our gear.

"Patience," she said, singing the word softly. Her magnifying goggles were back in place, and she was hunched over the holodisk on the table, ever so carefully touching it with the world's tiniest soldering iron.

"Fio!" I hissed, leaning in even closer. "If we don't go *right now...*"

We had passed the ten-minute mark thirty seconds ago, which was our scheduled go-time. My mom and Emi agreed that Henry never made empty threats. An execution team would be on their way, if they weren't already nearby, waiting on orders to attack. For all I knew, they could've been scaling the castle walls at this very moment, something I couldn't detect without concentrating. And right now, my sole focus was on getting Fiona moving.

"I just need one more—" Fiona sat bolt upright as a holographic globe appeared, hovering over the holodisk on the table, then vanished, there one second, gone the next. "Fixed it," she said, looking at me, distorted eyes blinking behind the lenses of her magnifying goggles.

I slid the holodisk to the edge of the table and onto my palm. The instant the disk made contact with my skin, the holograph of Earth reappeared. Heart hammering and blood electrified, I spun the globe around until I spotted the beacon marking the location of the elusive Omega site.

It was in Egypt—Cairo, from the looks of it. The coordinates were written in Olympian, making them gibberish to my throbbing, fractured mind. *But*, I still had the translation of the coordinates for the labyrinth in Brazil written in my mom's journal. We could use that as a cipher and at least translate some of the digits. Anything at all would help us hone in on the exact location.

I snatched the storage cube holding the other holodisks off of the table and gently tucked the repaired disk inside, then grabbed Fiona's arm and dragged her toward the door. We raced down the spiraling staircase and ran into the dark courtyard, skidding to a stop just a few steps onto the grass.

The van was there, but all the doors were open and some of the gear and bags were scattered about on the lawn. There was no sign of the others, and a heavy silence filled the courtyard.

I exchanged a look with Fiona. Her expression mirrored the confusion I felt. "Where did they go?" I murmured.

"Cora!" someone hissed from the doorway to the tower in the opposite corner of the courtyard. My mom peeked out from behind the door, only the upper third of her body visible. She was making a shooing gesture with her arm.

"What?" I said, standing there, shaking my head. Like an idiot.

"Get back inside!" she shouted, just a moment before the deafening *rat-tat-tat* of automatic gunfire drove her back behind the door. The shots had come from directly above me.

I backpedaled, extending an arm to push Fiona back as I craned my neck to peer up at the wall walk topping the wall towering behind me. A commando matching those I had encountered in the rainforest was peeking over the interior battlement, training his rifle on me.

I raised a hand above my head, willing an energy shield into existence at the exact moment the muzzle of the intruder's rifle flashed, and another deafening series of cracks cut through the still night. Three bullets ricocheted off the shimmering electric-blue barrier, quickly followed by dozens more, coming from all around us.

"Get inside!" I barked at Fiona, handing her the storage cube and shoving her back toward the safety of the tower behind us before drawing the retracted doru from the sheath on my back. I extended the golden staff weapon to its full length with a thought and lowered my shield just long enough to take out the threat directly above me with a quick energy blast.

Through the shimmering shield, I focused on the two commandos atop the far wall. I took a deep breath, then lowered the shield and sent a series of energy blasts in their direction. My aim was shit compared to Peri's, and I had to raise my shield again after only taking out one of my targets, along with mauling part of the stone wall. In those brief seconds, several more commandos had appeared on the wall walk, scattered about the perimeter of the castle. Even without concentrating on my psychic senses, I could tell more were closing in on us.

Maybe Peri would have been able to handle their growing numbers, but they were more than a match for me. Outnumbered, I retreated into the tower and dropped my shield.

Fiona huddled on the bottom stair, hugging the tower's central pillar. She watched me with owl eyes, her eyelids opened wide and unblinking. It was like she had never seen me before. Like I was some kind of monster. After the show I had just put on, I could hardly blame her.

"Let's go, Fio!" I said, grabbing her by the elbow and yanking her to her feet. She could be in shock later; right now, we needed to run.

I dragged her the first few steps, but soon enough, she was leading the way. We raced down the hallway spanning the length of the eastern wall, heading for the doorway to the northeastern tower.

Someone hurtled through the doorway, and Fiona screamed. We stumbled to a halt, my heart jackhammering in my chest, and Fiona clung to my arm as I awkwardly aimed the doru at our ambusher.

At Raiden.

I felt Meg approaching before she passed through the doorway, joining Raiden, closely followed by Emi and my mom. All four wore bulging packs and panicked expressions.

Relief flooded me, and I lowered the doru, skipping into a jog as I headed toward them. I gave my mom a quick hug and reached out to squeeze Raiden's biceps. "There's too many of them. They're everywhere," I said, exchanging a quick glance with Meg, who confirmed what I had sensed with a nod. I looked to Raiden, and then to my mom. "What do we do?"

"There's a hidden passage that leads down to the beach," Fiona offered. "Maybe we can swim, or—"

"They came by boat," Raiden said. "Meg sensed their approach while you two were up in the tower." That explained how the others had had the foresight to snag some of our gear from the van before clearing out of the courtyard. "We can use one of their boats to get away," he suggested.

"A few remained down on the beach," Meg added, her eyes

grew unfocused, just for a moment, and I sensed she was concentrating on gauging their numbers and position. "But just three," she said, her eyes met mine. "We can take them."

I nodded once, then turned to Fiona. "Where's this passage?"

Fiona gulped, then pushed past me. We all followed her through the base of the northeastern tower and into the great hall. She jogged to the far corner of the huge room, where a gigantic antique L-shaped cupboard stood tucked into the corner. The piece of furniture was so large, I thought it must have been built right here in this room.

"It's going to be dark," Fiona said as she opened one six-foot tall door, revealing empty shelves. She shut the door immediately, then cracked open the one beside it and stepped back, pulling the door open further to reveal an empty compartment with an open back. Beyond was only darkness. "We'll have to feel our way," she added, waving us into the cupboard.

"This should help," Meg said as she stepped forward, her hand held out in front of herself, palm up. A ball of brilliant, amethyst energy appeared in her cupped hand, and she stepped into the cupboard.

Fiona watched her go, a tinge of her earlier shock returning to her eyes. I could relate. Most of the time, I still felt like the world didn't make sense anymore.

My mom and Emi passed through the back-less cupboard after Meg. Raiden glanced my way, hesitating before following them.

"Go on," I said, flashing him a quick, closed-mouth smile. "I'll light up the rear." With a thought, I channeled a bit more energy into the doru, and the focus crystal glowed brighter.

Raiden stared at me for a moment longer, his eyes alight with the concern I sensed rolling off him in waves. He reached up, grasping my shoulder, and leaned in to press his lips against mine in a quick, heart-stopping kiss. "Hurry," he said as he pulled away, and then he turned and vanished through the cupboard.

"Go, Fio," I said, pointing to the cupboard with my chin, my cheeks on fire.

Fiona scampered after Raiden without a single teasing remark—a testament to just how shaken she really was—and disappeared into the darkness beyond.

I turned, giving the great hall one last scan. I sensed the intruders, several dozen highly trained and very deadly men and women scurrying throughout the castle like ants in an ant farm. A few were rushing down the spiral staircase in the northwest tower. I slipped into the cupboard and pulled the door shut mere seconds before they charged into the room.

I held my breath and ever so slowly backed into the hidden passage, the wooden floor of the cupboard creaking under my boots. Once the wood gave way to rough stone floors, I turned and hurried after the others, jogging to catch up. Soon enough, I was hot on Fiona's heels.

The walls were solid stone, giving the impression the passageway had been carved into the bedrock beneath the castle. The narrow tunnel soon gave way to steep, uneven stairs, which drastically slowed our escape. The deeper we burrowed underground, the cooler and danker the air grew.

Not five minutes after passing through the cupboard, I could smell the salty sea air and hear the muffled sound of the surf. My heart swelled with longing for home. I was about as far from my beloved island as I could get, and there was no saying when I would make it back. *If* I ever would make it back.

Up ahead, the passage curved to the left, then widened from two feet across to about six, and the mouth of the tunnel suddenly came into view between the thick bars of an ancient looking iron gate. The sandy beach had a faint silver sheen in the starlight, but the sea beyond was an expanse of inky darkness. Large, dark shapes stood out against the silvery sand. It took my mind a few seconds to recognize them for what they were: boats. Our way out of this mess.

Thankfully, I couldn't sense any human minds on the beach. The stray commandos must have been called up to the castle to reinforce their buddies after we proved we weren't going down without a fight.

As I drew near the gate, Raiden and my mom shifted off to the right side of the tunnel, heads bent close together as they strategized our next moves. Emi and Meg stood at the gate, both women clasping the bars and peering out toward the beach like prisoners catching a rare glimpse of freedom.

Panic fluttered in my chest at the thought that we might be stuck behind a locked gate, escape so close we could almost touch it, but just out of reach. That panic morphed into dread as I sensed one of the Order's commandos entering the secret passage through the cupboard in the great hall.

Meg spun around, one hand still clasping an iron bar, and her eyes locked with mine. She had sensed the new danger, too.

Fiona rushed ahead, pausing beside Raiden. "Pardon me," she said, reaching between Raiden and my mom. Metal scraped against stone as she retrieved a thick iron key from a small notch carved into the wall. Key in hand, she hurried to the gate.

I turned my back to the others, guarding the way we had come while Fiona worked on the lock. After a handful of tense seconds and some mildly shocking cursing, hinges screeched. I spun around just in time to watch Fiona pull the gate open.

Raiden raced ahead across the beach, making a beeline for the nearest boat. They were of the inflatable variety, still large enough to fit us all, but light enough for him to start dragging one back toward the water on his own.

By the time the rest of us joined him, he almost had the boat in the water. I tossed the doru into the boat, then helped him push it the rest of the way out, until the craft was floating, bobbing and lurching with the motion of the water. My mom and Emi raced from boat to boat, stabbing each one several times until all four were well on their way to being hopelessly unseaworthy.

Meg helped Fiona into our chosen boat, then climbed over the sides herself, while Raiden and I continued to push it farther out.

"Get your butts in there," my mom shouted, she and Emi splashing through the surf toward us.

With a grunt, Raiden jumped, hoisting his heavy body up and over the side of the boat like it was no big deal. The water was up to my waist, and I wasn't feeling so athletically inclined.

As Fiona settled by the engine attached to the stern, Raiden crossed the small craft and reached his arm out to help me. I grasped his forearm, and he did the same to me, pulling me almost completely out of the water with a single tug. He wrapped his other arm around my waist and dragged the upper half of my body over the boat's inflatable side. My legs were still dangling over the water when the engine roared to life.

I fell into Raiden, and his arms locked around me in a tight embrace. He pressed his lips against my temple, his quick breaths hot against my hair. I turned my face toward his, kissing him with all I had.

"Would you look at that," my mom said between huffed breaths.

Raiden and I froze, then separated like teens caught making out on the doorstep. Heat rushed up my neck, suffusing my cheeks, and I stared at my mom with wide, unblinking eyes.

She and Emi sat huddled together near the side of the boat, dripping wet and shivering, but both with proud, knowing grins plastered on their faces.

"Everyone ready?" Fiona said, giving the engine a warning rev before shifting it into gear.

I crouched, bracing myself. Raiden did the same.

"Off like a prom dress," Fiona sang, winking at me before turning the throttle and sending us speeding away into the night.

[32]

As I slunk down in my rickety airplane seat, my elbow brushing Raiden's, I was almost unable to believe we had truly escaped. That we were on our way to the Omega site. I wasn't naïve enough to think we were beyond the reach of the Custodes Veritatis, but we had cleared the latest hurdle. All that was left was getting into the Omega site and waking Hades from cryosleep.

If he was even still alive.

There was a real chance we would succeed. That I would survive. What had felt impossible yesterday was now just out of reach. So close, I could taste it.

The plane rattled, and I couldn't resist the urge to look out the tiny window. All I could see was water, the Irish Sea looking like a great vat of ink in the darkness of night. I gulped. At another notable rattle, my fingers became talons gripping the *Liber Veritatis*—my chosen entertainment for this flight. This plane was the smallest I had ridden on yet and far from new, but it was the only aircraft my mom's connection could get his hands on so quickly.

The plan was to fly low and avoid the air zones monitored by the various European countries' air traffic departments.

Apparently taking a swerving, zig-zagging route would help us avoid detection by the Order, but it would also tack on a couple hours to the trip. Even with the slight delay and my ever-worsening headache, our odds of success were higher than if the Order shot us down. After the siege at the castle, I wouldn't put anything past them, not even anti-aircraft missile launchers.

"Can we trade seats, Raiden?" my mom asked, standing in the aisle. Her fingertips created little indents in the cushion of Raiden's headrest. Her dark brown hair was pulled back in a low, messy bun, and the lines around her eyes and mouth looked more pronounced than usual. Like me, she had been on the run for a couple weeks, and she was clearly exhausted.

"Yeah," Raiden said. "Of course." I looked from my mom to Raiden, watching as he fumbled with the buckle of his seatbelt. It clicked faintly as he released the latch, and he reached for the top of the seatback in front of him. He stood, sidestepping out into the aisle and settling in one of the empty seats near the front of the plane. There were fourteen rows, with two seats on either side.

My mom slipped into his seat and patted my knee, her eyes endless pools of worry. "How are you doing, sweetheart?"

My head ached worse than it had the morning after Raiden and I snuck a case of wine from the cellar and attempted to drink our way through all twelve bottles in a single night. It was my sixteenth birthday, and I had had the brilliant idea that alcohol would dull my senses enough that my condition would go dormant. My plan had been to orchestrate the perfect first kiss—with Raiden—though he hadn't known that part. He had just wanted to help.

I shrugged, grimacing slightly.

My mom inhaled deeply, sighing as she released the breath. "That good, huh?"

I laughed softly, then winced as it made the pounding in my

head worsen for a few heartbeats. It was best if I just didn't move at all.

My mom gave my leg a squeeze. "Well, let's make the rest of this journey as easy on you as possible," she said. She held out her other hand, offering me the ancient storage cube. "Will you open this so I can take a look at the holodisk? I'd like to pinpoint our destination."

I frowned, my brow furrowing. I had totally forgotten about the holodisk. I reached out with one hand, moving slowly. The instant my pointer finger made contact with the polished stone, hidden channels beneath the surface started to glow, and the box popped open.

"It's this one," I said, tapping the disk on the far right with the tip of my fingernail. "I can't translate the coordinates anymore, but the translation for the location of the South America labyrinth is written in your journal. Maybe you can use it as a cipher?"

My mom nodded as she pulled the holodisk from the safety of the stone box. "Good thinking," she said, setting the holodisk on her upraised palm.

The holographic model of Earth appeared, hovering over her hand. It flickered slightly but stabilized after a heart-stopping moment.

"Em?" my mom said, not taking her eyes from the globe.

The top half of Emi's face popped up over the top of the seatback in front of me, her eyebrows raised in question. "Yes?"

"Can you hand me my journal?" my mom asked. "Thanks," she said when Emi handed her the leather book through the narrow opening between the seatbacks.

Without lifting my head from the headrest, I watched my mom flip through the pages one-handed. "It's before all that," I told her as she leafed through page after page of Peri's and my translations of Hades' logs. "Oh, there," I said when she passed it. "Go back a page."

She did, then freed the pen holding her hair back and quickly copied down the Olympian symbols marking the exact location of the Omega site. She double and triple checked the symbols against those on the blinking beacon before tucking the holodisk back into the storage cube and gently pressing it closed.

Cross-referencing with my translation of the first set of coordinates, she wrote out each of the numbers she knew for sure, leaving blanks marked by a line for the mystery symbols—those not present in the first set. When she finished, nine of the fourteen symbols had numbers written beneath them, while the remaining five were marked by blanks.

"Hmmm," my mom said, thinking aloud. "Unless the Olympians used additional integers beyond the standard ten, we're only missing the translation of a few numbers."

After a quick study of the first translation, I noted that it lacked both twos, threes, and sixes.

My mom jotted down nine variations of the coordinates using all the possible combinations, but quickly scratched out four of them. After another moment, she scratched out two more. She paused with the tip of her pen poised over another set. "Raiden, do you know the general coordinates for Cairo off the top of your head?"

"No," he said, "but give me a sec and I'll tell you."

I closed my eyes, picturing the world map hanging on the wall in my bedroom, directly over my headboard. I had been tracking my mom's expeditions on that map since I was eight years old. A small pin with a gold head about the size of a ball bearing marked each of her destinations. I used to stare at that map for hours at a time, imagining what my mom was doing and where I would go if I could just go *somewhere*. Anywhere would have made me happy, but Egypt was at the top of my list.

"Thirty degrees North," I said, reading the numbers on the map in my mind's eye. "By thirty-one degrees East." I opened my eyes, taking a moment to bask in the pride transforming my mom's face. "Approximately," I added with the tiniest of smiles.

My mom flashed me a grin, then looked down at the dwindling list of coordinates on the page, crossing out two of the remaining three. "And then there was one," she murmured. "Can I see your phone, Em?" she said, barely looking up to grab the smartphone Emi passed between the seats.

My mom opened the map app and typed in the coordinates, her eyes widening almost as soon as she hit search. "No way," she murmured, the two words filled with equal parts awe and astonishment.

"What?" Emi said, once again peeking over the top of her seat.

Raiden stood and started down the short stretch of aisle, and Fiona rose up to her knees, leaning over the top of her seatback. Meg was the only one who didn't react, but then, the sun was due to rise soon, and she was hibernating in her nun's habit to prevent life-threatening burns, so I could hardly blame her.

Curiosity momentarily overwhelmed the pain in my head, and I leaned forward to get a look at the phone's screen. The outline of the landmark marked by the small red arrow on the map was impossible to mistake. But it was also just plain impossible: the Great Sphinx of Giza.

"No way," I breathed, repeating my mom's exclamation of surprise.

"The Hall of Records," my mom said, voice almost reverent as she referenced the mythical library so many pseudo-archaeologists claimed was buried beneath the Sphinx. According to legend, the Hall of Records contained all the knowledge of Atlantis.

"There's a seed of truth to every myth," my mom said, her eyes meeting mine, glittering with excitement. "Haven't I always said the Sphinx guards undiscovered secrets?"

"Yeah," I agreed reluctantly, "but you also said that about pretty much every landmark, so…"

My mom smacked my thigh with the back of her hand. "Oh, Cora…" She shook her head in exasperation, but her mood had lifted considerably. All of our moods had. We had a destination. An endpoint. A real, tangible goal.

Finally, we knew exactly where we were going. Now, we just had to get there before it was too late. Before the damage to my brain was beyond fixing.

"So, here's what I'm thinking," my mom said as she stood, setting both her journal and the storage cube on the seat before moving back up a row to sit beside Emi. Raiden knelt in the aisle beside my mom's seat, and Fiona crossed her arms over the top of her seatback, resting her chin on her forearms.

Figuring I would only get in the way of their plotting and strategizing, I picked up the *Liber Veritatis* and flipped open the cover of the black, leather-bound book. The plane jiggled and jarred far too much for me to be able get any sleep, and at least this way I wouldn't just be sitting here thinking about how much my head hurt.

Besides, it wasn't like I had anything better to do.

[33]

A crimson spot appeared on the page I was reading, and for a long moment, I just stared at it. Until another crimson spot joined the first.

Hand shaking, I brought my fingertips to my nose. Thick, wet blood trickled down my upper lip. I wiped it away with a hasty swipe of my hand, looking up to make sure nobody was watching me. The last thing they needed was the added stress of knowing just how quickly the mental fracture was causing my health to deteriorate. Distracting them with this could cost me my life.

Through the crack between the pair of seats in front of me, I could see my mom was resting her head on Emi's shoulder. Beside me, Raiden sat slumped in his seat with his chin resting on his chest, snoring softly with each slow inhale. Across the aisle, Meg was hiding under a makeshift tent constructed of a couple of blankets draped strategically over two sets of seatbacks. Fiona sat a couple rows ahead of Meg, her head bobbing back and forth as she listened to whatever music blared in her earbuds.

I wiped the blood staining my hand onto the pants of my

hoplon suit, then did the same with the droplets marring the page in the *Liber Veritatis*. Pressing a knuckle to my nostril to stave the bleeding, I shut the book and stood, carefully stepping over Raiden's legs and out into the aisle.

I made my way to the set of seats behind mine and squatted down to dig through my pack. I fished out a T-shirt and a bottle of water, then tucked the *Liber Veritatis* into the bag, hoping nobody would want to look through it again before we reached the Omega site. It was hardly urgent reading material for our current mission, after all.

I unscrewed the cap on the water bottle but held it in place atop the bottle as we flew through a patch of turbulence, making the plane jump and jar unpredictably. The pilot apologized over the intercom and announced that we were about to start our decent, adding a warning that there might be some more turbulence coming.

I could see the others stirring, awakened by the pilot's announcement. I quickly wet the sleeve of the T-shirt, using it to wipe any remaining blood from my upper lip and dab around my nostril. The olive-green fabric came away stained bright crimson.

"Shit," I mouthed. The nosebleed wasn't stopping. It didn't even seem to be slowing.

The plane jerked up and down in a quick, violent burst of turbulence. Leaving me momentarily airborne and earning shouts of alarm from the others still in their seats. I landed on my butt in the aisle, clutching the nearest armrest.

"That was a good one," my mom said, stretching her arms straight up until her hands pressed against the curved ceiling. "Everyone all right?" She poked her head around her seatback, to check on Raiden and me.

When she didn't find me in my seat, panic transformed her features, and she stood partway. She froze when she spotted me sitting in the aisle.

I wadded up the T-shirt, hoping she hadn't noticed the blood, and flashed her a weak, closed-mouth smile.

"Cora!" She rushed into the aisle and dropped to her knees in front of me. "You're bleeding!"

Raiden burst out of his seat, hovering behind my mom, and Emi turned in hers, standing on her knees so she could see over the seatback.

My mom dabbed blood from under my nose with the cuff of her sleeve.

"I smacked the arm rest," I lied, thinking fast. "With my face…"

"I can see that," my mom said, eyeing the smear of blood on the armrest. It had come from my hand when I had gripped the armrest for stability, not from my nose, but she didn't need to know that. She curved a hand around the back of my neck, angling my head downward. "Em? Can you hand me the first aid kit?" A moment later, my mom unceremoniously stuffed a roll of gauze up my nostril.

At Emi's prompting, my mom moved out of the way so she and Meg could squeeze into the aisle together to examine me further. Their respective medical and psychic proficiencies trumping my mom's expertise in field medicine.

Emi's expression was blank as she lowered a stumpy pen light after dozens of questions and tests, but I could see the frown in her eyes. With my regulator activated, muting my psychic senses, I could only guess at the cause.

Meg knelt behind Emi, her eyes somber and watchful. For the life of me, I couldn't recall why they were both staring at me with such concern.

"How do you feel?" Emi asked, eyelids narrowing slightly.

I shrugged. "The same, I guess. My head hurts. Why?" I looked around suddenly, and at seeing where we were in the plane—as well as the worried faces of the others—an icy rush of fear spread through me. "What happened? What are we doing on the floor, and why are you all looking at me like that?"

Emi's eyes widened. "You fell, Cora. Don't you remember?" she said. "The turbulence—you hit your nose."

Brow furrowing, I brought my hand up to my nose. A roll of gauze had been stuffed into my nostril, which definitely corroborated Emi's story.

My eyes stung as tears welled on the brim of my eyelids. Holding Emi's stare, I shook my head slowly. "I don't remember," I said, my voice wobbly. "I was reading the *Liber Veritatis*, and…" I trailed off, chin trembling.

I couldn't remember anything after that. It was like I had blinked and now I was somewhere else. Like I had lost time.

"It's all right, Cora," Emi said, resting a hand on my shoulder. She pulled me in close for a hug, and I squeezed my eyes shut to block out the worried faces of everyone that I loved. "Everything is going to be all right."

But I didn't need to be able read her mind to know she was lying. Meg had mentioned two possible symptoms of the increasing damage to my brain caused by my fractured consciousness, besides the headache: memory loss and loss of consciousness. Looked like I had reached the memory-loss phase. I could only imagine what that meant for the state of my brain.

I inhaled shakily, then cleared my throat. "Are we close? I —" I squeezed my eyes shut more tightly, forcing out a few more tears. "I can't remember."

"We're almost there, sweetie," my mom said from further up the aisle.

I opened my eyes, meeting hers.

"You just have to hang on a little bit longer."

[34]

Time slipped past in fits and starts. I felt drugged, or just really, really drunk. I knew where we were going—the Great Sphinx—but I couldn't remember much of the in-between.

Holding a towel to my nose, I stared out the tiny oval window as the plane made its final descent. The change in air pressure made it feel like my brain was going to burst inside my skull.

I blinked, and I was in the back of a panel van, sitting across from Fiona, my head resting on Raiden's shoulder. Wearing her nun's habit, Meg huddled in the very back of the van, as far as she could get from the sun's rays flooding in through the front windows, her exposed face buried behind her knees.

At the sound of my mom's voice, I looked up toward the front of the van. She occupied the passenger seat, while an unfamiliar dark-skinned man sat behind the wheel, guiding us at break-neck speed down a sun-drenched desert road.

I blinked, and I was lying on the floor of the van, stretched out flat on my back. The pain in my head was white-hot, like my brain was too bloated for my skull, making the bones fracture.

This felt worse even than when the plane was landing, and I could hardly hold on to a coherent thought.

There was chaos all around me. Through the pain, it was difficult to make sense of what I was seeing and hearing. Shouting. Familiar voices. Screeching tires. Faces moved in and out of view above me. Emi. Raiden. Fiona.

"Move!" Meg ordered, pulling Fiona out of sight and pushing Raiden back. "I need space to work!" Meg climbed on top of me, straddling my waist, and pressed her fingertips into my temples. The pressure was too much, and I screamed as the agony whited out my vision.

The next time I opened my eyes, Meg's face hovered over mine, her features cloaked in shadow. Her hands formed a cage on either side of my head, and her eyes were shut tight, her face a mask of concentration. Sweat beaded on her brow beneath the brim of her sheltering headpiece, shimmering violet in the combined glow from our regulators, and her skin looked severely sunburned. Her regulator glowed a vibrant amethyst through the black fabric of her borrowed nun's habit, and the weight of her body was heavy on my middle, making it kind of hard to breathe.

"Meg?" I said, my voice scratchy.

Her eyes snapped open, her stare locking with mine. She looked utterly astonished, and for once, I couldn't sense a single thing through our bond.

I cleared my throat. "What's going on?"

"It worked," Meg said, sitting up and releasing her death grip on my head. "I can't believe it worked." She sighed, her relief evident, if not palpable, and her shoulders slumped as she let her head fall back.

"You can't believe *what* worked?" I turned my head slightly, looking first one way, then the other. So far as I could tell, we were in the back of a panel van, and we were alone. "Where are we?" After a brief moment, I added, "And where are the others?"

Meg took a deep breath, then scooted off me, kneeling close by. "We're parked on the road near the Sphinx," she explained, tugging her head piece off and tossing it onto the floor of the van. "You had a stroke shortly before we arrived, and I've been working for hours to isolate the damaged areas. I think this should buy us some time."

I sat up part of the way, propping myself up with my elbows, and swallowed past the lump of fear forming in my throat. "How much time?"

Meg shook her head, and a fear-tinged laugh trembled up from her chest. "There's no way to say." She reached behind herself for the door handle and yanked on it.

The door slid open along the side of the van, revealing a glorious, head-on view of the Great Sphinx of Giza, the front of the massive statue illuminated by spotlights, making the face of the weathered beast stand out in stark contrast against the night sky, golden against a sea of silvery stars. The sliver of the moon hung over the Western Desert, midway between the Sphinx's haunches and the dark triangular patch cut out by the colossal Pyramid of Khafre. Even larger still, the Great Pyramid of Giza —Khufu's ancient tomb—reached toward the stars, partially obscured by the rise of the land on the far side of the road.

I only had a moment to take in the view before Raiden appeared in the opening, crawling partway into the van. "Cora," he said, bowing his body to bring his face close to mine. His eyes scoured my features, searching for some sign of my well-being. "Are you all right?" He glanced at Meg, only taking his eyes off me for a split second. "Is she all right?"

Meg seemed hesitant to commit to anything regarding my health status, but her pinched mouth and guarded eyes said it all.

"She's fine," I said, then clarified with, "*I'm* fine."

Except, I couldn't sense any of Raiden's emotions, let alone his thoughts. The stone in my regulator glowed its usual electric blue. Meg must've had to deactivate mine in order to enable her own psychic abilities, as the two were linked. And yet, I couldn't sense any external thoughts or emotions. Not even Meg's.

My eyes widened, and I looked at her, opening my mouth and inhaling to voice my concerns.

"I had to isolate the areas surrounding the bleed in order to contain it," Meg said before I could start. "That included the area that controls your psychic gifts." Her face crumpled, and her head hung, her shoulders slumping once more. "I'm sorry. I tried to find another way, but…"

I supposed that explained why I couldn't sense her at all. The psychic quarantine must have been blocking our connection.

Slowly, I closed my mouth, pressing my lips together and swallowing with some difficulty. My throat felt as dry as the desert outside. I just hoped my psychic abilities wouldn't be required to get us into the Omega site. But then I remembered Hades had been coming and going over the millennia, so I figured it shouldn't end up being an issue. Besides, we had Meg, who was far better at controlling her psychic mojo.

"Is there water?" I asked, clearing my throat.

Meg twisted to reach for a water bottle somewhere behind her. She unscrewed the cap before handing it to me.

"Thanks," I whispered before taking a gulp. I chugged half of the bottle, then lowered it, breathing hard.

Both Raiden and Meg were watching me with guarded expressions, like they were expecting my head to explode at any second. I could hardly blame them; I felt the same. My brain was a time bomb, only we didn't know how much time we had left until the big *boom*.

I took another swig of water, then handed the bottle back to Meg. "Well, I suppose we should get moving." I flashed them a grim smile. "We don't have all day…"

Neither Raiden nor Meg looked amused.

"Tough crowd," I grumbled as I sat up the rest of the way and scooted toward the opening.

With Raiden's help, I was soon on my feet, standing on a sand-swept walkway paved with well-worn gray stone blocks. A low stone wall stretched out to the right, following the walkway back toward the road, and the pyramids beyond. A three-foot-high metal fence stretched out in the other direction, beyond which the lights from the city of Giza drowned out the stars. Parallel to the van, a metal gate stood open, not a security camera or guard in sight.

"Where is everyone?" I asked, leaning on Raiden's arm as I looked around for my mom and the others. My legs felt rubbery, like I didn't have full control over the muscles, and I wondered if Meg's neural quarantine was messing with my motor functions as well.

"Down at the Sphinx," Raiden said, snaking his arm around my waist to steady me as I took my first few steps.

Much as I wanted to tell him I could walk on my own just fine—thank you very much—I wasn't sure I actually could. I preferred accepting his help over making a stubborn fool of myself and falling flat on my face.

Beyond the gate, stone pavers gave way to a walkway of wood planks that emphasized every footstep with a hollow echo. Sand gritted underfoot, making the walkway a little slick. It couldn't have been more than a hundred yards from the gate to the front of the Sphinx, but by the time we reached the enormous left paw, my legs were trembling, and I was all but panting from the exertion.

Fiona spotted us as we made our way down the long, gradual wooden stairway and alerted the others. By the time we reached the bottom, my mom, Emi, and an Egyptian man I didn't recognize emerged from between the Sphinx's front legs. The three followed Fiona, meeting us on the wooden platform built directly in front of the Sphinx. The spotlights cast our shadows against the toes of the ten-foot-tall paw, turning us into a giant, spidery monster.

My mom pulled me close, hugging me tight before pulling back to examine me with even more concern and scrutiny than Raiden had. She brushed stray strands of hair from my face and tucked them behind my ear. "How do you feel, sweetie?" she asked, brow lined with worry.

"Like we need to hustle," I admitted begrudgingly.

My mom inhaled deeply, blowing out the breath through her nose. She didn't like the answer, but she accepted it for what it was. "All right," she said with a nod. She released me, leaving me to wobble unsteadily for a few seconds, and turned back toward the Sphinx. "I've studied just about every word ever written about the fabled 'Hall of Records'," she said.

Raiden slipped his arm around my waist once more, lending me his strength while my mom recounted what she knew.

"Campbell's Tomb and the surrounding passages are too far from the coordinates," my mom said, referring to the deep pit containing a sarcophagus discovered behind the Sphinx in the early 1800s. "And the shafts diving into the earth on either side of the Sphinx were long since proven to be dug by ancient treasure hunters."

My mom turned and started toward the trench between the beast's two towering front legs. "It's got to be here," she said adamantly.

Raiden and I followed her, trailed by the others. The Sphinx's head loomed high above, taller than most six-story buildings.

"When Eugène Grébaut was excavating this area in the late 1800s," my mom explained as she circumvented the stone altar directly between the front paws, heading into the trench, "he was surprised to find that the limestone floor had been removed at some earlier point."

She stopped halfway between the altar and the Dream Stele, erected directly in front of the Sphinx's chest three and a half millennia ago. She dropped to one knee beside a hole that had been dug into the earth, about three feet deep and three feet wide.

"The SCA excavated deeper years ago, of course, but the reports claimed that they struck bedrock just a few feet down." She gestured to the unbroken stone surface lining the bottom of the hole.

I frowned, brow furrowing. Raiden released me so I could move closer, and I leaned against the altar for support. "That doesn't make any sense," I said. "Why would the bedrock be so shallow here, but not at the sides of the Sphinx?" Those shafts dug by ancient grave robbers delved way deeper into the ground than this.

My mom grinned at me as she tapped the side of her nose with her index finger. "Exactly!" she exclaimed. "The report from the SCA claimed 'geological variation', but I'm calling bullshit on that."

She placed a hand on the ground and dropped into the hole. Crouching, she ran her hand over the smooth bedrock. "The stone is flawless. Not a single tool mark. Not even a scratch." She gave me a pointed look. "Do you really think the excavation team could have uncovered this *that* cleanly? Or that treasure hunters over the millennia wouldn't have tried to dig under the Sphinx here, or that they had tried, but somehow managed to avoid leaving behind a single mark?"

Realization struck at the same moment as I felt a tickle high up in my nostril. I ignored the impending nosebleed and rushed forward. "Because it's not bedrock," I said, right before my knee gave out and I stumbled to the ground. I barely managed to catch myself with my hands before tumbling face-first into the hole.

I watched, fingers gripping the edge of the hole, as a single drop of blood dripped from my nose and landed on the exposed bedrock. The stone seemed to absorb the drop of blood.

Without warning, the solid surface beneath my mom's feet evaporated, and with a yelp, she dropped out of sight.

"Mom!" I shouted, rising to hands and knees. I could hear her grunting and scuffling coming from within the pitch-black pit. "Mom! Are you okay?"

Another second or two of scuffling, and then my mom called up, "I'm all right!"

A moment later, the pit was illuminated with a faint orange light, and a steep stairway became visible. Not of stone, but constructed from some silver steel-like alloy, just like in the tunnel to the Beta site and in my—Peri's—memories of other Olympian structures. The artificial light from within the passageway grew stronger with each passing second until it was bright as day within.

I had been right. The stone wasn't bedrock; it was a hologram, and it must have been set to be unlocked by the presence of Olympian DNA. When my blood landed on the exposed surface, it vanished, revealing this hidden stairway underground.

My mom's face popped into view, one hand shielding herself from the stream of sand pouring into the passage from above. She was grinning from ear to ear. "This is *amazing*, Cora!" she exclaimed, holding a hand up toward me. "Get down here and see!"

Heart pounding, I shifted, sliding my feet and legs over the edge of the hole and causing more sand and small rocks to tumble into the opening. Adrenaline reinforced my wavering strength, lending me a modicum of stability. I stood on the top step and grasped my mom's hand. She helped me down several dozen stairs, and as soon as I could, I dipped my head to see below the bottom lip of the ceiling to the chamber that lay beyond.

"Oh my God," I said, my voice barely a whisper. In a daze, I leaned on my mom as we made our way down the final few steps.

The chamber beyond was like something straight out of a science fiction movie. It reminded me of the spaceship I had seen in Peri's memories: the *Tartarus*. I couldn't help but wonder if I was standing in part of the ship right now.

The room was shaped strangely, like a cone had been turned on its side and cut in half by the floor, with the narrowest point of the cone starting at the stairway where we were standing and the room broadening evenly from there. The ceiling arched overhead in a perfect arc, strips of light set into the metal, stretching out from the entrance at the base of the stairway like sunbeams. Everything was that same shiny, steel-like metal.

The polished surface of the far wall was unbroken save for an arched doorway blocked by a solid looking door. The chamber was maybe fifty feet from the entry point to the blocked doorway at the far wall. The bottom four feet of the two side walls was filled with all manner of futuristic screens and control panels, though everything appeared dark and dormant.

The floor was a solid sheet of metal grating, only broken up by a circle about eight feet in diameter, centered in the room maybe two-thirds of the way to the far wall. From my vantage point on the bottom stair, the circle in the floor looked like it was made of a thick sheet of ice.

The whole thing was so beautiful, and I felt completely overwhelmed by awe. This place belonged to my people, untouched by humans for as long as it had been in existence. Unlike the Beta site, this was ours, alone.

Tears snuck out from the corners of my eyes, and for once, I didn't have any qualms about being so openly emotional. These were tears of disbelief. Of joy. Of relief. I had earned these tears, damn it.

At the sound of the others descending the stairway behind us, my mom curled an arm around my waist and guided me off the final step and into the chamber proper. The instant our boots touched the metal grating, the glassy circle in the floor started to glow with an iridescent light.

"Oh my God," I repeated as the blurred shape of a humanoid

figure came into view through the fogged glass, backlit by the entrancing light.

I started toward the glowing, glassy circle in the floor, exhilaration and my mom's supportive arm the only things keeping me upright. By the time I reached the edge of the circle, the fog had cleared from the glass, and the figure's features were easily recognizable.

"That's him," I said, my voice breathy as I stared down at a familiar Olympian man garbed in a form-fitting gray bodysuit. "That's Hades."

And he didn't look dead. He looked asleep—or frozen, in cryosleep—but very much alive. The backup power core hadn't failed like he had feared, and from the looks of it, the auto-wake sequence had already begun, triggered by our entrance, just as Hades had written. All we had to do now was wait.

For the first time since leaving Brazil, I felt Peri stirring in my mind, like she couldn't resist the lure of seeing her beloved once more. Her activity caused a spike of pain in my head, and I winced. I rubbed the back of my neck, digging my fingers into the base of my skull as hard as I could in a vain attempt to alleviate the sudden influx of pressure.

My mom gasped, pointing down at Hades. "He moved!"

With some effort, I managed to focus on Hades' pale face and take in his cruelly handsome elven features, surrounded by a swath of silver-blond hair. To see his eyelids flutter, then open. To see the confusion clear from his ice-blue eyes, replaced by recognition. To see his lips begin to curve into a smile.

Another spike of pain in my skull made me double over. I cried out, clutching the sides of my head with both hands.

"Cora!" My mom grasped my arms, hugging me to her to keep me partially upright. "Meg!" she cried out. "Help!"

Knives stabbed repeatedly into my skull as I was lowered down to the floor, and darkness overtook my vision.

The voices all around me sounded warped and garbled,

fading in and out of hearing. Their next exchange was unintelligible, like I had dunked underwater.

Peri's voice whispered through my mind, her words the last thing I heard before the world slipped away.

"I'm sorry."

[35]

I stand in an enormous, empty space. There is darkness all around me, but a quick glance down at myself reveals two things: I am clothed in a black, form-fitting bodysuit, and I can see just fine. This place is not void of light; it is merely empty of everything but the darkness.

I take a step, and ripples cascade out from around the soles of my boots, as though the floor is somehow both solid and liquid. I watch the floor until the ripples are gone and it is once again smooth and glassy, and then I take another step.

Soft, sorrowful crying echoes through the air behind me, and I spin around.

A small girl stands a dozen paces away, her hands covering her face, her shoulders shaking as she weeps. She is pale and thin, and her long, dark hair is split into two braids pulled over her shoulders. She is wearing a blue cotton dress with tiny white flowers embroidered into the fabric, and her feet are sheathed in shiny, white patent leather shoes.

"Hello?" I say, taking a tentative step toward the girl. She is obviously upset, and I feel the urge to comfort her, but I don't want to frighten her. "Are you all right?"

She inhales shakily and lowers her hands. Her pale face is splotchy from crying, and tear streaks stain her cheeks. Her red-rimmed eyes make her aquamarine irises stand out in startling contrast.

"I—I'm lost," she says, her chin trembling as she takes another shaky breath. "My friend was supposed to meet me here, but now I can't find her. Will you help me?"

Moving slowly, I close the distance between us and crouch in front of the girl. "How about we help each other?"

The girl sniffles, fidgeting with her skirt, then nods.

"What's your name?" I ask, studying her face. There was something so familiar about her. I feel like I know her, and I wonder if she is someone I once met but have since forgotten.

"Cora," she says, her voice tiny.

"Cora," I repeat, thinking that, like the little girl herself, her name feels familiar. "That's a very pretty name," I tell her. "My name is—" I falter and furrow my brow, my own name perched on the tip of my tongue but somehow managing to evade me. I think it should bother me, not knowing my own name, but it doesn't. I mostly just feel confused. "You know, I can't remember my name," I admit, more to myself than to the girl.

Cora watches me with somber eyes. "Maybe my friend knows your name," she says.

"Yeah," I murmur. "Maybe." I straighten and look around. "You know, when I've lost something, I find the best place to start looking for it is the last place I remember seeing it," I tell Cora. "Where's the last place you saw your friend?"

"Um..." Cora's lips pinch into a tight rosebud, and she quirks her mouth to the side, thinking hard. Suddenly, her eyes widen, and she smiles. "The Tartarus!"

Without warning, Cora grabs my hand and starts running, and I have little choice but to follow her.

We haven't been running for long when the darkness surrounding us gives way to shiny silver, and the solid-liquid floor is hidden under metal grating. Cora slows to a walk, and I take the time to scan our new surroundings.

We've entered a trapezoidal passage, and the floor, walls, and ceiling all seem to be made of the same silver metal. Thick beams bordered by glowing strips of light break up the endless passage in a pattern that stretches on as far as the eye can see. As we walk, an opening appears in the left-hand wall up ahead, trapezoidal, just like this passage, and I assume it leads to another passage.

"Maybe she's in there!" Cora says, tugging on my hand to walk faster, and I pick up the pace.

We slow as we near the opening. Once I'm able to see what lies beyond, my mouth falls open and my feet drag until we stop altogether. The opening doesn't lead to another hallway; it is a doorway leading to another place entirely.

The metal grating on the floor gives way to soft, damp earth and leafy underbrush. Tall pine trees frame the opening on the other side, and a path cut through the forest leads to a large boulder overlooking a gorgeous bay view. Puffy white clouds hover in the bright blue sky, and the air smells of the sea.

The scene pulls on my heart, and I want to walk through the doorway. I want to climb the boulder and sit at the very top, staring out at the water. I feel as though I could sit there for hours. For days. Forever.

"She's not in there," Cora says, her hopeful expression falling, transformed by disappointment. "Come on, let's keep looking." Cora takes a few steps, then tugs on my hand when I don't make any move to follow. "Are you coming?" she asks.

When I look at her, I see that her eyebrows are raised, and her red-rimmed eyes are filled with hope rather than tears. I can't stomach the thought of being the reason her tears return, so I nod. "Yeah, kiddo, I'm coming."

The smile she flashes me lights up her eyes. "Great!" she says and starts walking.

This time, I follow.

Soon, another opening appears, this one in the wall on the right. Again, we speed up, only slowing as we draw near.

We stop in front of the opening, staring into a beautiful library that looks like it would fit in perfectly in a stately old mansion. A fire crackles in the fireplace, making the nearby armchairs all too inviting. As with the scene of the boulder overlooking the bay, I feel like the library is drawing me in, and I take a step toward the doorway. My hand slips free from Cora's as I take another step.

"Do you think Peri is in there?" Cora asks.

I pause mid-step, glancing at her over my shoulder. That name—Peri—tickles my mind, sounding so familiar. And yet, I can't place it. For a moment, I think that might be my *name. But then, Cora would have recognized me if I was the friend she is searching for. I shake my head, dispelling the curious thought.*

"You don't think she's in there?" Cora asks.

"I—" I return to gazing into the library, my heart filled with longing. "I don't know," I tell the little girl. I tear my stare from the enticing scene to look back at her. "Do you *think she's in there?"*

A wrinkle forms between Cora's eyebrows as she considers the question, and then she shakes her head.

I shoot one last wistful glance at the library, then sigh and turn my back to the doorway. "All right," I say, "let's keep going." Besides, I could always come back here, after I deliver Cora to her friend.

We continue walking, and it feels like hours pass before we come across another opening in the passage walls. This time, there's an opening on either side, directly across from one another. We jog ahead, not stopping until we reach the openings.

On one side of the passage, I look into a bedroom. The floors are glossy hardwood, and a stocky pit bull is curled up on the bed, snoring audibly. The windows beyond the bed display a view of the same bay I glimpsed in the scene with the woods and boulder. A single word forms in my mind: home.

The other scenes were alluring, but this one is a siren's call, pulling me in. I belong here, I know it.

I am one step from crossing the threshold when Cora catches my hand. I freeze, glancing back at her. And for the first time, I see what lies beyond the opening in the opposite wall.

It's another bedroom, only this one is smaller and about as Spartan as a bedroom could be, containing little more than a small bed and a desk, both constructed of the same metal as the walls, ceiling, and floor. A lone girl sits on the bed, wearing a simple outfit of gray, loose-fitting pants and a matching tunic. A pendant dangles from a golden chain around her neck, the stone in the pendant glowing a shocking electric blue. Her hands are clasped together on her lap, and she stares at the floor beyond her feet. Even with her dark hair pulled up into a tight bun atop her head, it's impossible not to notice the resemblance between her and Cora. They could be sisters. Or twins.

"That's Peri," Cora says, her smile not reaching her eyes. She releases my hand, turning away from me and stepping toward the opening to the stark bedroom. "She looks so lonely," Cora says, her shoulders slumping.

I shift my attention from Cora to Peri, and my eyes widen when I find that she is no longer a little girl. She is a grown woman, though she still sits in the same place, on the edge of her bed, and she still stares down at the floor. Her hair is the same, pulled up into a tight bun atop her head, but her outfit has changed; she now wears a black, form-fitting suit identical to mine.

But despite our matching outfits, that's not what draws me to her. She wears loneliness like a second skin. She looks as lost as I feel.

"Where should we go?" Cora asks, tugging gently on my

hand. Somehow, I know we must go together, and whatever we choose, the choice is final. No going back.

I stare down at her, my heart tearing in two. I desperately want to turn around and flee into the cozy bedroom with the slumbering dog. It's warm and inviting, and it feels like it's the place that fits me. That has shaped itself around me. The place where I belong.

And yet, the Spartan room, with its lonely occupant, calls to my heart. To my soul. I can't squash the sense that she isn't a stranger. She is my equal. My match. My other half.

The warm, inviting room may fit me, but she *can make me whole.*

Without meaning to, I take a tiny step toward the Spartan room. It's not inviting. It's not desirable. It doesn't look the least bit fun.

But she *is in there, and I can't stifle the sense that no matter how many comforts the other room provides to distract me from the emptiness, I will always feel fractured. I will always have a jagged edge. I will always be incomplete.*

I take another step toward the Spartan room. Then another.

I hesitate at the threshold, little Cora at my side. I look down at her, and she smiles up at me, like she knows I'm making the right decision. After one last glance back at the cozy, comfy bedroom, I face forward and step through the doorway.

Peri, the once-child-now-woman raises her head and looks at me. Relief transforms her face from hopeless loneliness to cautious optimism. "I thought you would never come," she says, standing.

I smile quizzically, not understanding her meaning.

She holds out her hands, one toward me and one toward Cora. "Will you join me?"

I reach for her hand, as does Cora, and the moment my skin touches hers, there is a brilliant flash of blue light, and the world fades away.

[36]

When I woke, I felt amazing, save for the remnants of the strange dream lingering in my mind. I rolled onto my back and stretched, pointing my toes and reaching my arms straight over my head until my whole body shook. Few things in life felt as good as a full-body stretch first thing in the morning. At least, I thought that was true. I couldn't actually think of any other things that felt good.

Or any other things, at all.

Confused, I opened my eyes, and then I sat bolt upright. I had no idea where I was.

The room was stark and silver, with nothing on the four walls or the ceiling save for the bands of light glowing from the place where the ceiling and walls met. I was on a platform of some kind, about waist-high from the floor. The platform was not quite wide enough for me to stretch my arms out completely, with edges that curved upward on either side of me—possibly to keep me from rolling off in my sleep—and the surface was covered in a thin, squishy pad.

I froze when I spotted the only other thing in the room —a man.

He was sitting in the right-most corner behind me, his legs curled up and his arms folded over his knees, his head resting on his forearms. He was big—muscular—and had tan skin, with black tattoos marking up one arm, disappearing under the cuff of his sleeve. I didn't recognize him. I didn't know if he was friend or foe, which made me hesitant to move.

After a few minutes of indecision, I figured it was inevitable he would wake, eventually—and more and more likely the longer I sat there. As quietly as possible, I scooted to the foot of the platform and eased down to the floor. The metal was neither warm nor cool against the soles of my feet.

I tiptoed to the nearest wall and studied the fuzzy image of a woman staring back at me in the polished silver surface, surprised to find I didn't have any expectations of what I would find in the reflection. Once again, I thought back to the strange dream. I hadn't been certain of who I was in the dream, either.

Leaning closer to the reflective wall, I turned my face this way and that. Long, dark hair. Pale skin. Blue eyes. Pleasing features.

I took a step back and looked down at my body. My build was slim, and I was wearing a loose-fitting, gray tunic and pants, both made of the same incredibly soft, thin fabric.

I glanced at the man in the corner. He was dressed very different from me—black and coarse-looking fabric. The contrast in our style of clothing made me uneasy. I bit my lip, unsure what to do. Should I wait for him to wake and ask him questions, or should I play it safe and take out the potential threat while his guard was down?

That thought made me frown. Had I just thought about killing someone? For no other reason than that he *might* be a threat? *Could* I kill someone? Was I capable of such a thing?

Less certain about my own identity than the man's, I returned to examining my reflection. A pendant with a softly glowing amber stone hung from a chain around my neck. I recalled seeing a similar pendant in the dream, only that one had been glowing with an electric-blue light.

Acting on impulse, I touched the pendant, tracing my finger around the stone. The amber glow faded to a vibrant, electric blue.

I blinked, surprised by the change.

All of a sudden, I was filled with a rush of joy and excitement.

"Cora?"

I spun around at the sound of the man's voice, my right arm outstretched in front of me, blue lighting dancing over the fingers of my extended hand.

The man froze, halfway to his feet, one hand on the wall.

"Who—who are you?" I asked, stumbling over my words as foreign thoughts and emotions flooded my mind. *This man's* thoughts and emotions.

His name was Raiden, and he knew me. Cora—that was me. Just like the girl in the dream. Raiden had strong feelings for me. I was important to him. My life mattered to him—more than his own did. He was overjoyed to see me standing, but fear and confusion were dulling his excitement. He was worried something went wrong. That the procedure didn't work.

I closed my eyes, trying to make sense of it all. A mental image formed in my mind's eye, and I was sucked into one of Raiden's memories.

I am seeing through Raiden's eyes. I am Raiden.

I cradle Cora in my arms as I run down a long corridor, following Hades. My mom and Diana are close on my heels, the others behind them. There are periodic openings in the walls on either side of the hallway, but I don't have the time or care to look. Everything within me is focused on Cora. On keeping her alive.

I can't lose her. If she dies here, now, that's it. I give up. I quit. I'm done.

"Hurry," Hades says, the single word heavily accented by his alien tongue. There is a translator implanted in his head that allows him to communicate with us, or so he explained when he first woke. After we convinced him not to kill us for bringing Cora—Peri—to him in such a sorry state.

Hades takes a sharp right into a small, barren room, and I follow, boots squealing on the floor at the sudden change of direction. I recognize the device at the center of the room. An asclypos. My heart sinks.

"This won't fix her," I practically scream at Hades. "Meg!" Frantically, I look over my shoulder, searching for Cora's shadow.

Meg stumbles in through the doorway after my mom and Diana, an arm around Fiona's shoulder. Meg has been deteriorating quickly since Cora collapsed, and the worse Meg gets, the sicker I feel.

"Tell him this won't work," I order, pointing to the asclypos with my chin.

Meg's skin has an ashen cast to it, and she looks like she's about to vomit. "It won't help with the discord between Cora and Persephone," Meg says, her voice weak. She swallows roughly. "But it will fix the bleeding..."

"She is dying," Hades snaps. "I did not wait twelve thousand years only to be reunited with a corpse. Put her in the asclypos, boy. Now!"

Feeling numb inside, I do as I'm told. I can already feel my heart hardening to the very real likelihood of a world without Cora. It is a world I want no part in. Robotically, I help Hades remove the hoplon suit, and then I step back, watching him erect a holographic field over Cora's barely clothed body.

She looks pale. Limp. Lifeless. Blood seeps from her nose

and eyes, and her lips are parted. Her chest isn't moving. She's not breathing.

A white band of light scans the length of her body, reminding me of a copy machine. A moment later, her entire body jolts, and I wonder if the machine is trying to restart her heart. The jolt happens twice more, followed by another light scan.

When the scan finishes, dozens of tiny laser beams flash into existence around her head, zigging and zagging, moving sporadically.

My mom and Diana clutch onto one another, watching with wide, terror-filled eyes, and Fiona and Meg are sitting against the wall off to the side of the machine. Meg's head lolls forward, as though she has lost consciousness, and Fiona is covering her mouth with one hand, tears streaming down her cheeks.

After a long moment of watching the light show surrounding Cora's head, Hades exhales heavily and takes a step back from the machine, turning to face me. "The asclypos has determined the damage can be fixed."

The ice hardening around my heart starts to thaw.

"It gives a thirty-three percent chance of success," Hades adds.

"Better than thirty-two percent," I hear myself say.

I'm not sure if I imagined it, but I think the corner of Hades' mouth just twitched with amusement. "If she survives this initial repair," Hades explains, "then we will be able to remove both consciousnesses and run her body through the asclypos again. The healing will be more thorough without the psychic interference, allowing the asclypos to return her neural structure to a more malleable state. The rest is up to Peri and Cora..."

"What do you mean, 'remove both consciousnesses'?" I say eyes narrowing. I can't even begin to imagine how such a thing could be possible. "And what exactly is up to Cora and Peri?"

The situation feels out of control—or maybe just out of my control—and it's frustrating to the point that I want to hit some-

thing. My hands ball into fists, and the tension in my muscles makes my body tremble. I need to understand at least some of what's happening, and right now, I simply don't.

"Raiden, dear," my mom says, laying a hand on my arm, "you need to calm down."

I hadn't noticed her approach. I had rage-tinged blinders up, and all I could see was Hades. This man—this thing*—was holding Cora's fate in his hands. I don't know him. He is a stranger to me, and I don't know why I'm trusting him with her life.*

"You're trusting him with her life because he loves her," Meg says, her voice weak. With Fiona's help, she manages to stand up.

I can't stop staring at Meg. She isn't Cora. She is nothing like Cora, but her life is linked to Cora's, so if she's doing better, then Cora must be improving, too. It takes a few seconds for the shock of seeing Meg awake and on her feet to wear off and for her words to sink in. Hades loves Cora—or rather, Peri. If Cora had known about this, she sure as hell hadn't shared it with me.

I think I should feel jealous, or inadequate maybe, after all Hades had done to be reunited with Cora. No, not with Cora—with Peri. How could I compete with that?

And yet, all I feel is relief. Because I love her, and I would do anything for her. Sacrifice anything. If his love for her is anything like mine—and I'm willing to bet it is based on everything he has done—then he is just as invested in saving her. In bringing her back from the brink. Just like me, he's all in.

Sure as shit, that's going to be an issue down the road—if Cora survives this—but I can't think about that right now.

The lasers in the asclypos extinguish suddenly, and all eyes shift to Cora's motionless form. We watch as Hades pulls up a holographic screen that hovers over Cora's shoulder and studies the readings. I hold my breath, terrified of what he's going to tell us.

After a long, tense moment, Hades grins. "The procedure was successful." He scans the room, making eye contact with each one of us. "Now, for the consciousness extraction…"

I opened my eyes, exiting the memory and returning to the present. To myself. The electric-blue lightning dancing around my hand faded away, and I lowered my arm. My brow furrowed as, once again, I recalled that strange dream. Cora and Peri—the little girl and the woman from the dream—were both a part of me. At least, according to Raiden's memory.

"Cora?" Raiden said, taking a cautious step toward me.

Unsure how to respond, I shook my head.

Raiden hesitated before speaking again, his expression guarded. "Peri?"

I looked at him, my eyes locking with his. "I don't know."

[37]

"We're almost there," Raiden said, walking by my side down a long corridor toward the arched doorway at the end, blocked by a polished metal door. "Everyone is going to be so excited to see you up and..." He seemed to struggle to find the right words, and though I had activated the regulator so the only thoughts and feelings in my head were my own, his uncertainty was impossible to miss. "Up and walking around."

I glanced at him sidelong, flashing him an uneasy smile. I knew who the people were he was talking about. I had seen them in his memory. Cora's mother, Diana, and Raiden's mother, Emi. Fiona, Cora's friend. Meg, Cora's I-don't-know-what-to-call-her. Hades, Peri's paramour. These were Cora's and Peri's people. Not *my* people.

At least, it didn't feel that way.

We stopped in front of the door, and a moment later, the metal barrier slid silently upward, revealing a long, almost triangular-shaped room. Three people stood with their backs to us, two women—the smaller one with a long, black braid trailing down her back, the taller with her wavy brown hair pulled up into a messy bun—and one man, standing head and shoulders taller than the women, his shoulder-length silver-blond hair gathered in a tie at the nape of his neck.

I recognized the two women as Emi and Diana. Both important women to me, according to Raiden's memory, though I didn't feel any sort of connection to either of them. I also recognized the man—Hades, one of two men I was supposed to be in love with, alongside Raiden. Though, as with Raiden and Diana and Emi, I didn't actually feel the feelings I was apparently supposed to feel.

With rapt attention, Diana, Hades, and Emi watched a massive screen on the left-most wall. It displayed a photorealistic three-dimensional map of the stars.

"You're sure it's them—these *Tsakali?*" Diana said, her head turning slightly toward Hades.

He nodded. "This telemetric system is keyed specifically to pick up on the Tsakali's technological signature," he said, his words accented differently from hers. "We built the system shortly before the siege that laid waste to Olympus. It is what allowed some of our people to escape before they destroyed the planet."

"Fascinating…," Diana said, nodding slowly. "Maybe they haven't noticed us yet. It could just be a coincidence, right? They might just be passing by?"

"Much as I would prefer to believe that, I cannot," Hades said. "This energy signature is too immense for a simple scouting drone. My guess is something on this planet has already tripped a scouting drone's sensors, and the Tsakali have sent a recon fleet to inspect the planet more thoroughly." He sighed. "And I am afraid there is no question as to their destination. They are heading straight for us, which can only mean one thing."

"I'm guessing it's a bad thing?" Diana said.

"Indeed." Hades gestured toward the screen, and the image changed from a model of the universe to a three-dimensional model of Earth. *"Search for chaos signatures,"* he said, and it took me a moment to realize he had spoken in an entirely different language than before. A language I understood perfectly.

A glowing grid surrounded the holographic planet and slowly began to rotate around the stationary globe.

"What are we looking for?" Diana asked.

Her question surprised me. For a moment, I wondered if she hadn't heard his command, but then I realized that, unlike me, she must not have been able to understand the other language he had spoken.

"Chaos signatures," Hades told her. "Chaos is a unique form of energy created from an element not native to this solar system —my people call it orichalcum." He turned toward her partway as he explained. "The element can be super condensed into a hyper-productive energy source called a chaos stone. Chaos opens the door to interstellar travel by powering faster-than-light engines, as well as a myriad of other advanced technologies."

"Maybe I'm misunderstanding," Diana said, "but wouldn't the discovery of this 'chaos' be a good thing for us mere earthlings?"

"In theory," Hades said, returning his attention to the screen. "But the Tsakali are greedy, scavenging parasites. Their sole purpose is to hunt for and hoard chaos stones, destroying any and all who stand in their way."

"Surely there must be some way to reason with them," Emi started, speaking for the first time since my unnoticed arrival. "Or—"

In an instant, the grid vanished, and a blinking beacon appeared over western Europe.

"What is that—France?" Diana said, more to herself than to the others. She touched Hades' arm. "Can you zoom in?"

The holographic model of the planet became much larger, until only Europe, the Mediterranean Sea, and a little sliver of northern Africa were visible on the screen.

"More," Diana said, then added, "please."

Again, the three-dimensional map zoomed in, until no ocean or sea was visible at all, only continental Europe. The beacon blinked over a point just to the left of a crescent-shaped lake.

"That's Lake Geneva," Diana said. She looked around the man to speak to Emi. "Do you think it's CERN—that *Atlantea Project* that's been all over the news?"

"It must be," Emi said.

Raiden cleared his throat. "Mom," he said. "Diana…"

All three heads turned our way.

Overwhelmed by the attention, I averted my gaze to the floor. In my peripheral vision, I could see the trio heading for us. For me. One pulled ahead of the others—Diana—her walk turning into a jog that didn't slow until she was almost to me.

She stopped just out of arm's reach. "Cora? Sweetie?" She took a step closer. "Sweetheart, look at me. Please." Her voice was thick with emotion, and the sound tugged at some instinctive part of me buried deep inside. I was a moth to a flame. I couldn't help but respond to her plea.

I raised my gaze to her face. The moment my eyes locked with hers, flashes of memories flitted past my mind's eye, moments from Cora's life, and all she had experienced with Diana. With her mom. A rush of warmth flooded my chest, and my heart swelled with love, making my eyes sting with welling tears. The rising tide of emotion sent cracks snaking through the damn in my mind.

Chin trembling, I took a tentative step toward her.

She threw her arms around me in a desperate embrace, and with that contact, the dam in my mind broke, unleashing a flood of memories. Not Cora's memories. *My* memories.

"Hi Mom," I said as I wrapped my arms around my mom, shutting my eyes and squeezing her just as tightly.

Diana Blackthorn may not have been my biological mother, but she was my mom in every way that mattered, and our connection ran deeper than blood. Our hearts were connected by invisible strings that could never be severed. She was the one who brought me into this world, and it seemed fitting to me that she was the one to trigger my rebirth. My awakening.

The hug was long, and much needed, and I really didn't want to let go. But as with all good things, it couldn't last forever. My mom's arms loosened, and following her cue, I released her.

She took a small step backward, reaching up to wipe the tears from my cheeks with tender hands. "You look good, sweetie," she said, flashing me a watery smile. "How do you feel?"

"Great, actually," I said, laughing softly, like my answer surprised me. In a way, it did. A moment ago, I hadn't known who I was. Now, I was *me*, and I felt awesome.

I turned to Raiden, standing at my side, and reached for his hand. Fresh tears streamed down my cheeks as my eyes met his. "Thank you," I said, meaning those two words with all of my heart. For coming back to me, and for never really leaving. For loving me, just as much as I loved him. For being there, always.

Raiden stepped closer, wrapping his arms around me in a tight embrace. I pressed my cheek against his shoulder, inhaling his familiar, masculine scent. This was, quite possibly, the happiest moment of my entire life. I was desperate to angle my face up toward Raiden's and press my lips to his, or better yet, to sneak off to some secret corner of this alien base together and finish what we had started back at Fiona's castle, but I was very aware of the other people in the room. My mom and Emi.

And Hades.

Suddenly self-conscious, I released Raiden and took a small step backward. I held his stare for a moment longer, smiling gently, then turned back to my mom.

She flashed me a hesitant smile before biting her lip. "And you're...*you*?"

"I..." My gaze slid past her to land on Hades, standing a

dozen paces behind her. My heart gave an excited *thud-thump*, and I suddenly felt flushed all over.

Hades watched me, his expression guarded. Everyone else disappeared, and for long seconds—for eons—we were alone, frozen and staring at one another.

"Peri," he said by way of greeting, more than a hint of a question in his voice. Was I Peri? Was I *his* Peri?

I stood a little taller and squared my shoulders.

And then I nodded.

I was Peri, *and* I was Cora. I was, once and for all, wholly and completely *me*.

⬚

Thanks for reading! You've reached the end of Fate of the Fallen, *but the story continues in* Dreams of the Damned.

Go to authorlindseysparks.com/sacrifice to grab a free copy of Sacrifice of the Sinners, the Atlantis Legacy prequel.

ECHO TRILOGY

Echo in Time

Resonance

Time Anomaly

Dissonance

Ricochet Through Time

KAT DUBOIS CHRONICLES

Ink Witch

Outcast

Underground

Soul Eater

Judgement

Afterlife

ATLANTIS LEGACY

Sacrifice of the Sinners

Legacy of the Lost

Fate of the Fallen

Dreams of the Damned

Song of the Soulless

Blood of the Broken

Rise of the Revenants

<u>ALLWORLD ONLINE</u>

<u>AO: Pride & Prejudice</u>

<u>AO: The Wonderful Wizard of Oz</u>

<u>Vertigo</u>

<u>THE ENDING SERIES</u>

<u>The Ending Beginnings: Omnibus Edition</u>

<u>After The Ending</u>

<u>Into The Fire</u>

<u>Out Of The Ashes</u>

<u>Before The Dawn</u>

<u>World Before</u>

<u>THE ENDING LEGACY</u>

<u>World After</u>

For more information on Lindsey and her books:

<u>www.authorlindseysparks.com</u>

Join Lindsey's mailing list to stay up to date on releases

AND to get a FREE copy of *Sacrifice of the Sinners*.

<u>www.authorlindseysparks.com/sacrifice</u>

To read Lindsey's books as she writes them, check her out on Patreon:

<u>https://www.patreon.com/lindseysparks</u>

ABOUT THE AUTHOR

Lindsey Sparks is a bestselling Science Fiction and Fantasy author who lives her life with one foot in a book—so long as that book transports her to a magical world or bends the rules of science. Her novels, from Post-apocalyptic to Time Travel Romance, always offer up a hearty dose of unreality,  along with plenty of history, mystery, adventure, and romance.

When she's not working on her next novel, Lindsey spends her time hanging out with her two little boys, working in her garden, or playing board games with her husband. She lives in the Pacific Northwest with her family and their small pack of cats and dogs.

www.authorlindseysparks.com

Facebook: www.facebook.com/authorlindseysparks
Facebook Reader Group: www.facebook.com/
groups/lovelyreaders
Instagram: @authorlindseysparks
Pinterest: www.pinterest.com/authorlindseysparks
Newsletter: www.authorlindseysparks.com/join-newsletter
Patreon: www.patreon.com/lindseysparks